I0728996

A Divergence of Conductors

Book 2 in The Conductors Trilogy

Sydney Ducharme

First Edition

A Divergence of Conductors ©
Copyright © 2023 SKD Books

All Rights Reserved.

The characters and events portrayed in this book are fictitious. Any similarity to real persons, living or dead, is coincidental and not intended by the author.

No part of this publication may be reproduced, stored in a retrieval system, or transmitted, in any form or by any means, electronic, mechanical, photocopying, recording or otherwise – without prior written permission of the publishers.

978-1-7780827-4-0
978-1-7780827-3-3
978-1-7780827-5-7

Place of Publication: Lacombe, Alberta, Canada
Printed in the United States of America & Canada

Cover Design by AM Selig
Edited by MN Boven

Table of Contents

1

The Chase

Daisy sprinted through the dense forest; her feet pounded the ground like a drum. Her ears rang. Her heart raced. The sound of her laboured breaths echoed in the silence of the forest. She darted left; suddenly a massive tree appeared in front of her, stopping her dead in her tracks. Daisy's eyes rose to the top of the tree, and the tree began shaking. Daisy barely had time to process what was happening when the tree started swinging its mighty limbs towards her. She jumped, barely avoiding the branch. Quickly, she reached out a fisted hand and ran the knuckles of her other hand across her fist, causing sparks to ignite. As she opened her hand, a large fireball came alive. Without a second thought, Daisy hurled the fireball towards the flailing tree which ignited instantly into a towering wall of flames. Daisy shielded her face with her arms in a desperate attempt to protect herself from the intense heat.

However, Daisy knew she couldn't stop. It was crucial for her to keep pushing forward.

Keeping her face protected, she ran past the inferno. Once she knew she was far enough away from the dangers of the tree, she snapped her fingers and doused flames.

No reason to set the whole forest ablaze, she thought. Daisy continued running. Her feet hurt, and her legs burned. Exhaustion was starting to set in. Daisy was not sure how much longer she could continue, but knew she had to keep going.

She ran, picking up her speed even as the foliage grew denser, and her legs grew weaker. Daisy had never reached this part of the forest before, but she didn't have time to take in her new surroundings. She ran. The further she ran, the thicker the underbrush became, and the thicker the underbrush became the harder it was to run. She willed the trees and shrubs to move, but her attempts seemed futile. The shrubs and bushes refused to budge. Daisy started to panic, but she continued sprinting as best she could. Her desperation to continue running overshadowed the pain in her legs and the burning sensation in her lungs. Right as the foliage started to thin, Daisy stepped in a hole and tumbled to the ground. Just as her hands reached the dirt, without any warning, the earth beneath her hands jumped up and launched Daisy above the treetops and high into the sky.

Daisy now found herself free falling, hurtling down towards the hard packed earth. Without panicking, Daisy slowly moved her hands in small circles to encourage the air to slow her descent. It was not nearly as effective as she had hoped, and, before long, Daisy slammed face first into the dirt. She groaned and punched the ground. Hard. She took a deep breath and gingerly rolled onto her back. Slowly, she opened her eyes and stared at the slivers of blue sky poking through the dense canopy. She had failed.

Again.

Soon after, the unmistakable sound of footsteps grew near. Daisy didn't move; she wasn't concerned now. She had failed and nothing mattered anymore. She closed her eyes and prepared herself for the inevitable as the footsteps got louder and closer; finally they stopped. Seconds later, a light kick to her ribs encouraged Daisy to open her eyes.

A familiar figure, silhouetted against the sun, stood above her. His blonde hair was short, curly, and untamed. Exhaustion was apparent on his face as dark, heavy bags sat underneath his blue and purple eyes. His appearance was tired and worn, and Daisy understood it all too well; the constant training and running had taken its toll on both of them. Evander had been training her from sunrise to sunset nearly every day for the past year. If she felt drained, Daisy could only imagine how he felt.

"You used fire against earth. You're not supposed to be able to do that," Evander stated matter-of-factly.

"Wood burns. It doesn't just blow away in the wind. Fire made more sense to me at the time," Daisy retorted, feeling even more annoyed that she had not succeeded. Evander shrugged and offered a kind smile.

"You're not wrong, but you're still not supposed to be able to do that. It shouldn't be effective," Evander remarked as he extended his hand to help Daisy up. Daisy rolled her eyes but accepted his hand. "That was a rough landing, too."

"I wasn't expecting you to make the ground jump," Daisy responded. Evander let out a quiet chuckle, clearly pleased with his ingenuity. Daisy dusted herself off as they began walking back to their encampment.

"That's the whole point of this training. Expect the unexpected and never assume that the same things will happen."

"You would think with me doing the exact same assessment over and over that your brain wouldn't remember the past and would keep doing the same tactics."

"Ah, but you are also different each time you enter the assessment, so I adjust accordingly. It doesn't matter about my memory." Evander paused; his brow furrowed and a look of confusion came across his face. "How many times have you lived this day? How many times have you done this assessment?"

Daisy sighed and averted her eyes. While she often struggled with the quick use of other elemental forces, she was exceptionally good at manipulating time, the force she created. Since the emergence of this sixth force, Daisy was able to do things like no one else. She was able to rewind time, stop time, and selectively age things, animals, and people. It was both fascinating and terrifying. Her powers were so unknown that everything was exciting but also frustratingly unpredictable. While Daisy's mastery of the time force was impressive, Evander insisted on her practising the other forces as well. Besides, they were at war. Every single Conductor needed to be ready to fight.

"Two hundred seventy-three," Daisy finally whispered. Evander stopped dead in his tracks.

"Two hundred and what now?" Evander asked; his surprise was palpable.

"I have done this assessment two hundred and seventy-three times, and you have beaten me every single time." Evander let out a slow and low whistle.

"This whole time force is unfathomable to me." He shook his head in disbelief. "I advance at every other force, but your time force just makes no sense. Are you lying to me? Have you made all this up?"

Although slightly offended, she could understand where he was coming from. Daisy offered a soft smile. "I would never lie about such a thing."

"You excel in all of the forces though. You've achieved more things in one year than I did in a decade. I don't understand it to be honest. You are truly baffling to me."

"I don't really understand it either. I get these visions that show me how to conduct differently. When I relax into it, it's like forces conduct me rather than me conducting them. I don't know how to explain it, but it's like the forces have been waiting for me."

"You might actually be better than me someday, but today is definitely not that day." Daisy rolled her eyes as Evander grinned.

They continued their way through the forest discussing the various assessments until they came to a small clearing. A tiny, simple log cabin sat in the middle of the meadow. A blanket of bright, green moss grew on the roof and the exterior walls were covered with weathered logs that had greyed with age. A small porch with a few mismatched chairs adorned the front of the cabin. Daisy smiled as she saw Brighid, the youngest Conductor, and Rosie, her best friend, sitting on the porch. As they approached, Rosie smiled and waved, but Brighid came running towards them and embraced Evander in a hug.

"I was worried Daisy was going to wipe you out this time," Brighid announced, though her face was buried in Evander's shirt which muffled her voice.

"She may be good, but few can out match my skills. Even the inventor of a new force seems to be no match for me," Evander proudly remarked. Daisy scoffed. Even over the past year of being on the run with these Conductors, Daisy had not grown fond of Evander's overconfidence. He was intelligent, anyone could see that, but he was also cocky and never missed an opportunity to arrogantly highlight his own perceived superiority. In all honesty, Daisy found him infuriating, but she knew she had few other options for training partners.

"How did the assessment go today?" Rosie asked from the porch. Evander and Brighid took that as a cue to leave and entered the cabin. Daisy moved to the porch and threw herself down into the chair beside Rosie.

"I did not pass," Daisy stated flatly. She let out a heavy sigh and ran her hand through her hair. She felt frustrated and was losing patience. "I excel with the time force and do well in practice with the other forces, but once my skills are tested and there is pressure, I get sloppy and lose focus. The slightest thing can throw me. I also don't follow the rules which infuriates Evander, and I am sure it is slowing my progression. Perhaps using the opposite force would be more effective. I don't know. I got launched into the air today because he made a mountain grow underneath me. How does that even work?"

Rosie laughed, which earned her a stern glare from Daisy. "I'm sorry, but I can only imagine you flailing through the air as a random mountain appears. It's rather humorous."

"I can assure you that it was anything but humorous," Daisy stated emphatically and quickly changed the subject. "You can still choose to learn, you know. You could become a Conductor. You could wield the elemental forces and join us to help us fight this war." Rosie gently placed her hand on Daisy's arm with a soft and sympathetic smile. Daisy knew what this meant.

"My calling is not to be a Conductor. I wasn't drawn to this world like you were. I don't want to age slowly or have more power than I was born with. I already have enough battles to fight that I don't need to add learning magic to the list."

Shortly after they had gone into hiding, Rosie disclosed to Daisy why she was sent to Dame Agatha's School for Young Women. Rosie had quickly become the ideal lady, a picture of perfect decorum, and excelled in all her courses, but her family would not accept her, for she loved women rather than men. Because of this, she would never marry nor have any children. Many people would not accept Rosie as she was, and she was often cast aside and alienated when her personal truth came to light. It broke Daisy's heart to think that who someone loved would make them any less deserving of love, but Daisy found many things in the world confusing.

"Two hundred seventy-three!?" There was a muffled exclaim from inside the house, and Daisy groaned knowing what was to come. The door to the cabin violently flung open. Exiting in a mad fury was Alina. "You have done today's assessment two hundred seventy-three times?! Why would you do that? Why would you waste so much time?"

Daisy stood up from her chair, adjusted her posture to face Alina directly, signalling her determination to stand firm. After leaving Daisy's family estate and Abe to the Grand Master, Alina sunk into a deep depression that had only recently started to ebb. Now, an abundance of pent-up anger resided within her, which she frequently unleashed upon Daisy. Alina attributed the entire responsibility for the group's predicament to Daisy. She believed that Daisy was solely to blame for the loss of Abe and their current circumstances of constantly running and hiding.

"It is not a waste of time," Daisy venomously spat back. "I have to be better at this. If I can't beat Evander, then how can I ever be expected to beat Azalea! I need to repeat the exercises over and over until I get it right. I need more time and, luckily, I can ensure I get that."

Alina stepped closer to Daisy; she was mere inches from Daisy's nose, but Daisy knew not to back down. When it came to Alina, any sign of weakness would be exploited.

"The Grand Master is an expert, and you…" she looked Daisy up and down, "…you are a joke." Alina paused to let the weight of her words settle, but Daisy remained unphased. In comparison to the horrific treatment and incessant torment inflicted by her mother, Alina's abuse seemed pale and insignificant to her. "We don't understand your new force. To be honest, we've had hardly any evidence you can even control time. Perhaps you've made this all up. Perhaps you're pretending and your farce has cost us Ames for nothing! It should have been you! She should have taken you!" she exclaimed with a pointed finger digging into Daisy's chest. Daisy remained stoic on the outside, but a fire raged within her.

Alina often spoke as if Abe was dead; she was certain that the Grand Master would have killed him as soon as she had had the chance. Alina's resolve and acceptance of Abe's fate drove Daisy insane. Somehow, for some illogical reason, Daisy knew Abe was alive, but not entirely himself. Daisy had no doubts that he was physically unharmed. She just had no idea what kind of mental state he was in or if he was even in control of his own mind at all. She felt it deep in her soul that he was alive but had no facts or reasoning to back up her intuition. She just knew in her heart that he was.

"This doesn't help us, Alina! Nothing you are saying or doing is a productive use of time or energy!" Daisy yelled back. She was losing her temper. She was tired of being called a fraud, being told repeatedly that Abe was dead, and that their situation was entirely her fault. In a moment of rage, she grabbed Alina's wrist, raised her other hand above her head, and snapped her fingers in a circle. A sprinkle of silver light washed over Alina and Daisy, signifying time was rewinding.

Daisy had gotten used to the immense tension building in her stomach as time shifted. The first time she had experienced it purposefully, she promptly threw up. Alina appeared to experience the same reaction. As time settled, Daisy released Alina's wrist. Alina did not have the time to process what had occurred before she vomited all over the porch.

"Ew! Gross!" Brighid yelled from her chair on the porch. Daisy had only gone back a few minutes, but she felt it was enough to prove her point.

"Where did you two come from?" Rosie questioned over the sounds of Alina vomiting.

"About five minutes in the future," Daisy stated. Alina righted herself, wiped her mouth with her sleeve, and glared at Daisy.

"You've never transported another person through time with you," Alina said angrily. She was right. Typically, when Daisy moved through time, she was the only one that remembered it. Because no one was ever aware of the time changes, they had never seen or experienced the time force. In an attempt to dispel further accusations from Alina regarding Daisy's abilities, Daisy decided to test a theory about bringing someone through time with her. In the moment, she believed it was the only way to quell Alina's dissent. "You should not have done that! How dare you experiment on me! Who do you think you are? You are nothing but an inbred swine that emerged from an accident. You… you… strumpet!"

Rosie and Brighid inhaled sharply. Daisy clenched her fists at her sides. Her jaw tightened as she attempted to rein in the rage boiling within her.

"I am tired of you calling me a fraud," Daisy muttered through clenched teeth. Daisy could feel all the pent-up emotions and frustrations bubbling to the surface. "I am tired of you doubting the decision Abe and I made. I am tired of you hating me and blaming me for all of this. I am tired of how you treat me and act like you are superior in every way to me. We've been gone a year, but I know…I know in my heart Abe is alive. I've given you proof of my powers, of what I can show you proof of. Can you give me some grace? I am trying to master all of these forces so I can help you. Help Abe. Help all of us!"

Alina stared doe-eyed at Daisy. Clearly, Daisy's response was unexpected. Rosie and Brighid watched in fascination from behind Alina. Daisy, at the very least, appreciated having witnesses to the altercation. However, instead of responding to Daisy, Alina stormed off into the woods in a huff. Just as Alina disappeared in the treeline, Evander strode out of the underbrush unaccompanied. He seemed undeterred, but confused at the same time.

"You disappeared," Evander shouted across the yard, "I was just about to blast you with a mountain and you just vanished."

"I did a bit of an experiment," Daisy responded. "Alina was doubting my abilities and honour, so I decided to bring her back in time with me."

"So that's why she just ploughed through me on the path? She seemed in a foul mood."

"A fair assumption," Rosie chimed in sarcastically.

"Well, in the meantime, shall we review today's training?" Evander offered as he took a seat across from Daisy and Rosie.

Up until the 1400s, there had never been a new force. However, when the Grand Master was faced with death, she created a fifth force that controlled the mind. The creation of this force created an imbalance in the forces. Ever since then, no one knew if another force would ever appear and bring balance back to the elements. That was until Daisy met Abe, and the Conductors' whole world changed. Somehow, Daisy had created the sixth force, time, and, as it had never been used before, Daisy had to learn the inner workings of the force to figure out how it could be used and manipulated.

Naturally, as is typical when learning new things, there were hiccups now and then. For example, one issue was how draining the force was. It took a hard toll on Daisy to repeatedly use it. She would be drained for days and unable to do much after these intense training sessions. Bigger time spells would take even more energy. It was hard to learn when she was always exhausted.

Another issue with time force seemed to be that she could not exist in two different places at the same time. While this was not a major issue when she was training with the other Conductors, Daisy could see how it could present problems should she need to go back further in her timeline. She could end up pulling herself from her own past. The time force was still messy and unknown, but Daisy was trying to make sense of it all. Besides, the only teacher available to her was Evander, and he technically wasn't even a graduated Conductor. The only full Conductor Daisy had access to was Alina, but she often refused to even talk to Daisy, let alone teach her. To Daisy, Alina often acted more like a child than Brighid. Alina was supposed to guide them, but she was lost in her grief and anger, so Evander stepped up to continue their education and aid Daisy in her training.

Unlike Alina, Evander was eager to see Daisy's skills grow. He liked a challenge, and a new force presented many. Although he had no memory of most of the redos and time jumps, he was still fascinated by each of Daisy's retellings. He would scribble notes in the back of a worn looking journal every time Daisy described her powers. Although he repeatedly stated it was just for reference, Daisy was certain he was trying to learn the time force as she developed it.

Daisy reviewed a few of the major events as Evander scribbled in the tattered looking journal he carried with him at all times. She reviewed the last session in the most detail as it was freshest in her mind. When she relived the same moment several times, her memories blurred and merged. It became harder to separate things. As she told her stories, the evening faded and the stars started to speckle the sky, but Alina had not yet returned.

"It's getting late," Brighid said with a yawn, "and Alina isn't back. Should we go look for her?"

To Brighid, Alina was like a mother. Brighid was dependent on Alina in many ways, and Daisy knew how important Alina was to her. Although she did not like Alina, Daisy would never wish her harm and her continued absence was concerning considering they were constantly being hunted by Azalea's followers.

Daisy smiled and extended her hand to Brighid. "We should probably split into teams and search the woods. Maybe she got lost on the path."

Brighid smiled happily and quickly stood up. She interlocked her hand with Daisy's and started skipping towards the forest. Rosie followed Daisy and Brighid while Arlo and Evander took off in the opposite direction.

In the heavy trees, nearly all remaining light was blocked out. Daisy and Brighid sparked up fireballs to help light the way. They followed the path for a while before Rosie noticed a broken branch with a piece of cloth snagged on it. The piece of black silk was similar to the clothes Alina wore. A sudden sense of alarm bubbled in Daisy's stomach. Something was wrong.

"Rosie, take Brighid back to the cabin," Daisy stated, trying to keep her voice level, so she wouldn't alarm Brighid. Rosie kept a flat expression, but nodded her head in a knowing manner. Brighid need not know that anything was wrong.

"But we haven't found Alina yet," Brighid protested.

"It's getting quite late, and we should get you to bed. Tomorrow is moving day, so we all need to be well rested," Rosie insisted in an attempt to aid Daisy's cause.

"Quite right," Daisy agreed. "Let Rosie take you to bed. I will make sure Alina checks in on you when we return."

Brighid looked between Rosie and Daisy. Their faces showed no signs of negotiation, so Brighid let out a large sigh before crossing her arms and stomping away back towards the cabin. Rosie gave Daisy a supportive squeeze on the arm before following Brighid.

Just as the two passed out of sight, Daisy heard a twig snap behind her. She turned towards the sound but could see nothing. She cast a larger fireball to increase her range of vision, but still nothing showed. She swallowed hard. Her skin crawled as she felt like a thousand eyes suddenly fell on her. Daisy had no idea what was happening, but she knew something was terribly wrong.

2

Things that Go Bump in the Night

Daisy kept a fireball lit and proceeded further down Alina's trail. Every once in a while, another snapped branch or a snagged piece of cloth would tell Daisy she was on the right track. She tried to move as quickly as possible while maintaining some semblance of stealth. Eventually, Daisy found herself in a clearing. Daisy had been here earlier in the day, but now the ground was black with soot. The few remaining trees were bared and charred. Some small bushes continued to smoulder, and standing in the middle of destruction was Alina.

Alina was usually well-composed and perfectly manicured. She maintained exceptional decorum even when lashing out at Daisy. This Alina, however, was nothing like normal. Alina had her back to Daisy, but Daisy could still tell something was terribly wrong with her. Alina's shoulders were hunched and her hands were held like claws. Large, heaving breaths shook her whole body. Her dark hair was dishevelled and resembled that of a lion's mane. Dirty, tattered clothes hung lifelessly off her body.

She was even missing a shoe. Daisy could see a large cut on Alina's calf that was gushing blood. Daisy was terrified to see what her face would look like.

Slowly, Daisy crept forward trying to not startle Alina. Daisy maintained her focus on Alina, vigilant for any sudden movement. Her intense focus on Alina distracted Daisy from paying attention to her footing. Amidst the darkened terrain, a solitary stick remained; Daisy accidently stepped on it, resulting in a loud snap.

Alina whipped her head towards the sound. Blood ran from her mouth and dripped off her chin. Instead of her usual purple and red eyes, Alina's eyes shone yellow like a wolf's. Daisy barely stifled a scream of horror at Alina's new appearance. Her stomach nearly revolted, but somehow Daisy prevented her dinner from ejecting itself. Alina cocked her head in a hawk-like manner, as if she was setting her eyes on her prey. She moved towards Daisy with a crow-like hop, reminiscent of a bird chasing after a worm. Daisy gradually enlarged her fireball which casted an ominous orange glow over her and Alina. Daisy had hoped the light would attract the attention of Evander and Arlo.

"Alina..." Daisy said softly; Alina flinched as though Daisy had yelled at the top of her lungs. Daisy lowered her voice to barely above a whisper. "Alina, I am here to help you. I come as a friend. I want to make sure you are okay."

Alina hissed and slashed her claw-like hand towards Daisy. Instinctively, Daisy jumped back and raised her hands; her fireball vanished and so too did its light. As quickly as possible, Daisy reignited her fire even stronger than before, but Alina had vanished. Daisy turned in a slow circle looking for any sign of where Alina may have gone but found nothing. Suddenly, there was a rustling of branches behind her. Daisy whipped toward the sound and saw a shadow dart away. Then another rustle on the other side of the clearing and another shadow. The figure was moving inhumanly fast.

Daisy's heart pounded. A high pitched hum buzzed in her ears. She felt like a trapped mouse being relentlessly hunted by a cunning cat. An eerie cackle echoed through the air sending shivers up Daisy's spine.

"Oh little Daisy. Come to play?" echoed a voice from the shadows. It was raspier and shriller than Alina's voice. Daisy wasn't even sure if this was Alina she was facing anymore. "Pathetic child thinks she can compete with Alina. Barely a woman and yet steals the hearts of men."

"Alina, I mean you no harm. Let me help you," Daisy pleaded.

"Help me?!?" the shadow laughed. "What could little Daisy do to help poor, broken Alina?"

"Maybe if you tell me what is wrong, we can come up with a solution together." Alina snickered malignantly. Daisy tried to keep calm, but the situation was growing intense and it appeared no one was coming to aid her. Daisy needed to come up with some type of plan.

"Alina is broken. Her mind is broken. Abe fixed her. Was fixing her, but he's gone. Dead. Dead. Dead. So very dead."

"Abe isn't dead."

"LIAR!" Daisy felt a sudden violent gust of wind, which knocked her off balance. She stumbled and tried to catch her fall, but another gust of wind pushed Daisy to the ground. She fumbled to get up, but standing over Daisy was a deranged looking Alina.

"Let us help you. Let's go back to the cabin and let's get you help," Daisy desperately pleaded. Even though she felt like Alina was beyond rational thought, Daisy was certain she would lose in a fight against Alina.

"No! We can't bring this to Brighid. Precious Brighid can't see this. Precious Brighid can never know. Poor Brighid. Precious Brighid."

For a moment, Alina seemed lost in her thoughts. Daisy heard a snapping branch and looked towards the sound. Through the clearing, came Evander and Arlo. Daisy momentarily relaxed knowing help was on the way.

Suddenly a searing pain lashed through her throat; Daisy clasped her neck. It was hot and wet. Daisy looked back at Alina and, in the low light, she saw dark liquid dripping from her hand. Blackness painted the edges of Daisy's vision. She heard a squeal like a pig and, just before she lost consciousness, she watched as something wrapped around Alina.

***

Daisy scrunched her nose at the dim light landing on her face. She was not ready to wake up, but the sun's warmth tickled her cheek, forcing her from the darkness and into reality. Her whole body ached. She opened her eyes to the glaring sun and flinched, causing a spark of pain to shoot through her skull. Her whole body suddenly ached and she felt completely weak. She tried to groan from the pain, but noticed barely a whisper came out.

"Daisy?" Rosie whispered. "Oh my goodness. I didn't think… you're awake. Good God, you are alive!"

Rosie stood and dashed towards Daisy's bedside. Gingerly, Rosie picked up Daisy's hand. A bright smile grew across Rosie's face. Daisy wished to return the gesture, but found smiling uncomfortable.

"I didn't think you were going to make it. I am so glad you are alive! I'd never be forgiven if something happened to you," Rosie exclaimed while running a gentle finger along the back of Daisy's hand. "As much as I want to celebrate, I said I would inform Evander of any changes immediately. I will be right back."

Rosie scurried out of the room and gently closed the door behind her. Daisy attempted to sit up but the vertigo was overwhelming. Her stomach was knotted and her throat was sore. She tried to remember what happened, but very little came to mind. All that her mind could recall was blackness, fear, and pain… so much pain…

Rosie quickly returned with Evander in tow. His skin was pale and his shirt was covered in blood. Was it his own? Or someone else's? He placed the back of his hand on Daisy's head. After a moment, he grabbed her wrist and felt for a pulse. Rosie stood over his shoulder, chewing on her fingernails and watching Daisy intently. Daisy was confused about their reaction. What had happened?

"Her pulse is almost normal and her colour has come back. She doesn't have a noticeable fever so likely no infection yet. These are good signs," Evander explained. "She has come around well. Glad to see you pull through, Daisy. You had us worried for a while."

"Ek -" Daisy tried to speak but found she could barely make a noise. She had questions that she needed answered, but her voice evaded her. A distant, but horrible memory flashed across her mind. Daisy reached her hands to her neck and felt heavy bandages wrapped around her throat. Evander quickly pulled her hands away.

"Don't touch. It's still healing," Evander chided. Daisy squirmed on the bed and flailed her arms. Pain ricocheted through her body, but she didn't care. She was angry and confused and no one was helping her. Two sets of strong arms pinned her to the bed. Evander was holding one arm and Rosie the other.

"If you move too much, you will reopen the wound," Evander dictated. Daisy tried to ask what wound, but nothing came out. "Allow me."

As if guessing what Daisy was trying to do, Evander moved one arm and gently touched Daisy's temple. A sudden rush of memories re-emerged, and Daisy was reminded of the previous night's horrors. The quick image from before became surrounded by context, and Daisy understood all too well what happened. She wanted to scream, but now knew she couldn't speak. Alina's attack had completely opened Daisy's throat. As Evander pulled away and the memories dissipated, Daisy realised the blood on Evander's shirt was likely hers. It was an immense amount of blood. She was certain she barely survived.

"We weren't entirely sure what happened," Evander indicated. "When we arrived, there was a lot of blood and you were on the ground, but as I watched your memory, it appears she just slashed your throat with her bare hands."

Evander began pacing the room. He stroked his chin. Eventually, he stopped at the end of the bed and faced Daisy. "I have one more idea. I will try one more force on the wound to see if we can further heal your throat, but I am not sure it will work. It's the best I can do with the information provided. Is that okay?"

Daisy realised she did not have much choice. Her voice was a requirement for some conduction and she knew she would need strong conduction to save Abe. Whatever could lead to her voice returning, she would do it. In response to Evander, she gave a quick head jerk to give him permission. Evander began baring her neck.

"Can you go grab Arlo please?" Evander asked Rosie as he eyed Daisy's wound. Without saying anything, she left the room and returned quickly with Arlo. "I will need you to hold her still as I perform this. It may be painful. Rosie, grab something to put in her mouth. The last thing we need is for her to bite through her tongue."

Rosie handed Evander a wooden spoon. He gingerly placed the spoon in between Daisy's teeth then made direct eye contact with her. His brow furrowed and his lips were tight, but quivering. He lifted his hands which shook slightly. His eyes begged for forgiveness and Daisy knew this was going to be unpleasant. She steeled her nerves, preparing for the worst, but hoping for the best.

Evander began moving his hand in an intricate pattern around Daisy's neck. Sparks of various colours floated down. As they touched Daisy's skin, she could feel them burn like hot coals. She instinctively flinched, but Arlo and Rosie's hands held strong. More sparks fell and Daisy could smell her flesh burning. Blood began to trickle down the side of her neck. Evander swore loudly before stopping the spell and applying pressure to her neck with clean gauze. They began frantically moving about. Rosie grabbed strips of cloth and gauze as Arlo and Evander pressed bandages against Daisy's neck.

"That was my last idea," Evander shouted at Arlo who shook his head. Both of their faces paled. Daisy could feel Evander's hands shaking against her neck. In the past year, Evander always seemed to have the answers, but as Daisy looked at Evander now, he seemed scared, defeated, and lost.

Daisy closed her eyes as a weakness started to overcome her. In doing so, she saw silver sparkles dancing behind her eyelids. She eased into the sparkles and let them overcome her mind and being. Between one breath and the next, a vision appeared to Daisy of a time force spell. A repeated figure eight across the wound in a counter clockwise fashion could rewind the time of a specific section or thing while leaving the rest in the present. She had gotten accustomed to these quick visions, telling her how to use the time force and other forces, but this conduction seemed exceptionally strong. She wasn't sure if it would work, but it was worth an attempt.

Daisy's eyes flashed opened. With what little energy she had, she lifted her arm and placed her hand on Evander's face. Quickly, she transferred her knowledge in hopes that he could perform the spell. His hands stopped applying pressure and began performing the correct hand motions. Daisy could feel her skin knitting itself back together as time was rewound. Slowly but surely, she could breathe easier. The pain subsided and the dizziness in her head lightened. She even felt herself smile slightly.

Evander fell to the floor with a loud thud. He breathed heavily, and his whole body shook. Dark, purple bags painted beneath his eyes. His lips were nearly white, and his pupils were tiny pinpricks. Even his cheeks were sunken and his hair greyed at the edges. He looked completely drained, and guilt overwhelmed Daisy. Perhaps it was too much for him. Daisy reached a hand out to him. He intertwined his fingers with hers and smiled. A bit of light seemed to come back to his face.

"Better?" Evander inquired weakly.

"Much," Daisy muttered. Her voice was raspy and felt harsh in her throat. "Are you alright though?"

"A bit drained, but you are alive which is what matters," Evander answered.

"We were scared you weren't going to make it," Rosie explained. "You were bleeding really bad when they brought you back last night."

"What happened?" Daisy questioned.

"Well…" Evander started and looked at Arlo who nodded slightly. "We went looking for Alina and you found her. When we saw your fireball blazing, we came running assuming that meant you found Alina. Which you did…"

Evander seemed to struggle with saying more. Arlo stepped in and said, "when we got to you, we were worried we were too late. Alina was over top of you and blood was dripping from her hands. You were clutching your throat and bleeding profusely. I quickly lassoed Alina with vines to subdue her and Evander went to you."

Daisy stared at the people surrounding her. She had never felt so much care and concern over her wellbeing. Even after the incident at the Solstice Ball when Daisy was tested, she had not felt such compassion and love. She barely knew Abe then and she was still becoming acquainted with Rosie. Now, Daisy had known all of them for nearly two years and been living with them for the past year. Clearly, they had grown to care for Daisy during that time. Feeling overwhelmed with emotion, Daisy started to cry. Even her own family had never shown such concern and love for her. This was something different. Unlike her family who felt an obligation to Daisy, these people had chosen to love Daisy.

"What's wrong?" Rosie asked as she moved to sit beside Daisy on the bed.

"You all care," Daisy managed between tears. Evander cocked his head in a confused manner. "You didn't have to save me. I was as good as dead, but you did. You saved me."

"Well, yeah…" Arlo stated while rubbing the back of his neck and staring at the floor. "You're one of us now. We'd do anything for our family."

"You're stuck with us now," Evander joked. Daisy smiled. The room fell quiet which Daisy found uncomfortable. The previous moment was tender, and it appeared no one knew what else to say.

"So what happened to Alina then?" Daisy inquired.

"She is currently in a cage of my design," Evander said with a smile while puffing his chest out with pride. "Should be nearly impossible for her to escape. I had been designing it for the Grand Master, but in Alina's current state… she is better in the cage."

"But what happened to her? She wasn't," Daisy paused while trying to find the right words. "She wasn't human last night."

"Evander was saying it might be mania," Rosie offered. Evander nodded his head solemnly.

"What is mania?" Daisy asked.

"Mania occurs when someone's force connection is broken. I don't know if you remember Abe telling us about early Conductors learning the elder tongue? If a Conductor learns the elder tongue before their forces can support it, their conduction becomes broken. They can't properly connect to the forces," Evander explained.

"But Alina said that the magic just becomes confused. You try to cast a fireball and instead throw dirt. She didn't say it would turn you into a raving, murderous animal," Daisy exclaimed.

"Yes and no. I've been reading through Abe's notes -"

"What do you mean you've been reading through Abe's notes?" Daisy interrupted and narrowed her eyes at Evander who suddenly became very quiet. After a moment, he dug through a pocket on the inside of his jacket and revealed a tattered notebook. It was the same book he would record Daisy's experiments with the time force in.

"This isn't my notebook. Abe gave this to me on the hill. He told me to help you all, but I thought he meant to train you. I've had to translate some sections. He switches between languages and combines others. Now that I can read some of the older sections, I am learning more about Alina and her… condition."

"What exactly happened?"

"It turns out that Abe was teaching Alina the elder tongue. They were working on one of her primaries, the mind force. Her task was to remove a strong emotional memory from Abe's mind. Abe had selected a particularly strong moment which he described as…" Evander looked at Daisy with uncertainty on his face.

"Please go on," Daisy encouraged.

"He describes it as the moment he fell in love with Alina." Daisy felt her stomach drop. She knew they had been together, but Abe made it seem like it wasn't anything serious. It seemed like he had never loved her, but it was the timing, the moments, and the stories that brought them together. Abe always made it seem like it wasn't really love. But these were Abe's memories in his own words, written at the exact time of the event. This would be a more personal and intimate recount. These were his stories, and he said he loved Alina.

"What happened?" Daisy stated, trying to act like the admission did not impact her. It's in the past. It doesn't mean he loves her now.

"The conduction went wrong. Her spell backfired and her ability to connect with the forces snapped. The miss-fired spell actually damaged Abe's memories permanently. Abe stated in his journal that his ability to love her vanished. He could tell there was something there once, but going forward, he couldn't convince himself to love Alina anymore. Even in more recent accounts, he stated he still couldn't find the ability to love Alina. Sometimes, it was like she was even a stranger to him. It's like he lost his ability to love anyone." Evander continued talking, but Daisy could no longer hear him. Her mind latched onto one statement.

Lost his ability to love anyone.

The words echoed in Daisy's mind. Perhaps it was all an illusion. Perhaps it was just a story which Daisy was now a victim of. Perhaps Abe never loved Daisy.

3

A Prison for One

The past year was painful as he watched his body follow the Grand Masters' every command.

No. Not the Grand Master anymore. Azalea.

Abe sat in the back of his mind watching his body perform tasks he would never have done under any other circumstance. As they searched the world for Daisy and the others, Abe was forced to torture a family for information, kill another Conductor that spoke out against the Azalea, capture children to brainwash, and other deeds so terrible that his mind blocked them out in order to protect himself. Each act destroyed a piece of his soul and diminished any hope that he'd ever be released.

Despite the crushing despair, Abe constantly tried to break through Azalea's hold. There were moments of lessened intensity, like when she was asleep, where Abe had some freedom of his mind. It was never enough to do anything though. He couldn't speak or move. He couldn't leave Azalea though he desperately wanted to. He was frozen, watching the world burn in front of him, helpless to do anything to stop it. She was more powerful than him and he didn't understand why. All he knew was that he was completely helpless to stop her or be free of her.

In these moments of reprieve, where he wasn't horrified by the atrocities he had committed, he often found his mind wandering to Daisy. He tried to keep his thoughts of her suppressed, so Azalea wouldn't mutilate the purity of his memories. It was all he had left of her. However, there were moments where Azalea would come to Abe and wander through his memories of Daisy. Azalea seemed curious about Daisy as a Conductor and Abe held such memories. He tried to protect his memories, protect Daisy from Azalea learning more, but Azalea always prevailed and he always lost.

Over the past year under Azalea's control, Abe searched for Daisy and his family while also recruiting other Conductors to the supposed cause. Abe was still confused as to what the cause was exactly, but what he did know was the Grand Master was building an army and planning something big. She always seemed to keep Abe at an arm's length whenever discussing anything big or important. Or, at the very least, suppress his memory of anything discussed. Even updates on Daisy's whereabouts were kept as quiet as possible, but Abe clung to any whisper or rumour about Daisy and his family. He desperately hoped they were okay and safe. As long as they were out of Azalea's grasp, there was still a chance to defeat her.

"Abe, come here," Azalea whispered in his mind. His limbs started moving which he fruitlessly tried to fight.

He left the room he was often placed in when he was of no use and walked down the hall. He made several turns to navigate the labyrinth of tunnels, but eventually the halls started to converge and widen. Finally, the hall opened into a room where a large round table sat in the middle. Azalea stood at the table looking down at the papers strewn across its surface. She braced herself against the table. Her brow was furrowed and her nose was scrunched up. She idly tapped her fingernails on the table top in a syncopated rhythm. Usually, when she was this focused Abe would be given some unpleasant task.

Instead of focusing on the likely tortuous task, Abe focused on the other people in the room. He took notice of any signs of mind control. Usually a flat expression and slight purple tone to the eyes were good indicators. However, no one in the room showed any signs of mind control. Abe wanted to scream for help, but was unable and knew it would be pointless. The three other people in the room were all Azalea's minions.

Henry was a large man that towered over everyone. He was built like an ox and had brown, shaggy hair to match the description. A scruffy beard hid most of a large scar that disfigured his face. Azalea seemed to connect with him most. Abe often wondered if it was because they shared the same primaries: mind and fire.

In contrast, Kotravai was a petite and beautiful woman. Her skin was deep brown like bronze, and her hair was onyx black. Although she was petite, her personality more than made up for it. She was a strong woman who had no issue expressing her mind. She was bold, outspoken, and incredibly clever. Abe found her annoying, and was surprised Azalea had not forced her into silence. However, Abe liked having her around for one reason and one reason only. She has gold eyes like Daisy. Whenever Abe saw her eyes, Daisy jumped into his mind. She was annoying, yes, but a needed reminder of what he was fighting for sometimes.

The last advisor to Azalea was a balding, old man. He was hunched over and often moved at a snail's pace. Everything on him was white as snow. He looked frail, like a slight breeze would knock him over. He often wore long robes and cloaks. His eyes were milky and unmoving, but the faint colours of blue and brown peaked through. Abe had to look really close to see any colour at all. The colour was incredibly faint. Abe originally thought he was blind, but he could often see things no one else noticed. He made Abe uncomfortable in the few interactions they had had. Abe felt lucky that his interactions with him had been kept short, but this also meant Abe knew very little about him. He didn't even know the man's name. Most of their interactions were transactional and, unlike Henry who was always around, the old man would only pop in every once in a while with updates that Abe was never allowed to hear. The uncertainty and ambiguity surrounding this man made Abe even more uncomfortable.

Abe often thought the combination of advisors was unusual. Henry certainly had military experience, and the old man seemed wise on many topics, but the addition of a non-conductor was even more intriguing. Kotravai was able to do actual magic, which Abe couldn't figure out. He only knew of very few people who could do magic, and most of them were not human. She was an intriguing addition, but Abe couldn't figure out what about her was different. He often tried to think on it, but found Azalea would steer his mind away from further analysis of her. Azalea often steered his mind off many topics when he started to look at anything closely. It was infuriating.

"Glad you can join us," Azalea muttered without looking up from the papers on the table. "There were reports of a large fire in the Grey Root Pines Forest three days ago. As quickly as it started, it seemed to be put out. We expect this is a group of Conductors on the run. We have not had verification if this is my sister and her protectors."

My family, you mean. Abe thought, wanting to scream at Azalea for her lack of consideration.

"I am sending you and Henry on a mission to investigate the area for any additional signs of Conductor activity and determine who may be in the area."

Abe cringed inward. He hated being sent on missions especially when it meant he might run into Daisy. He did not want Daisy to see him like this. He wanted Daisy to love him and was terrified that Azalea would make Daisy hate him. She was cruel and harsh, but Abe knew Daisy was the only soft spot for Azalea.

"If you don't find anything useful, head to Felderelsy. It's the closest train station and major centre to that area. If it's Daisy, she will be looking for some way out of there."

Azalea waved her hand and Abe's feet immediately began to move. Henry followed behind. While Henry was Azalea's closet minion, he could also act as conduit. Usually, the mind force had a certain range. When a subject went out of the range, the connection would break. However, two mind force primaries could interact outside of the normal parameters. As long as Abe remained close to Henry, Azalea could control Abe through Henry. Azalea tried to explain conduits to Abe when the mind force was in its early emergence, but it confused him more than anything. All Abe knew was that leaving Azalea did not mean losing her control over his mind.

They started towards a wall in the room. There were no windows and the walls were chiselled stone. Abe tried to note anything of use, but could never find anything to indicate where they were in the maze of Azalea's fortress. He counted steps and noticed uneven stones, before Henry stopped him and placed a burlap sack over his head. Azalea never trusted Abe and wanted him to remain unknowing. Henry guided Abe down the rest of the hall. A door clicked and Abe could feel a cold breeze brushing his cheeks. Henry pulled him along for about an hour before stopping and unbagging Abe's head.

"I believe you know what to do," Henry stated. His voice was deep and gravelly. Abe hated it.

Abe was always taken to some new spot in the woods whenever he was allowed out. From here, he was expected to transport his attendant to wherever Azalea had directed. Unlike any other Conductors, Azalea and Abe could teleport. It appeared that their connections to the forces and the universe gave them one extra benefit. He snapped his fingers in a purposeful triangle. A melodic tune of chimes and flutes hummed through the air until the spell was complete. With the end of the song, Abe and Henry appeared thousands of miles from their original position in the Grey Root Pines Forest.

Henry reviewed a map and note about the reported incident. He looked at the sky to determine direction before taking off in a specific direction. Abe trailed behind while wishing he could get his feet to stop moving. Henry idly whistled a tune while checking the map and navigating towards some point.

Eventually, they came to a river. The water was clear and crisp, but lower than usual. The water line on the river banks were exposed and parched. This forest was often damp and humid, but it seemed oddly dry. While the forest was called Grey Root Pines Forest, there were hardly any pine trees. The forest mostly consisted of large and ancient redwoods with extensive underbrush of ferns and fallen lumber. These trees often captured moisture and grew in more wet environments. For this forest to feel so arid, something drastic must have occurred.

Henry trudged through the water without missing a single note in his tune. Abe begrudgingly followed. The water was cold and unpleasant. With soaking wet shoes, they continued through the foliage. Eventually, they came to a clearing that was obviously the target site. Everything here was charred to complete ash.

As Abe stood in the middle of the clearing, realisation dawned on him. He knew what this was from. His stomach immediately began to churn. He tried to bury the thought in hopes that Azalea and Henry wouldn't pick up on his realisation. However, this proved useless. Henry spun on his heel to face Abe. He extended his hand, which Abe knew to mean a truth conduction.

"What do you know about this?" Henry asked. While Abe was forced to tell the truth, he could still withhold information in some minor capacity.

"I have seen this before," Abe muttered. He rarely spoke these days, so his voice was weak and mottled.

"Useless. What do you know about this type of destruction?" Henry demanded. Abe felt Henry's conduction run deeper into his mind, pulling at the information and nagging at the truth.

"When I last saw this, it was when someone's conduction broke. They tried to speak the elder tongue too early and caused this same level of destruction."

"Do you know who did this?"

"I've seen similar castings before but I cannot guarantee who did this."

"Tell me who it is," Henry demanded. Abe tried to resist. He pushed back as hard as he could but with each morsel of resistance, Henry furthered his reach into Abe's mind. "Tell me who caused this now"

"Alina," Abe sputtered. "It was likely Alina."

A surprised look painted Henry's face. There was a slight release in his hold on Abe which Abe basked in. A bit more freedom and space inside his own mind.

"Alina has broken conduction?" Henry enquired with an oddly impressed smirk. "But she was always such a strong contender when we fought her in the past. Tell me more. No, show me more."

Henry touched Abe's temple, allowing him to push further into Abe's mind and pull at memories Abe wished he could have forgotten. Henry pulled at a single thread until the memory came to the forefront of Abe's memory.

Abe and Alina stood in a field of tall grass. They often came here when learning the elder tongue, as there was limited potential for casualties. The occasional grass fire that could quickly be extinguished was really the only risk. She smiled at Abe over her shoulder as she turned in a slow circle, tracing her hands over the long grass. She giggled as she danced away from Abe, who tried to pull her focus back to the task.

"Alina," Abe stated, but his voice was full of joy and pleasure. "Come on, Alina. We must focus."

She skipped towards him and wrapped her hands around his neck. Her body pressed against his. Slowly and tenderly, Abe ran his hands down the sides of her body feeling every curve beneath his fingers. She stood on her tippy toes and kissed his cheek lightly.

"I rarely get you alone anymore. We always have the other studies with us. Can't we waste the afternoon with something more fun?" She kissed his neck then his collar bone. Abe let his head hang back as he dissolved in the sensations of her touch.

"As wonderful as that sounds, we must prepare for your third and final exam, but to do so, you must learn the elder tongue and its ways."

"Always the teacher first." Alina dropped her hands from his neck and took a step back.

"Succeed with today's lesson, I will make it up to you tonight. I promise," Abe offered. Alina smiled and nodded in agreement. "You have one last spell to learn for your primary force. However, there is a reason I have left this spell to last. It will cause you and me pain."

"You are not selling me on completing this spell."

"I am not trying to, but I am trying to warn you that it won't be easy. I have seen this spell go wrong and it is horrible."

"Elder tongue is never easy or pretty," Alina remarked while placing her hands on her hips and shifting her weight to one leg. Abe smiled at her before becoming serious again. He needed to stay focused. He couldn't let him distract her with her wit and womanly charms.

"This spell is about removing strong memories and emotions. Our emotions are often tied to memories, so by removing memories, we can change a person's emotions."

"But removing memories is not advanced for Conductors with the mind force. We learn to do this early on and easily I might add."

"Yes and no. You learn to remove memories, but not large segments and certainly not memories with strong emotional connections for you and your target. I want you to think of the worst thing that could happen to you."

"Losing you." Alina didn't miss a beat. She was quick to respond and with such strong resolve. However, this shattered Abe's heart. He knew which memories to extract from her and which memories she would extract from him. The fear was screwing up the extraction.

"Alina," Abe pleaded. "Is that really the only strong emotion you can think of?"

"It's the only one that matters. If I am going to do this, I want to do it to the fullest extent."

"When you extract another's memories, they become yours. Your target will have no memory of whatever you took. If you don't put it back properly or fully intact, you can corrupt that person's memories, or worse, their mind."

"My family is dead. You are the only thing that matters to me. I have nothing to lose but you. So yes, you are my strongest memories."

Abe sighed and ran his hand over his face. This was not what he was expecting or wanting to happen. He thought she would have something else to use for this, but she had made it clear there was no other option. He braced himself and tried to lock in whatever memories he could of

Alina. He wanted to preserve their connection in case this went wrong.

"I will demonstrate first. I will enter your mind and remove your memories that made you fall in love with me," Abe explained, but Alina flinched. He knew she had never been loved properly by anyone before him. Abe tried to remain composed. "I will hold them in my memory for you to feel what it is like without them. Then, I will return your memories to you intact. Understand?"

"Yes, I understand," Alina replied with a head nod.

Abe ran one finger down the side of her face. He cupped the side of her head and placed his thumb over her temple. Slowly, he moved his head forward until his forehead rested against hers while repeating, "Abi hace mentes memorias solviture. Detrahes praeteritums doloremi ets faci meums."

A connection clicked like a piece of rope being pulled tight. Abe grabbed onto one end and pulled himself into her memories. Images suddenly flashed through his mind.

He saw his own smile with a level of amazement and adoration he had never felt before. He saw the way he brushed back his hair when it got too long. He saw his half laugh when something was uncomfortable. He saw the way he ran his hand over his face when he was frustrated or disappointed. All the little pieces that made up who Abe was. All the small details that Alina had picked up on and slowly grew to love. It wasn't any large act of courtship that drew Alina's attention. It was small details that encompassed Abe in his entirety.

He pulled away and looked at Alina. Her memories swam through his mind making his head feel fuzzy and cramped. Alina was dazed momentarily before blinking repeatedly and coming back to the moment. The joy Abe had become used to her having was completely dissolved. She seemed a hardened shell completely void of passion. Abe hated it.

"How do you feel?" Abe asked her. She turned her head to the side, eyeing Abe with a puzzled look.

"I know you, but I don't *know* you. It's unusual. I can tell there is something about you, but it's foggy and empty," Alina responded.

"With time, the fogginess would fade and the memories would come back, but this spell with the elder tongue can take years, even decades, to fully fade. Now, I will restore your memories."

Abe tapped her temple three times and muttered the spell from earlier. With each tap, he could feel the weight of the memories dissipate. Having watched the memories, they now remained in his mind, but through his own lens of interpretation.

Alina relaxed as her memories and emotions returned. Her light and joy refilled her body which eased the tension in Abe's chest. She smiled up at him and could feel her love for him exuding from every inch of her. Abe stroked her cheek gently. She closed her eyes and moved towards his hand.

"How do you feel now?" Abe questioned.

"Better. Normal." Alina responded and opened her eyes.

"Are you ready to try?"

"Can we try it on something less important? What if I make a mistake?"

"This particular spell only works with strong emotions and it's the last spell you need to learn for your exam. We can't avoid it anymore."

"Okay. I shall try."

"Now remember, it must be a strong emotion for both you and me."

"So your love for me?" Alina enquired with a jab to the ribs in a playful manner. Abe smirked, but knew she was right.

"Yes, that would be an appropriate option. Go ahead. I trust you."

Alina repeated the same motions and words that Abe had done earlier. Abe felt the same connection as she wiggled her mind through Abe's memories before locking onto those that Abe and Alina both felt strongly about. Unlike Alina, there was one moment that caused Abe to love her. Abe watched as Alina passed her second exam and showed such great passion and excitement. Abe's heart crumpled and he felt a rush of affection and pride. It showed Alina's true inner-self to Abe.

The image dissolved and so did the feelings. There was a snap in the connection. Abe felt something fracture but he hardly had time to respond. His eyes flicked open and he stared at Alina. There was no love this time, but instead an engrossing fear.

Alina was shaking her hands as black flames licked her skin. She screamed in pain and her entire body became quickly engulfed in flames. Abe tried to reach her to cool the flames, but she started running away. Abe chased after her, calling for her to stop and wait. She stumbled and fell to the ground. Abe reached out and tried to touch her, but in doing so, a sudden explosion occurred. Abe was tossed backwards and smashed his head on hard earth. His ears rang, and blackness painted his vision.

When Abe came to, Alina sat in the middle of a blackened clearing. Abe approached her cautiously, unsure of what exactly had happened. He touched her shoulder. She flipped around and hissed at Abe. Her eyes were like a wolf's, yellow and beady.

"Oh Alina," Abe pleaded. Immense pity and grief overwhelmed him. He had caused this. "I am so sorry."

"Pain," Alina whimpered and clutched her head. "Much pain."

"I know. Let me help you." He tried to reach out and place his hand on her head. She flinched away. "Please Alina, let me help you."

She eased herself closer like a beaten dog trying to trust a human again. Abe slowly and softly rested his hand against Alina's temple. He repeated the same spell, but removed the memory of harming Abe, of casting the spell, of speaking the elder tongue. He held the memories and embedded them in the back of his mind. When Abe opened his eyes, Alina stared back at him, but with her normal ruby and plum eyes. She looked terrified but otherwise restored.

"Wh - what happened, Ambrose?" Her voice was small like a child's.

"I failed you," Abe stated. "The spell backfired. I - I... Alina, I am so sorry."

"Something is missing. I can't feel it. I can't feel the forces. Did I... am I... is my conduction broken? Did I fail? Am I broken? What happened to me?!" Alina started to cry. Abe could feel her pain, but was unsure how to help her.

"I am sorry Alina, but I think your conduction is broken. I tried to pull the memory to delay the mania, but it's only temporary. We will have to be careful."

"But... the memories... I- you- do you still love me?" Abe stopped and searched his mind. The emotion was gone. All he felt for Alina was pity and guilt.

"Alina, let's focus on getting your conduction fixed then we can fix my memories." Alina started to sob. Abe held her to his chest and tried to comfort her.

Suddenly, Abe felt the release of the memory and he was back to the present. Henry glared at him with suspicion. Abe wanted to punch him in the face. Henry had invaded Abe's thoughts and learned more than he should have.

"I am guessing you never fixed her then," Henry scoffed and let out a bellowing laugh. "You are pathetic."

Abe groaned, but instead of internally, a small whimper escaped his lips. A short opportunity for freedom. Abe held on to it and moved into it.

"What was that?" Henry sputtered.

"No," Abe managed to exclaim. Henry moved closer. Abe seized the opportunity and punched him square in the jaw.

4

Healing a Devil

Daisy struggled to get out of bed, but eventually made it to her feet. Evander strongly advised against it, but Daisy insisted on immediately being taken to Alina in her cage. Daisy hobbled down the hallway, her bones aching and muscles screaming the entire way. Rosie supported Daisy with a soft hand on her elbow.

As they came to the main area, Daisy's eyes were immediately drawn to the large contraption in the middle of the sitting room. It consisted of many layers of bars made from various materials. One even glistened like water. It was large and moved like a living being. Each layer seemed so meticulously designed. Daisy couldn't even imagine the time and skill this level of creation required.

Alina paced inside the cage, dragging her claws across the innermost bars with an ominous ticking sound that sent shivers up Daisy's spine. Alina hissed at Daisy, and her animalistic eyes flared like two fires sparking to life. Daisy swallowed hard. Her throat burned with the memory of last night. She struggled to move towards Alina.

With a slight head shake, Daisy took a step back and felt a strong hand gently grasping her shoulder.

"I know, Daisy," Rosie stated softly while gently squeezing her shoulder. "But they need you. She needs you."

Rosie pointed towards a bundle of cloth sitting closely to the bars, but just out of Alina's reach. But it wasn't clothes. Brighid sat in the corner hugging her knees, tears silently streaming down her cheeks. To Brighid, Alina was like a mother. Daisy couldn't even imagine what this situation was doing to Brighid. Daisy froze, weighing her options, trying to suppress her fear.

"Does Abe's journal mention anything about how to fix her?" Arlo asked, breaking through Daisy's panic. Evander started flipping through the journal before stopping and reading a page.

"It says he would use the elder tongue to pull the memory out of Alina's mind which would temporarily revert and delay the mania, but it doesn't solve the problem," Evander answered. He flipped several more pages. "Because it was the mind force that caused her connection to break, there had never been a way to reverse it. With time, the effects wear off, but unlike the other forces, there wasn't an opposite to negate its effects."

"Until now..." Daisy whispered. Although her force was new and experimental, she understood that the time force was opposite to the mind force.

Daisy took one shaky step towards Alina's cage. A low, growl echoed from Alina's throat. Daisy was the only option to save Alina. She took several deep breaths to calm her nerves. In her mind, Daisy knew she could help Alina, but in the back of her head, a thought nagged: *If the roles were reversed, would Alina do the same?* Daisy was nearly certain Alina would not do the same, but Daisy wasn't going to let that stop her.

"I think the time force will allow me to reverse this," Daisy stated, trying to sound confident, but her knees buckled. She hoped no one noticed.

"Potentially," Evander pondered. He stroked his chin while reading later parts of the journal. "But your skills and force are still untested."

"The time force might not be well known, but the answers often just… come to me. It's like a dream with all the answers in it. I don't know how to explain it any other way, but I know I can help her." Daisy rolled her shoulders back and lifted her chin. As much as she wanted to run away, she wasn't going to back down. The room fell quiet as everyone seemed to assess Daisy's offer.

"We don't have many options here," Arlo voiced.

"You are right, but there are risks here. Grave risks," Evander indicated.

"Like my conduction breaking?" Daisy interjected. "This requires strong conduction, maybe even elder tongue and I know very little of it. My conduction could break while trying to fix hers."

"You're not like the rest of us, Daisy," Evander stated. "You created a force. The only comparison we have to you is Abe and the Grand Master. As far as we know, they can't be broken like us. They are predisposed to be able to use the elder tongue. We can assume you are the same."

"But I don't know any of the words."

"Abe has a dictionary of sorts in his journal. It may not be exact, but I think we can piece something together. If you are willing to try, that is."

Daisy looked at the faces before her. Evander seemed eager and willing to try. Rosie looked concerned and Brighid looked terrified, though she was looking at Alina and not at Daisy. Arlo seemed intrigued, but he rarely expressed large emotions. He was often difficult to read and kept mostly to himself. She was the only answer they had, and who was she to deny them of their friend, of their family.

Daisy let out a deep breath and closed her eyes for a moment. *In and out. In and out.* She focused on her breathing and slowly calmed herself enough to think clearly. With her eyes closed, she couldn't see Alina. Her heart slowed. She turned her back on the cage and thought of the vision that gave her the spell to fix her neck. She needed some direction in how to proceed. Then a realisation dawned on her. Daisy's neck injury was severe and life threatening; perhaps the same spell could repair Alina's mind and it wouldn't require the elder tongue.

But would it be strong enough? Was Daisy strong enough to do this?

"I am going to try to fix her, but I don't think I need elder tongue for this. Let me try something first," Daisy stated.

She slowly moved towards the cage. Alina hissed and swiped her elongated claws at Daisy, but Daisy didn't feel fear this time. She was calm. She needed to feel capable and fear only diminished that. Alina continued slashing towards Daisy, but she didn't step back this time. Instead, she moved her hands in circles beside her waist and froze time. The eerie silence of nothingness encompassed Daisy. It was oddly welcomed as it allowed her to focus more. It even eased some of Daisy's fear with getting closer to Alina.

Daisy opened the cage with a quick flick of her wrist and approached Alina. Each step was slowly and carefully placed. Although Daisy knew Alina was frozen, Daisy still feared Alina lashing out again. Subconsciously, Daisy grabbed her neck with one hand. She could feel the ridges of a nasty scar. As Daisy got closer to Alina, Daisy could see the same fear and pain of an injured predator caught in a trap. Daisy almost felt sorry for Alina, but that quickly passed. She needed to repair Alina's injury.

Just like before, Daisy traced a repeated figure eight in a counter clockwise direction. Since there was no obvious injury, Daisy traced the shape across Alina's forehead. There was a tingle in Daisy's arm that slowly extended into her hand. Silver sparks danced across Alina's head before absorbing and disappearing into her skin. Daisy could feel time rewinding in Alina's mind until there was a sort of click and Daisy knew she could let go. To ensure her safety, however, Daisy stepped out of the cage and resealed it before unfreezing time.

Rapidly, Alina's eyes softened and turned back to their regular red and purple. Her hair smoothed of frizziness and her nails retracted to a normal length. She straightened her posture and appeared completely human. Brighid ran towards the cage and reached her arms through the bars towards Alina. Gently, Alina grabbed hold of Brighid's hand before rushing into a hug through the bars.

"I am so sorry you had to see that," Alina sobbed. She stroked Brighid's hair who was also crying. "I never intended for this to happen."

"You may have not intended it, but you almost killed Daisy. I think you need to explain yourself," Rosie snapped. Alina released Brighid and turned towards the others. Alina's eyes looked towards the floor and her shoulders hunched forward. She looked like a scolded child which Daisy oddly enjoyed. Alina never seemed deterred by much, but this outburst appeared to have changed her.

"You're right. I do have to explain, but I would be more comfortable talking outside of the cage," Alina pleaded.

"Daisy, what did you do to Alina? Is this temporary?" Arlo questioned. Daisy was surprised to hear him speak. He rarely joined the conversation unless it encouraged him to be lazy or… protected Brighid. Daisy assumed it was the latter option.

"I used the same conduction Evander used on my neck, but on Alina's mind. I honestly don't know how long, or if, it will hold. I cannot determine the extent of her injury," Daisy responded. Alina looked toward Daisy. Her mouth was opened and her eyebrows raised.

"You - you saved me?" Alina sputtered. "After everything I did, you still saved me?"

"I am not a monster, Alina. I help those who need it," Daisy retorted.

"But I nearly killed you. In fact, you should be dead."

"Are you surprised or disappointed?" The room fell completely silent in response to Daisy's remark. It was almost like time had frozen, but Daisy knew that it hadn't.

Everyone looked at Daisy, horror struck, and she knew she said the wrong thing. She couldn't take it back now, so she crossed her arms and challenged anyone to speak out. Alina seemed to come out of her shock first with a head shake.

"Surprised. I am surprised," Alina defended. "I have only fragmented memories of my manic episodes, but I know I hurt you badly. I wasn't in the right mind frame."

"She is sick, Daisy," Evander interjected, but before he could continue, Daisy held up her hand to silence him.

"So your conduction is broken and you never thought to tell any of us?" Daisy asked angrily, completely ignoring Evander's comment. She clenched her fists at her side and left out a huff of air. She had nearly died, but somehow, Alina was becoming the victim. "What did you expect to happen when you started experiencing mania? What if it had been Brighid instead of me?"

There were gasps about the room. Daisy knew she was stepping further and further across the line, but she couldn't seem to stop herself. The built up anger from Alina's constant belittlement and exclusion of Daisy appeared to have surfaced at last. Daisy looked around at the shocked and accusatory stares. Clearly, there was no winning here. Daisy groaned and ran out of the room. She needed air. She needed space. She needed to be away from everyone else.

She stopped on the deck and looked at the heavy forest surrounding the cabin. Bracing herself against the railing, she took several slow, deep breaths to calm herself. Memories of her mother flooded her mind and pained her heart. It was like being back at home all of a sudden. Daisy began to cry. She needed to be alone. She took off running into the forest.

"Daisy!" Rosie called just as Daisy entered the woods, but she didn't stop. She needed to get away, so she just kept running and running and running. Her feet carried her through the forest. Tears poured down her cheeks. She kept moving forward, not knowing where she was going, but knowing it was away from Alina and the others.

The past year was exhausting. Daisy needed to learn from the others, but Alina was always there with her scrutiny and harsh words. Daisy had grown up in a similar environment, but something about Alina was worse. For some reason, Daisy craved Alina's approval. Having known more of what her sister did to her parents, their torment somehow hurt less. Alina's torture was optional, however. She chose to treat Daisy poorly, and the choice was worse than the hundreds of lashes that criss-crossed Daisy's back. The scar on Daisy's neck would be an enduring remainder of Alina's cruelty.

Daisy ran blindly, tears blocked her vision while anger and pain clouded her mind. She ran across the river. Her lungs burned. She wanted to stop, but her body just kept moving. Eventually, her tears dried and legs stopped moving. She collapsed on the ground. Her chest heaved as her lungs struggled to take in enough air. With a few deep breaths, she steadied her breathing. She stood and began aimlessly walking through the forest. Her emotions had subsided some, but she was still not ready to go back to the group. A distant train whistle meant she was approaching the small town close to their cabin. They occasionally needed supplies that nature could not provide so they often set up around small communities.

She could hear the hustle and bustle of the town. It was inviting, intoxicating almost. The town made Daisy feel normal again, human even. It reminded her of everything before she became a conductor. Right now, it felt like exactly what she needed. Usually, she went with someone else at a minimum. It was safer to travel in pairs, as someone was always on guard. It was likely a dim-witted idea for Daisy to go to town by herself, but in the weeks they had been here, they had never come across another conductor. The probability of that changing today seemed minimal, and Daisy desperately needed to be away from the others and feel some semblance of normalcy.

Daisy headed to the town hoping for a distraction, for something that would pull her temporarily out of her pain and sorrow. The small market often had plenty of fresh fruit and vegetables, but also many unique treats and pleasures. She had been to the market many times with the others, but never by herself. Daisy often enjoyed idly browsing and chatting with the merchants, while Evander or Arlo kept guard. She thought it would be a great distraction and the needed time to reset, but she also knew it wasn't exactly safe to be by herself. She just needed to feel normal again. Although not always wise, it was often the small pleasures of ordinary life that allowed Daisy to slow down and remember where she came from. Since she became a conductor, it was often hard to remember that she was still human.

The others often compared her to Abe and Azalea, but they weren't exactly human either. They had taken human form, but weren't entirely human. Daisy, however, was human. She was born to human parents and lived a human life before any of this. It was an unnerving comparison. She oddly wished she wouldn't be compared to them. She had always been compared to her sister by her parents, but she was always seen as less. Now that she was seen as an equal to Azalea, it was uncomfortable, but simultaneously freeing. She had the opportunity to break free of her sister, but constantly found herself being sucked back into comparison. She just wanted to be separate.

"Looking for anything in particular?" a merchant enquired, breaking through Daisy's reverence. Daisy glanced at his eyes and noticed two plain green eyes staring back at her. She felt herself relax minutely. *No signs of other Conductors yet.*

"Nothing in particular. Just browsing," Daisy replied. She quickly glanced around her at the crowd, looking for any signs of anything amiss.

"Ah, so spending money you shouldn't spend on things you don't really need," the merchant suggested with a wink. Daisy lightly laughed and flicked her hair behind her shoulder. "What a lovely ring. Shouldn't you be accompanied by its giver?"

Daisy looked sadly upon the golden stone shining on her finger. She could see her eyes reflecting back at her: silver and gold. An unusual combo even for a conductor.

"He is... indisposed at the moment," Daisy whispered.

"Ah. I see. Well, if you see anything you wish to purchase just shout." The merchant turned away. Daisy picked up a trinket and idly turned it in her hands.

"He's right, you know. You really should be accompanied," muttered a stranger behind her. His voice was gruff like he was recovering from some illness. Daisy didn't look up from the trinket she was surveying.

"I am quite alright on my own, thank you," Daisy retorted, hoping the stranger would take the hint and leave her alone. She needn't be told by anyone what she should or should not do. She also knew she shouldn't talk to anyone for too long. Long conversations meant questions and Daisy didn't want to answer anything unnecessarily.

"You may be alright on your own, but that doesn't mean you should be alone." Annoyed, Daisy threw down the trinket and turned to the stranger with an exasperated sigh.

"Look -" she was cut short. Staring back at her were two eyes, one blue and one green. A small scar just above the lip and a mess of black hair took her breath away.

Abe.

5

A Break in Time

Abe's fist smashed into Henry's face. Henry fell backwards, but stopped mid air. The world silenced and everything stilled. Time had stopped, and if time had stopped … that meant Daisy was near.

His heart sped up at the thought of seeing Daisy, but his stomach immediately dropped. When time unfroze, Henry would awake and his connection with Abe's mind would reconnect, throwing Abe back under Azalea's control. Abe didn't understand the time force at all, but it seemed not to impact him as it did other Conductors. Either way, this was his opportunity to try and run. He turned to bolt, but as soon as he started to run, time was released. There was a large thump as Henry slammed into the ground. A painful snap cracked inside of Abe's head, and he found himself trapped back in his mind. Whatever chance he had of breaking through and getting away crumbled with the release of Daisy's spell.

Henry sat up and stared at Abe looking dumbfounded. Blood trickled from a small cut on his lip. He spat to the side then wiped away blood from his mouth.

Henry's eyes locked on Abe. His jaw clenched and his hands formed fists. He grunted before standing up and trudging towards Abe.

"You broke through," Henry snapped, extending his hand in twisting motion and pulling the truth from Abe's mind. "How?"

"Connection to my family," Abe responded through clenched teeth. "This space brought Alina back to my mind and temporarily released my consciousness."

"Huh." Henry circled Abe with a heavy gaze. "I will have to report this to the Grand Master."

After several moments of staring at Abe, Henry returned to investigating the blackened earth. He eventually stopped in the middle of the field where there was a deep reddish brown splotch. Abe had seen enough battlefields to know it was blood. There was enough blood that likely the victim did not survive. Alina likely killed someone in her mania.

Guilt washed over Abe. Had he been there, he could have prevented this. Back at Daisy's family estate, he sacrificed himself to allow the others to get away from the Grand Master. In doing so, he left Alina open to mania. Abe had given Alina regular treatments to keep the elder tongue from plaguing her mind. Over the past year, Alina wouldn't have received any treatments. This was likely an outburst of mania. Abe only hoped that her victim had been an animal and not another human.

"Do you see anything of use? Any direction to follow?" Henry enquired. This was at least something Abe could answer without giving away anything.

"Truly, I do not. The fire damage is intense, but I can't see any footprints or broken tree limbs."

"Agreed. Shall we head to town then?" Abe paused. He knew Daisy was close but he didn't know how close or which way to go. He didn't know if she was in town or out in the woods. All he knew was that she was here. He felt the pull of the mind force making Abe support Henry's suggestion.

"Yes. That's an option."

Henry looked to the sky to determine their location and took off in a particular direction. Abe reluctantly trailed behind. They walked for a while until the distant blow of a whistle indicated the town was near. Henry continued plodding along right into the centre of town.

The vibrant commotion of the market enveloped Abe's senses; he enjoyed being around people. Besides the odd mind controlled mission, he had barely been around people in the last year. Azalea mostly kept him in a room and locked the door. She would sometimes release his mind while she slept, but the room was locked with magic that he could never escape. But really, by being trapped in the room and under mind control when out, he never got to interact with people. Abe liked being around other people, even with his mind trapped. Some even smiled and waved at him. It was refreshing.

Henry moved ahead and spoke to some merchants about the fire last night. Abe lingered behind. He found he had some freedom to move his head and was able to survey the market. Abe assumed Henry gave him freedom to watch out for threats, but Abe liked the ability to move his head willingly.

He looked down the one aisle and saw a swish of sandy blonde hair that seemed familiar. He focused on the hair and felt a strong compulsion to move towards it. His feet started to carry him forward towards the hair and away from Henry without Abe even noticing. There was a light laugh that made his heart speed up. He found his feet moving quicker. Like metal to a magnet, he couldn't help moving towards the woman.

She was wearing a white blouse with a plaid dress overlay. A tight corset cinched her waist in. Brown leather walking boots completed her look. Effortless curls tumbled down her back with a blue daisy comb pinning back some wayward pieces. She flicked her hair behind her shoulder and Abe noticed a large yellow stone adorning her hand.

Daisy.

Clear as day, standing in front of him, was Daisy. So innocent and pure and completely oblivious to what was going on around her. His heart jumped and he could feel a fuzziness in his mind dissolving the connection with the Grand Master. *Could Daisy break through the connection?* Then a hand clenched his shoulder and the connection slammed back into Abe's head.

"Well, the Grand Master said she wanted you to find her sister. I am guessing that is her," Henry stated. "The Grand Master placed some elder tongue spell on you that would draw you towards her should you ever sense her. When you vanished, I assumed that was why. And when you broke through at the clearing, I figured we must have been close to her sister. I just didn't realise how close."

Abe felt fear grasp his heart. He was manipulated yet again, and now Daisy was in danger. He tried to move, but with Henry's grasp, Azalea's hold was stronger.

"Shall we capture her then?" Henry suggested and Abe could start to feel his feet moving. Abe tried to struggle against Henry, but nothing changed. Henry kept pushing and Abe kept moving forward.

"No," Abe managed. There was a brief moment of freedom and Abe leaned into it. "Let me convince her to come with us. It will be easier."

Henry glared at Abe. His brow furrowed and his eyes narrowed.

"I will be watching. One wrong move, and I will end you… and her." Abe nodded. "Don't forget that we control your mind. I still have a say in what you do and what you tell her."

Abe started to walk towards Daisy. He tried to plan what he was going to say and do. When he thought of their reunion, he thought he would be in full control of his mind. He thought he would be able to tell her how much she meant to him, how much he loved her, but instead his mind was corrupted and his options limited. He could feel Henry and Azalea sifting through options in his mind of what to say and do. It pained him that he found her and it nearly killed him that he was being forced to take her with them. He had to avoid this ever coming to fruition.

Abe listened carefully as she talked to the merchant. He commented on her ring and Abe's heart fluttered. She still wore it, his engagement ring to her. *Did that mean she still loved him?* Abe quickly glanced around and saw no signs of his studies or Alina. Daisy was likely alone, and obviously not paying nearly enough attention to her surroundings.

"He's right, you know. You really should be accompanied," Abe managed. The force of trying to break through the mind force and his lack of talking made his voice sound harsh and unfamiliar to even his own ears. Daisy didn't even look up.

"I am quite alright on my own, thank you," Daisy retorted and flicked her hair over her shoulder. She barely even turned to look at who was talking. He knew his voice was raspy and weak, but *couldn't she tell it was him?*

"You may be alright on your own, but that doesn't mean you should be alone." Abe tried it as a warning, but knew when she tossed down the trinket it had failed. She spun on her heel to face him.

"Look -" She stopped. Her mouth slowly opened as realisation dawned on her. Abe feared what she may do next. *Would she run? Would she attack him? Would she hug him?* Instead, she lifted her hand and jabbed him in the ribs. Abe flinched.

"Ow!" Abe exclaimed. "What was that for?"

"You're real. You're actually *here*." Daisy looked around him at the passing faces, before coming back to stare at him. Everyone around them was quickly moving away.

"Yes."

"How?" Daisy's eyebrows drew together. She began looking around for anyone with him. Abe could see Henry circling Daisy in his peripheral vision. "No. You shouldn't be here."

"Daisy, it's me." She stepped away from him and bumped into the merchant's table. A knick knack fell off the table and smashed against the ground. Daisy's chest rapidly rose and fell. Her eyes were wide and Abe could feel her intense anxiety. He wanted to tell her to run, but he couldn't manage to get the words out.

"No. No, it's not." She stumbled backwards. She looked around, whether for a way out or some type of support, Abe wasn't sure. She needed a way out, but Henry was closing in. She was running out of time and opportunities. Abe's hand reached out towards her. "You can't be here. It's just not possible that you broke away from her."

"You're right," Henry stated from behind her. Before Daisy could react, Henry wrapped his arm around her waist, pinning her arms to her side. In one hand, he held a sharp knife pressed harshly against her throat. Abe wondered why no one around them reacted, but as he glanced around, he noticed the market was empty. Somehow, Henry had enchanted everyone to leave, and Daisy was so distracted by Abe, she never noticed. Henry stared at Abe. "We tried your way. Now, it's my turn."

"Let go of me!" Daisy screamed and squirmed in his grasp. The knife nicked her collarbone, and a small drop of blood dripped down onto her chest. She winced and stopped moving. "You bastard!"

"Now, move quietly," Henry spat and started pushing Daisy forward.

They exited the mayhem of the town and entered the quiet of the woods. Hardly anyone even glanced at the trio. Abe could only assume Henry was casting some glamour or mind control that caused passers-by to avert their eyes and ignore their presence. Daisy tried to squirm one more time to free herself, but Henry promptly cut her throat and Abe heard her scream. She clutched her throat as blood welled between her fingers. Henry grabbed Daisy and Abe's hands.

"Now," Henry screamed. Abe conjured the transportation spell. They all started to fly and suddenly landed in the same clearing Abe had originally left from. Daisy immediately pulled her hand away and started running. Before she got too far, Henry cast a root spell, tripping Daisy. She fell flat on her face and did not move. She appeared unconscious, as the blood trickled onto the ground beside her. Henry picked her up and swung her over his shoulder like a sack of flour.

"Bag yourself and let's get going," Henry instructed, which Abe was forced to oblige. They began walking back to Azalea's camp with Daisy unconscious and Abe under her control.

He had officially stolen Daisy, and he felt awful about it.

6

Cold Trails

Rosie waited for a few minutes to see if Daisy would come back. She knew that Daisy needed time to process and chasing after her would not help. When it became clear that Daisy was going to be gone for a while, Rosie entered the cabin. She always felt uncomfortable in the presence of the other Conductors without Daisy and this time was no exception.

"Where is Daisy?" Brighid enquired.

"She went for a walk. I think she just needs time to reset," Rosie replied.

"Where did she go though?" Evander interjected.

"Into the woods. She will be back soon. I am sure of it," Rosie stated, mostly trying to convince herself that Daisy would come back. In the past year of harsh training, Daisy had never run off. Something about this situation felt off, but Rosie would never mention that. She couldn't let them doubt her. She needed them to trust her.

"Did you actually speak with her?" Alina asked from inside the cage.

"Not exactly, but she will be back. She has to come back eventually," Rosie said.

"She just performed strong conduction and it can have lasting effects. Damaging effects. She may have even used elder tongue. We really don't know what she did, but either way, this conduction could have severely damaged her. You should have gone after her. This is not the time for her to be alone." Alina slammed her hands against the cage to reinforce her point. Rosie was surprised by Alina's reaction. It was almost like Alina cared about Daisy.

"She seemed fine when she left," Evander added. "According to Abe's journal, mania shows quickly, so we would have seen the signs before she left."

"You are making a bold assumption, Evander. You have hardly any proof, and you should be more concerned about Daisy," Alina snapped. Rosie was befuddled and hurt by Alina's comment. *Was Alina suggesting that no one cared?*

"How dare you!" Rosie spat. "We all care about Daisy. We all care about this family. She saved you. Evander convinced her to save you, and she did. Without her, none of us would be here, and you have the nerve to suggest that we don't care! How dare you!?"

The room fell silent. Alina looked around at the faces in the room before resting her eyes on Rosie. A small tear hung on the corner of Alina's eye. Rosie placed her hands on her hips, beckoning Alina to challenge her.

"Rosette. That is not what I am saying. I am suggesting that someone should have gone after her to make sure she was safe and alright. The elder tongue and strong conduction can change people even if they don't experience mania. It can impair judgement or slow their reactions. Neither of which would be beneficial to Daisy when she is alone."

Arlo stood from his seat in the corner and moved in between Rosie and Alina. "I will go. I will make sure Daisy is fine then I will come back. Okay?"

Alina glared at Rosie before nodding her head. Rosie agreed. He left the cabin and headed for the woods. Rosie watched through the window until Arlo disappeared into the forest. Evander continued flipping through Abe's journal while Alina and Brighid talked in hushed tones through the cage.

Rosie paced alongside the window waiting for any sign of Arlo and Daisy. Rosie was starting to get anxious. Arlo had only been gone for a few minutes, but Rosie couldn't sit still any longer.

"I think we should go look for them," Rosie announced. Evander barely looked up from his book while Alina and Brighid remained talking. "I said, we should go look for them."

"I am sure they are fine," Evander stated and absentmindedly flipped another page. "Although lazy, Arlo is quite competent and Daisy seems to hold herself well enough."

"When Alina went missing, she went crazy and nearly killed Daisy. Are we really assuming that they are fine? Something feels off and I don't like it."

"She's right, Evander," Alina interjected. Rosie was baffled by Alina's sudden amenability since Alina was often quickly dismissive of Rosie. "You should go look for them. Something could have happened."

Evander sighed, stood from his chair, and snapped his book shut. He grabbed his coat off a hook. Rosie quickly followed him, eager to do something.

"I will stay with Alina," Brighid announced.

"You could let me out and I could go with you," Alina offered. Evander stopped in the doorway and looked back.

"Until we are sure whatever Daisy did worked and you are stable, we have to keep you in there. Brighid, she must stay in the cage. Under no circumstances will you let her out of the cage," Evander said sternly. Brighid looked as though she wanted to protest but then she thought better of it and nodded her head meekly.

The door slammed shut behind them as Evander and Rosie made their way out to the forest. The sun was just starting to set, casting strange shadows on the ground. Evander seemed less concerned and more irritated by the situation. Rosie showed Evander where Arlo and Daisy entered first to start their search mission. Luckily, neither of them seemed concerned about covering their tracks. Footprints were heavy and branches were snapped, making tracking both of them relatively easy.

Eventually, they came to a river. Rosie knew the town was just on the other side of the river which Daisy enjoyed visiting. It was likely where they both were. Rosie hoped they were having a drink at the bar or enjoying the market, but something about that idea felt wrong.

"Shall we cross?" Evander suggested.

"SHHHH!"a voice hissed from the nearby bushes. Evander and Rosie turned towards the sound. Arlo stuck his head out of the bush and indicated to them to crouch down.

They both bent down and made their way over to the bush where Arlo was hiding.

"What is the meaning of this?" Evander whispered. Arlo waved his hand at Evander indicating they should be quiet. They sat in silence for a long while. Arlo let out a heavy sigh and relaxed into a posture of defeat. It seemed as though whatever Arlo was waiting for was not coming.

"It was him. He was here," Arlo explained. Rosie looked at him perplexed.

"Who was here?" Rosie asked.

"Abe was here," Arlo stated as though that should have been obvious. "Abe was here with someone else. I saw them cross the river towards town and I thought he might come back. I thought he would come back to us. I couldn't cross. I couldn't go after him, but I thought maybe… maybe if he came back… maybe I could do something. Maybe I could save Abe."

There was a desperate sadness to his voice that Rosie had never seen him express before. In general, Arlo was pretty flat. He would occasionally smile when he made Brighid laugh, but otherwise he was even and inexpressive. This amount of emotion was abnormal and made Rosie even more uncomfortable.

"Are you sure? Are you positive it was Abe?" Evander inquired.

"As sure as day," Arlo replied unwaveringly. He puffed out his chest as if challenging any further questions. "Black hair. Green and blue eyes. It was him. His voice was his voice. He even walked like himself, but something was odd. He wasn't himself. I think the Grand Master still holds his mind."

"How is that possible? I thought a conductor had to be close to control someone's mind," Rosie added.

"Yes and no," Evander started. "The Grand Master has more range than the average conductor. Her powers outweigh all others, so her use of the mind force has far more reach than all others. It is also possible that she is using a conduit."

"What is a conduit?"

"A conduit is another conductor with the same primaries. A piece of their powers can be transferred to each other or one conductor can act through the other. Distance doesn't seem as crucial when a conduit is in place. It's like a special type of connection. Like how true love doesn't waver over time or distance, a conduit doesn't seem impacted either."

"So Azalea could have hundreds of conduits out there doing her bidding and using her powers and we wouldn't know."

"Yes," Arlo and Evander replied at the same time. Evander looked surprised at Arlo.

"You aren't the only one that pays attention to Abe's lessons. I just make it less obvious," Arlo stated. "Conduits are terrifying because it's essentially agreed upon mind control that provides extra benefits to the host."

"So the person with Abe was likely a conduit then? Or are we assuming Azalea is close?" Rosie inquired.

"I doubt the Grand Master is close," Evander suggested. "I would better assume that she is well guarded and using conduits or enslaved minds to do her bidding."

"Wait," Arlo interjected. "Why are you two here?"

"You had been gone a while and had not returned with Daisy. Rosie was getting worried."

"I was tracking her and noticed she crossed the river towards town. I was trying to find her tracks on the other side when I saw Abe."

"You mean to tell me that Abe and Daisy went in the same direction?" Rosie asked venomously. A horror-struck look painted Arlo's face as realisation dawned on him. Even Evander looked concerned.

"He's got her hasn't he?" Arlo whispered.

"I think that is a correct assumption," Evander stated. Rosie promptly punched him in the shoulder for his carefree tone. "Ouch! What was that for?"

"If Abe was with a conduit, that means he is under Azalea's control. If he is under Azalea's control, that means Daisy left with Azalea and not just Abe. That means Azalea now as all the creators of the forces in her control. Do you understand now?" Rosie's temper flared at his lack of consideration.

"We need to warn the others," Arlo said panicked and took off running towards the cabin. Rosie and Evander were quick to follow. When they arrived at the cabin, Alina sat on the floor of her cage. Brighid had brought some pillows and blankets and made a bed beside the cage. She was softly snoring and Rosie hated to wake her.

"You have returned without Daisy," Alina said quietly and stood to move as far away from Brighid as possible. The rest followed her lead. "Where is she?"

"Abe got to her," Evander provided.

"Abe is here?" Alina asked eagerly.

"Was here," Arlo stated. "He was under the control of a conduit. Daisy and Abe both went in the direction of town. When neither came back… I assume he has captured her."

"This is not good." Alina began pacing inside her cage.

"We understand that Daisy being a prisoner is not ideal, but -" Evander started

"No," Alina interrupted. "I don't think you do. Together, the embodiment of the forces have extra powers. Since the emergence of the fifth force, they have been out of balance and unable to properly harmonise. With Daisy in their grasp and the forces being rebalanced…. I am terrified to think of what the Grand Master could accomplish if she tried."

Evander paled. Even with his knowledge, it seemed like the thought had not occurred to him. Rosie was starting to feel even more anxious than she already did.

"So what do we do then?" Rosie asked.

"We get an army and we fight," Alina stated and pounded her fists against the bars of her cage. Brighid stirred and Alina immediately lowered her voice. "We must free both Daisy and Abe before anything worse happens."

"Where do we get an army?" Arlo asked. A sly smile crossed Alina's face that made Rosie shiver.

"I might have a few ideas."

7

Be our Guest

Daisy awoke feeling groggy and swore. She could feel the burning sensation of an open wound on her hand and neck. As she moved to feel the cut on her neck, she found her hands shackled to the wall. Even more concerning was the fact that her feet were also chained together meaning she could not run. She could barely even move. She rattled the chains to assess their strength but found the movement taxing and painful.

Looking around, she noticed she was in some type of cell. There was a barred door on one wall and a straw mattress opposite it. She sat on the floor in between the door and the bed, with her back propped up against the wall. The walls were covered in deep scratches, the origin of which was unknown to Daisy. Daisy assessed the possibility of conducting her way out of the cuffs, but she felt completely drained. It was like her connection to the forces was empty. *Where was she? How did she get here?* Her mind raced through her memories trying to remember exactly what happened that caused her to be here.

Abe.

She found Abe in the market. She immediately knew something was off about him, but she couldn't stop herself from wanting to be with him. Abe found her, not Azalea. *But was it Abe's doing? Or her sister's?* It was obvious now that Abe was still under Azalea's control, but she had hope. Maybe now with her here, she could free Abe, bring down Azalea, and liberate the Conductors from Azalea's oppressive and overreaching rule. It seemed nearly impossible, but Daisy wanted to stay optimistic. She had to have hope that she could do something or else all would be lost.

"You're awake," said a deep voice from the shadows. When he stepped into the light, Daisy recognized him as the man who was with Abe in the market. He had thick, messy hair and a beard. He had red and purple eyes like Azalea, but his face was disfigured by a long, red scar.

"Yes, and I find myself chained to a wall," Daisy retorted while shaking the chains binding her. Her wrist and arms ached from the motion.

"You're a prisoner."

"That's obvious. If you treat your guests like this, I imagine you'd have very few friends." He scoffed and walked away from Daisy's cell.

Daisy rested her head against the wall. Her wrists felt raw, her head ached, and her whole body felt weak to her very soul. Something about this place drained her powers and her energy. She couldn't even feel the forces to connect to them. Azalea had clearly done her research to ensure Daisy had limited opportunities for escape. She pushed against the chains one more time.

"They won't budge," announced a soft voice with a familiar accent from across the hall. "They seem indestructible. Even with the powers some people have used against them, they don't ever seem to break."

"That is not what I wanted to hear," Daisy muttered. "Have there been many other people here?"

"Yes, most are in worse shape than you." Daisy flopped her head to the side. Across the hall was the outline of a person sitting in a cell. She could not make out many features besides short, red hair and a skinny body. "What is the world like outside? I've been here for many, many months. I don't even know the season or the day. What is it like?"

"I wouldn't know. I've been in hiding for about a year, so my perception of the outside is limited."

"I miss the outside. I miss my family. I miss my daughter." There was a deep sadness to the voice. Daisy wished to comfort her cellmate, but all she could do was talk.

"What's your family like?" Daisy inquired but never got the chance to hear the response. The man returned and unlocked the cell. He reached over Daisy and detached her chains from the wall.

"Stand up" he commanded. Daisy thought about refusing, but she did not want to stay in the cell any longer than she had to. She stood and the man started pulling her chains which dug even more into her wrists and ankles. Daisy winced from the pain but followed the man. She quickly looked back at the resident of the other cell, but did not get a better glance.

They wound through a series of rough cut, stone hallways that looked more like tunnels. Daisy quickly became lost, but felt as though they were gradually climbing upwards.

"What's your name?" Daisy asked groggily. He looked sideways at her with suspicion.

"Henry," he replied curtly.

"And where, if I may ask, are we going?"

"The Grand Master wants to see you," Henry replied while forcefully pulling on Daisy's chains urging her forward.

"How long was I out?" The man grunted, seemingly irritated with Daisy's questioning. It was clear he was not in the mood for idle chit chat.

"Several days. There are runes to prevent your Conductor's healing. You seemed especially susceptible to the runes and took extra long to wake. Now, hush. Your jabbering is awfully annoying."

Daisy fell silent, and Henry continued to drag her through the twisting halls. Eventually, the ground flattened and the hallway opened up to a large round room. The roof was upheld by sturdy wooden beams, while a sizable stained glass window projected peculiar shadows and colours throughout the room. Another hallway branched off the other side of the room. A heavy circular table sat in the middle of the room and was covered in papers. Several people, all of whom Daisy didn't recognise, stood around the table. As she moved further into the room, they all turned to stare at her. A shiver ran through her body, raising goose bumps across her skin from the weight of the stares.

Henry tugged on her chains and moved her to one side of the room. Three chairs sat in a row. The two side chairs were high-backed and adorned with ornate carvings in their wood. Deep red fabric covered the cushions. The middle chair however, was more like a throne. It was on a raised platform to elevate it above the other two. Precious stones were embedded into the gold plated wood. And, lounging on the throne, looking completely bored, was Azalea.

Her golden hair nearly matched her chair. Thick, luscious curls draped down her back. Her eyes were like a perfect garnet and amethyst. Her lips and cheeks were a lively pink. She wore a black dress that clung to every curve of her body and made her skin look like china. She was hauntingly beautiful. Daisy couldn't look away.

As they approached Azalea's throne, Henry stopped and locked Daisy to a metal circle stuck in the ground. Daisy became aware of how weary and feeble her legs were in the absence of strain on the chains and the cessation of movement. She collapsed on the ground in front of Azalea and felt completely pathetic. This was not how she had planned her reunion with her sister or Abe for that matter.

Azalea eyed Daisy. She ejected herself from her throne and moved closer to Daisy. She walked around Daisy in slow circles. Daisy lazily tracked Azalea with her head. Suddenly, Azalea clapped her hands and all the other people in the room turned their immediate attention to Azalea.

"Leave us, now," Azalea commanded. Everyone put down whatever they were working on and made their ways towards the hallway opposite to the one Daisy had entered from. They were now alone. Daisy turned her head towards her sister who stood over her.

Azalea immediately fell to her knees and levelled with Daisy. Before Daisy understood what was happening, Azalea wrapped her arms around Daisy in a suffocating hug. Daisy was frozen in place, unsure of what to do. Azalea pulled back and looked Daisy in the eyes. She smiled so big that even her eyes crinkled. Daisy didn't understand Azalea's reaction. It was certainly unexpected.

"I am glad to see you here," Azalea gushed. She pushed a piece of hair back from Daisy's face, tenderly tucking it behind her ear.

"I cannot say that I am glad to be here," Daisy hissed and rattled the chains. "Not exactly a warm welcome, Azalea."

Azalea stood and moved back to her throne. She threw herself down and stared at Daisy. She sighed before saying, "I wasn't sure if you would be friendly, or if you'd try to kill me."

"I haven't decided yet."

"Well, not exactly a warm welcome then either."

"I am a prisoner. Why would I welcome you?"

"I thought you would be excited to see me."

"Perhaps under different circumstances, with less chains and deception, our reunification would be different."

"Perhaps." Azalea snapped her fingers, and Henry came back into the room. "Take her back to her cell, Henry. I have some thinking to do."

Henry unclipped her chains from the floor and guided her back down the twisting tunnels. Daisy was too exhausted to analyse their path and had to focus all her energy on staying upright and moving forward. They came to the cell, and Daisy was thrown into it. While she was not attached to the wall, her bindings were still attached to her.

"You're back," said the same voice from earlier.

"Yes, it was not a particularly good journey," Daisy responded.

"I am sorry to hear that." There was a pause, and Daisy was not sure what to say.

After a few moments, Daisy broke the silence: "Why are you here?"

"Leverage," the voice whispered. Daisy could barely hear the response at all. "But you should get some rest. I am sure Henry will be back soon to fetch you."

Daisy suddenly felt the exhaustion overwhelm her. She moved towards the mattress and passed out. Daisy wasn't sure how long she slept, but she was rudely awakened by a kick to the ribs.

"Get up," Henry bellowed. Daisy pushed herself into a seated position. "The Grand Master has requested you join her for a meal."

Henry started pulling on the chain, practically dragging Daisy out of the cell. Her sleep must have been short for she still felt bone tired. Henry tugged on the chains as Daisy trudged behind him. They came to a simple door which Henry opened. The room had nothing but a table and two chairs in it. There was another door, but otherwise the room was completely empty. Henry moved Daisy to one of the chairs and attached her chains to the table. He exited through the door they came into, leaving Daisy alone in the room.

She tested the chains to see if she could escape, but they held firm. After a while, several people started bringing food in. Various platters of decadent food that smelled fantastic, but made Daisy's stomach twist. The thought of eating was nauseating. When the final dish was placed down, Azalea entered the room.

She wore a similar dress to the last time Daisy saw her but, this time, it was a deep green with gold embellishments. She sat in the other chair and started grabbing different foods from the platters.

"Are you going to eat?" Azalea enquired. Daisy rattled the chains in response. "He was supposed to give you enough slack to eat."

"I won't eat in chains."

"You'll get hungry eventually." Azalea picked at the food on her plate. "I just wanted to enjoy a meal with you, like we did when we were young."

Even though their family wasn't close or even really civil, they always ate together. Their parents often discussed the estate and political affairs. During these moments, Azalea and Daisy had brief moments of childhood bliss where they joked and made fun of each other. It was some of Daisy's favourite memories with her sister.

"We aren't young anymore," Daisy responded.

"You are right," Azalea said sadly. They sat in silence for a while before Azalea spoke again. "What is that ring you are wearing? I noticed it when they brought you, but I don't remember you owning it before you went to finishing school."

Daisy looked down and smiled at the silver band with a rough, yellow stone. She ran her thumb across the back of the band. Since Abe left, she had never taken it off. It was a reminder of what she was fighting for and of Abe's love of her. Or what Daisy had interpreted as love before learning about Alina's accident. Her smile faltered.

"It brings you mixed emotions. What is it for?" Azalea asked again.

"Shouldn't you know? You've held Abe's mind captive for over a year," Daisy spat. Her sister could read minds, and Daisy didn't wish to divulge every piece of her life to Azalea.

"Just because I control his mind often, does not mean I am actively involved in it. Only when I send him out into the world do I take active control. Otherwise, it's just passive. I don't look in his memories. They wouldn't be of much use anymore. He's been in hiding and away from most Conductors since Isabetta's death. His memories provide nothing of substance besides images of you. I just prevent him from thinking and acting on his own desires. He does what I need him to, but I am not in his mind constantly. I am not actively watching his memories and monitoring his thoughts."

"That's almost worse." Daisy was horrified at the thought. While Daisy was in a literal prison filled with bars and chains, Abe was a prisoner within his mind and body. He was a shell of a man. Hollow. Empty.

"Hardly. Now, do I need to dig deeper into his mind or shall you just tell me the story of the ring?" Daisy weighed her options. She could imagine the torture Abe had endured and did not wish to cause him more.

"Abe proposed to me. We were on the train back to the family estate, and Abe came up with the idea of us getting married, so I could leave with the Conductors. To become a Conductor. You had died, and I didn't think our parents should lose us both in the span of a year. I needed a reason to leave, and Abe came up with a solution."

Azalea let out a wicked, high pitch laugh that sounded maniacal. It reminded Daisy of Alina in the clearing right before Alina slashed Daisy's throat open. Daisy flinched, but her sister did not seem to notice.

"I forgot about that," Azalea said. "I've died so many times that everything just blurs together."

"Well, I have not forgotten it. I mourned you. I grieved for months and could barely keep my head up. Becoming a Conductor saved me. Abe saved me."

"You're welcome then, I got you here."

"In a horribly cruel way." Azalea looked completely unfazed and actually bored of the discussion. It made Daisy even more enraged.

"So about this betrothal. Was it not all a ruse? Why do you still wear the ring?"

"It was a reminder of what I am fighting for."

"Fighting? Is that what you think you're doing? Ha! Oh darling, my forces could have crushed you and your small band of *warriors* months ago, but I needed to ensure you were safe; I certainly didn't want you accidentally killed. Honestly, I could have captured you many times, but this happened to be the perfect opportunity to acquire you without having to fight a soul."

"Who says it's just us? How do you know we haven't recruited others?" Azalea snapped her head toward Daisy and narrowed her eyes while tapping her fingers against the table top.

"Well, you are either incredibly brave or incredibly stupid, but you're clever and, as you know, I can't get into your mind to see which it is." Daisy had actively been working on preventing mind control as well as additional safeguards against it. It was exhausting, but she was putting all the energy she had left into preventing her sister's intrusions. The time force was the opposite to the mind force, but Daisy was still learning all its quirks. Sometimes, it seemed like the ideas would just pop into her mind, like someone whispered the secrets of the time force to her. It never quite made sense to her, but she accepted whatever she could learn, as no one else could teach her.

"Does that bother you?" Daisy spat. Azalea suddenly stood from her chair and moved to the door. She whispered to someone who quickly scurried off. Azalea returned to Daisy with a deeply self-satisfied smile; Daisy desperately wanted to punch that look off her face.

Henry returned and detached Daisy from the table. Azalea led the way back to the main hall with the large table and throne. Daisy was quickly attached back to the floor. Her legs vibrated from exhaustion and she collapsed to the ground. Each time she was forced to move, she felt even more exhausted. It was becoming harder and harder to prevent Azalea from having access to her mind.

Azalea sat back on her throne and picked at her nails all the while watching Daisy attentively. After a few moments of silence and an uncomfortable stare down, Abe entered the room. He moved as if he was sleepwalking. Daisy could tell that everything about him was off. His mind was not his own and that hurt Daisy more than she expected. Even though she watched Abe intently as he crossed the room, Daisy tried to keep her expression flat and show no change from Abe's arrival.

"Do you want to marry him?" Azalea asked. Daisy looked at Azalea with an open mouth and wide eyes. The forwardness of the question was off-putting and unexpected.

"I- I... I don't know," Daisy stumbled.

"How do you not know? This should be a relatively straightforward question. What is there to not know? Do you want to marry him or not?"

"This is not my Abe. This is but a shell which you have corrupted. I want to marry *my Abe*, not this Abe."

"What if I freed him? Temporarily, long enough to marry. Would you marry him then?"

"Why do you care?"

"I am trying to show you a gesture of good faith. Something to show you that I am not the monster you have created in your mind. I want to give you something you truly desire. I want you to see me as your sister and not this power-hungry, murderous beast that Abe has professed me to be."

"A gesture of good faith? How about my parents not being dead? That would suffice." Azalea cackled like a hyena in response to Daisy's suggestion.

"Some points become fixed. Once a life has passed on, not even the strongest conduction can repair the damage. I, nor anyone else for that matter, can bring back the dead. So what would you desire instead?"

"To be free and not pursued by you. I just want to live without your shadow diminishing my light."

"I do not pursue you. You are now my guest, or my prisoner, but that option remains yours to choose. If you want freedom, join me. It would be easier that way anyways. Now quit with this useless banter and tell me what you want."

Daisy sat in silence to contemplate the question. Her true desires were to be with her family and to be free from her sister, but clearly those were not acceptable. *In a different world where she did not fear her sister, what would she want? What were her desires?*

Abe.

She was crushed when she learned of Abe's love for Alina and how their stories were interlaced. She feared that when Abe was free of Azalea's grasp, that his memories would come back and he would choose Alina over her. She worried that it was all a front and her love for him was unrequited. But regardless of what or why or how, Daisy knew she loved Abe and wished beyond all reason that he felt the same.

"Abe…" Daisy whispered. His head slightly turned towards Daisy. She could have sworn she saw some glimmer in his eyes, some attempt to break through the hold. "I want to be with Abe for the rest of my days."

Azalea clapped her hands making Daisy jump. Azalea squealed like a young child and stood up from her throne.

"How delightful," Azalea exclaimed. "I always love a good wedding!"

"A what?" Daisy asked confusedly.

"A wedding of course! If you are betrothed and you want to be with him, then you shall be wed."

"But I don't want to marry him like-" Daisy stopped not wanting to say the rest. She looked towards Abe with his dazed and vacant stare. Her heart hurt at the thought of him being forced to marry anyone. She loved him, but for all she knew, maybe he loved Alina. Maybe he was supposed to be with Alina.

"Finish your sentence."

"What?" Daisy had become lost in her thoughts and clearly Azalea did not like being left hanging.

"You said you didn't want to marry him like - but then you didn't finish. Why don't you want to marry him?"

"I want to marry him, but I want him to have the choice. If you want us to be wed, he needs to have his own mind. He needs to be able to control what he does." Azalea began pacing the room while stroking her chin. Daisy still thought it weird that her sister was even considering this. *After all, wasn't Azalea also in love with Abe? Wouldn't this matrimony separate Abe from her permanently?*

"I will consider this." She sat back down on her throne and tented her fingers in front of her mouth. "For now, take her back to her cell."

Azalea snapped her fingers and Abe started moving. He unfastened Daisy's chains from the floor and waited for her to stand. She had not realised how long she had been sitting until she stood up and nearly fell over from the numbness in her legs. Somehow, Abe caught her and righted her back to standing position. Daisy looked over her shoulder at Azalea. *Did Azalea tell Abe to catch Daisy? Or did something else happen?* Azalea gave away no indication, as Abe led Daisy out of the room and down the hall into the depths of the fortress.

8

Sagacity

For the first time in a long time, Alina's mind felt clear. She felt more like herself than she had in years. Whatever Daisy did, had worked wonders, but she would never admit it. She would rather remain in the cage, then openly state Daisy had cured her. Her brain finally felt healed, but, based on the looks everyone was giving her, they all thought her insane.

"What do you mean you have ideas?" Rosie snapped. Alina found Rosie annoying; she often found herself wishing Rosie had never tagged along. Even worse, Rosie was often a liability rather than an asset. She was truly useless in a fight and refused to learn or even attempt any conduction. Alina fought not to roll her eyes at Rosie.

"I have been working with Ames for years. He has many groups of loyal studies. Some know more information than others, but I believe they will come to his aid if called upon. At this point, the five of us are not enough. We need reinforcements," Alina explained.

"I agree with you, but how do we find all these studies?" Evander remarked. Alina understood his apprehension. The idea of Abe having other studies, while expected, probably seemed unusual. For Evander and the others, this little family was all they knew. They had all come to Ames and Alina when they were young. At this point, the whole group had been together for thirty years.

"I know the last location of three different groups, and I am hoping they may know the location of the other groups. We can start building our defence in little pieces which will hopefully gain momentum and grow."

"But you don't know where the groups are currently?" Rosie demanded.

"Well…they don't move much. Like Ambrose, they typically hole up in an area for years at a time. They stay well hidden; Ames certainly instilled a deeply rooted fear of the Grand Master within them. He was a very different teacher then." Alina explained. Brighid seemed surprised at the idea of Ames being anything other than kind and stern. Alina gave her a reassuring smile before returning to Evander and Rosie. Arlo seemed less interested and almost asleep, but Alina knew he was listening intently.

"So you are suggesting that we leave our cabin of safety to venture into well hidden areas hoping to find other Conductors that may or may not be loyal to Abe and willing to help. Correct?" Rosie said rather sassily. Alina longed to slap her across the face but, so far, managed to contain herself.

"It's not safe anymore," Arlo stated. As Alina expected, he was paying more attention than his appearance gave away. "They know Daisy was here, and they know we were with her. It's highly likely that the Grand Master will send more people to this area to investigate further. They *will* find us here. Maybe not today or tomorrow, but our days of safety here are numbered."

"He's probably right," Evander offered. Rosie looked insulted that she was being challenged. Alina appreciated the support.

"We need to leave and we need support. I think this is the best plan," Alina stated. Evander stroked his chin and scrunched up his nose. Rosie looked irritated. Arlo appeared to agree with Alina and Brighid was nodding her head excitedly.

"I don't think we have many alternatives. I think this is the wisest option considering all that we have right now," Evander agreed.

"We should leave immediately. If Arlo is right, the Grand Master's forces will soon be upon us," Alina added.

"I am sure we can wait until morning. Get a good night's rest before starting this journey," Rosie pleaded. Alina did not understand why Rosie wanted them to stay. *Could she not see the urgency of the situation? Was she truly so daft?*

"I don't think that wise," Evander stated.

"What about Alina though? Can she be trusted out of the cage? What if her mania hasn't passed yet? Are we putting ourselves in greater danger by letting her out?" Rosie continued.

"This is the sanest I have ever seen her," Arlo added. Alina was slightly taken aback, but Arlo gave her an apologetic glance that eased her anger.

"What about Daisy? We are assuming that Abe has her, but we don't know that for sure. What if we leave and she comes back?"

"If we leave and she comes back then she will be caught by Ames anyways. Assuming that she is with Ames, regardless of evidence, is probably safer for everyone,"

Arlo replied. Rosie crossed her arms and let out a heavy sigh. Alina couldn't help but roll her eyes in annoyance.

"We leave as soon as everyone is packed," Evander stated matter-of-factly. He immediately moved towards Alina's cage and began dismantling it. It wasn't a traditional cage, but a Conductor's cage. He had briefly made a door for Daisy, but as soon as it was used, it disappeared. Now, Evander had to take it apart piece by piece. Rosie left in a huff to begin packing.

As the final piece of the cage dissolved, Alina stepped out of the cage, feeling reborn and alive for the first time in decades. Brighid immediately ran towards Alina, enveloping her in a hug. Alina kissed the top of Brighid's head before gently pushing her back to look her in the eyes.

She had gotten taller over the last bit. Brighid was growing so quickly, and Alina worried that eventually Brighid would not be so dependent on her. Her hair had deepened in colour from a rusty orange to a burnt chestnut. She had noticeable freckles and a narrow nose. Everything about her was delicate and gentle. Her soul was pure, and Alina was desperate to maintain Brighid's child-like innocence for as long as possible.

Brighid turned away and skipped down the hall towards her room. The house was a flurry of activity as they packed in preparation for their departure. Instead of packing, Alina pulled some maps down from a shelf and began plotting their journey. Although trains were the fastest route, they were not necessarily the safest. Alina was positive the Grand Master had spies in the train stations. However, the first leg of their journey was long and a train was really the only option. It was risky, but Alina hoped the risk was worth the reward.

Eventually, everyone was packed and ready to go. Over the past year, they had become quite good at packing lightly and quickly. Evander herded everyone out of the cabin and started towards the closest train station.

"Are you sure we should go to the nearest station?" Rosie asked.

"We need to leave as quickly as possible," Alina stated. She did not have time to argue with anyone and certainly not Rosie of all people.

"I understand that, but that would be the closest station to where they found Daisy. Wouldn't it be wiser to distance ourselves from that area and head to, let's say, the next town?" Alina paused to consider Rosie's statement. She had a good point, and Alina hated it.

"What do you suggest then?" Everyone stopped walking and looked at Rosie. She stood doe-eyed with her mouth open.

"I think," she said tentatively, "that we should walk to the next town over. From there we could take a carriage to the next town and jump on a train from there."

Everyone seemed to ponder her suggestion for a moment before turning towards Evander. Alina was taken aback for a moment that Arlo and Brighid turned to Evander rather than herself. Over the past year, she and Daisy had been guiding the group. Alina reluctantly shared the duties with Daisy. Afterall, Daisy was equivalent to Ambrose and the Grand Master or so the others kept reminding Alina.

In this moment, as her studies turned to Evander, Alina had realised she had lost them. Her mania had shaken their faith in her, and it broke her heart. They were like her children and suddenly, she wasn't their guiding leader. Not telling them about her condition meant losing their trust, and Alina felt the weight of that decision.

"It's not a bad idea, but the next town is a three-day walk," Evander explained as though he had been making decisions for the group for years. "I say we steal a carriage from this town and use it to get to the next town."

"I don't think stealing is the right idea," Brighid added.

"Fine. I have some coin. We will *encourage* someone to give us a very good deal on a wagon."

Having decided on Evander's plan, they took off towards the stables on the outskirts of town. Rosie went ahead to scout for any signs of other Conductors as she was the least likely to be noticed. Alina would have preferred anyone else to go as Rosie was hardly trustworthy. However, their reasoning made sense which Alina found infuriating. Rosie didn't have the tell-tale signs of conduction and could blend in with common people. Rosie finally had a use and it wasn't Alina that figured it out. It felt like the group was moving on without her and she was struggling to find a new place in this team. It baffled Alina how quickly her status changed.

Rosie eventually returned and stated there did not appear to be any Conductors in the stable. To keep attention to a minimum, Evander and Rosie headed back to the stables to obtain a horse and wagon. Alina, Arlo, and Brighid kept watch, from a safe distance, as Evander and Rosie had a quick conversation with the stableman. He was a bulky man with a thick black beard and a bald head. Even from a distance, Alina found him oddly attractive. He led Rosie and Evander around the back of the stable. After a few tense moments, they emerged with two large black horses and a matching barouche. The man shook Evander's hand before he departed leaving Rosie and Evander standing in front of the stable with the horses.

Alina, Arlo, and Brighid quickly made their way towards Evander and Rosie. Brighid seemed incredibly excited about the horses and bounded straight to them. The one horse tilted its head towards Brighid in a curious fashion. Alina found them terrifying and wanted to pull Brighid away from them to protect her, but she resisted. She allowed Brighid to be excited and amazed by the powerful beasts.

"What are they named?" Brighid asked in complete awe.

"This is Lyla and Storm," Rosie introduced while pointing to each respective horse. "They are a well-matched team and should meet our requirements."

"This whole setup seems slightly ostentatious and expensive," Alina interjected.

"Friesians are strong and incredibly agile for their size. They have the endurance we need while also providing the speed and strength," Rosie informed.

"Because you know so much about horses, do you?" Alina retired with an eye roll.

"I know a fair bit actually; my uncle was a breeder, " Rosie boasted. Alina scoffed at Rosie's remark; she didn't like this plan and wanted it to be known.

"And the barouche? We could have just done with a buggy which would likely have been more discreet."

"The buggies they had would not fit all of us. We need something that would partially cover us while still being light for quick travel."

"Alina," Evander interrupted, "this is the best option. We simply do not have time to discuss this any longer; we must leave immediately."

As if Evander had somehow predicted it, a small group of people rounded the corner. The group seemed monotonous at first, but Alina quickly noticed sparks of forces igniting as they approached. Everyone came to the same realisation and piled into the barouche in a panicked fashion. Alina was the last one in. As soon as she stood on the platform, Evander set the horses off causing Alina to fall over onto Rosie's lap.

They sped off out of town. The loud thundering hooves deafening the sound of the elements exploding around them. Evander expertly steered the horses trying to avoid various fireballs and rocks and roots being thrown their way. Alina righted herself and took aim at the pursuant. It was the first time she was going to cast a force since Ames left. Furthermore, it was the first time ever she was going to cast the forces in front of her studies. She hoped beyond reason this would work, that Daisy had somehow fixed her conduction and this would work. Alina desperately needed it to work.

9

Love's Sharp Edge

Daisy walked in front of Abe with her chains rattling across the ground. She seemed almost drunk as she waddled. Under other circumstances, he might have found her walk humorous, but right now, he was horrified. They descended down the spiralling hallways, passing multiple doors and passageways. It was a maze that even Abe didn't understand. It also seemed to change often. The only way he had any idea of where he was going was Azalea controlling his mind.

Daisy tripped on her chains. Abe felt his hands move to catch her, but he wasn't fully able to move. Instead, Daisy face planted into the ground in a mess of tattered skirts and chains. Abe's chin didn't even move to look at Daisy. Out of his peripheral vision, he watched as Daisy tried to untangle herself. Each time she tried to stand up, she would trip on her chains or skirts and fall back down. Abe longed to help her, but he couldn't control any of his limbs. Daisy flopped on her back and let out a frustrated sigh.

"Any chance you could help me?" Daisy snapped. "This does not seem to be working."

It was like Azalea was listening and allowed Abe to help Daisy up. She seemed even more irritated as she was righted. While brushing her dress off, she turned to face Abe.

"Are you aware of what's going on around you?" Daisy inquired as she softly poked Abe on the shoulder as if assessing the situation. "You can't respond to me, can you? You don't even seem to be able to look at me. You seem completely stuck…trapped… I don't even know what to do with you like this."

Abe tried to reply, to explain, but Azalea kept a tight hold on his tongue. Azalea then forced Abe to place a hand on Daisy's shoulder to turn her around and continue walking down the hallway. He could feel her warmth radiating through his hand. He could even feel the slight ridges of the scars that painted her back through her thin clothing. Her shoulder grinded slightly as she swung her arms. Abe disappeared into the odd comfort of her shoulder. He even found himself closing his eyes and listening to the slight click of her shoulder bone every once in a while. She rolled back her shoulder to account for the weight of the chain.

"There are breaks sometimes," Abe muttered in his voice with his own power. Daisy looked sideways at him. He held tighter onto her shoulder, focusing on the ridges and the clicking he could feel. "Little moments of freedom where her claws release just slightly."

"Like now?"

"Yes, like now." But the moment passed as quickly as it came. Azalea clutched his mind more and suddenly took over the conversation. "It's not all that bad."

"How is not having any control over your mind good? You can't say what you want or do what you want… feel what you want." The pain in Daisy's voice crushed Abe. He knew what she was trying to say, but she wouldn't actually say it. Surely, she wanted to know what had changed over the past year with him, with them. *Did she still love him?*

"Sometimes, not having to think is freeing. Someone else makes the decisions, and I can just live without concern or decisions. I don't have to worry about tomorrow or what comes next. I just exist."

"But what is life without mistakes or choices? If everything was decided, we would all be the same. Life would be boring and meaningless."

"Perhaps, but it could be free from harm and pain. There is always more than one story to any event or idea."

They arrived in the hallway of cells. There were several other residents in the hallway. There were several young Conductors crammed in one cell. Another cell housed a middle-age woman who often just silently sobbed. The cell across from Daisy housed an older gentleman with olive skin, fading red hair, and matching light green eyes. He was obviously not a Conductor, and Abe often wondered why he was trapped in the cells. It was a miserable space, and Abe did not want to leave Daisy here. However, he had no choice. Abe unlocked the cell and walked Daisy in. He closed the gate behind them and unlocked the shackles. Red burns were etched into her wrists. The marks almost looked like symbols, but Abe couldn't quite make them out. Daisy rubbed her hands where the chains had chaffed.

"Maybe you should try it," Abe offered as he watched as his hand rise to grace Daisy's cheek. He gently stroked her cheek in a loving manner that he envied. He wanted this to be on his own accord, but it was forced and unnatural.

"I like having my own mind, and I would like you to have yours," Daisy sighed. She moved away from his hand and turned her back to him. She walked into the far back corner of the cell, wrapped her arms around herself, and whispered: "I think… I need to be alone right now."

Abe wanted to stay, but not as Azalea's pawn. He wanted to be himself, and he never wanted to leave her. Finally, after all this time, she was here with him again, but there was nothing he could do. He wanted to tell her the truth, to make everything make sense, but he couldn't. He fought as Azalea started to guide his feet away from her and back to the main hall. Eventually, Azalea won out and he moved out of the cell, locking it behind him. He looked up from the lock; Daisy remained in the corner, as far as possible from the door, with her back facing towards him. He struggled for a moment, and broke through Azalea's hold briefly.

"I do love you," he managed to say. Daisy looked over her shoulder at him with a sad smile and a tear in her eye.

"I am sure you do," Daisy replied as a single tear trickled down her cheek. She did not believe him. It broke his heart. He longed to scream at the top of his lungs that it was him and that he did love her. He opened his mouth, but no words came out. He managed to hold on just a moment longer before the Grand Master forced his feet to move.

As he wound his way back up through the various tunnels, he found his mind wandering. He thought of his Conductors, his studies. He worried about Alina and her condition. He wasn't there to help or heal her. He worried that Evander was not being challenged and getting into trouble. Evander needed constant stimulus and new things to learn or his mind would run wild. Arlo, on the other hand, might thrive under less supervision and more freedom. Perhaps he would rise to the occasion to be more for Brighid. Then there was Brighid. Abe worried she wouldn't be protected and something would happen to her. He wanted her to stay a child as long as she could, but the world was fighting him every step of the way.

Then there was Daisy. His beautiful, little Daisy. Her hair was like golden summer wheat and her eyes were silver and gold. Her skin was fair and delicate but marked by so many sorrows. Whippings, slashes, near death occurrences, all left scars on Daisy; however, she wore those marks with pride now. They were symbols of her strength and all she had overcome. She had matured over the past year; she had found herself. Being separate from her sister seemed to catapult her personal development. Abe wanted to know this version of Daisy more. He wanted nothing more than to remain in her presence, but Azalea had other plans.

The hallway opened up to the main room. Azalea stood at the table in the centre reviewing the various papers on it. She held a letter that seemed very intriguing to her, only putting it down when she realised Abe had arrived. Abe wanted to turn and run away but knew he had no chance. As he came closer to the centre of the room, a root erupted from the ground and wrapped itself around the entirety of Abe's body. He could barely breathe; the root squeezed him as though it was an anaconda waiting patiently for its prey to cease breathing. Azalea turned and slowly walked towards him. She placed her palm on his nose with her fingers fully extended. She pulled her hand together until all her fingers touched just in front of his face. Suddenly, Abe found his brain a little less foggy. He felt a clarity that was unfamiliar and yet so welcomed.

"You have a moment to speak freely. I have questions to ask you and I want your honest opinion rather than trying to interpret your mangled thoughts," the Grand Master explained.

"My thoughts are only mangled because you keep my mind suppressed. A bit more freedom might be useful in that respect," Abe managed to say through gritted teeth as the root continued its relentless hold. He was angrier than he expected. Obviously, he was upset with Azalea, but with a bit more control over his thoughts, he realised how truly furious he was with her.

"Having more freedom temporarily does not give you grounds to be disrespectful." Her hand tightened at her side, causing the root around Abe to constrict even more. He desperately gasped for air. After a painful moment, the root eased slightly. "Keep that in mind," she remarked threateningly.

"What do you want to know then?"

"Daisy."

"What about her?"

"Do you love her?"

"Yes," Abe responded without hesitation or doubt. He knew it to be true now. Seeing her again, being close to her, and hearing her voice, reignited every feeling he had ever had for her. He desired nothing more than to be with her, truly with her in his own mind.

"Daisy fixed Alina's mind from corruption which means your memories should return," Azalea said with a flick of her wrist towards the table covered in papers. "With your memories and mind repaired, your emotions should also have come back. Do you not love Alina?"

Abe stopped for a moment to search his mind. Being as old as the universe, meant billions of memories to wade through. With time, some of those memories wore and became hard to recall. His mind was only able to remember so much, and he often focused on the more recent and important thoughts. He strained his brain to remember Alina as they were when they were together. The Grand Master was right, the memories were there, but Abe didn't feel the same way.

It was like watching someone through a window. He understood what was going on and could feel the emotions of the moment, but in the present, those emotions were distant and foreign. Alina was now more a sister and a partner than a lover. Abe and Alina had grown a lot and those people in the memories barely existed now. There was a different type of love for Alina. She was family and he didn't know what he would do without her, but she was not his heart's desire. Daisy held that in a way no other ever had or would.

"I love Alina as family, but that is not the same love I hold for Daisy," Abe stated. Azalea paced in front of him with her hands behind her back and her eyes looking at the ground. She pursed her lips and let out a long hmmm.

"I see this is true in your mind, but it is not what I expected," she stated.

"People change with time. Alina is not the same person today that I fell in love with all those years ago. Nor am I for that matter. We evolve and have become good partners, but we don't need romance anymore. My heart belongs to another."

"Hmmm." The Grand Master stopped pacing and looked at Abe. "Is that how you feel about me now?"

"No. I think you are a murderer. I think you are cruel and evil, and I think you have a terrible plan that you have very clearly been keeping me in the dark about." Azalea assessed his answer, before shrugging and turning back to her papers.

"You're not wrong, but you think I do this because I want to. The truth is that the people I've killed were not good people. Have you seen the scars across Daisy's back? The people who gave her those scars were terrible people. How could you say they deserved to live?"

"It's not your place to decide that."

"Maybe not yet. I do, however, understand what you mean about loving an old idea, but the person changing. You have changed a great deal. You are not the same person I loved. It's strange, but I do understand what you mean."

"You don't love me anymore?"

"Not in the same way. You've proven to be a very useful tool in my plans. Perhaps, I love what you can do for me more than loving you for you. I certainly don't feel the same way I used to. It's not really love anymore. It's more about utility." Abe cringed at the thought of being used for evil, but his options were limited. She held his mind. Now, he had an opportunity.

"I don't know what you are planning, Azalea, but keep Daisy out of this."

"Daisy! Right!" It was like she suddenly remembered something very important.

"What about Daisy?"

"She wants to be with you for the rest of her natural life apparently," Azalea sounded bored, but the thought of this made Abe's heart speed up and his hands sweat. During the earlier meeting with Daisy, Azalea had made it so he could not hear what they were discussing. He watched in a blind panic as Daisy spoke with Azalea. "You've made it quite clear you won't be with me willingly, nor do I desire to be with you anymore, but I do want my sister to be happy, so I have an offer for you."

"I don't know if I can trust you."

"You don't really have much choice, do you?" Abe paused and swallowed hard; he felt the root tighten ever so slightly.

"No, I suppose I don't."

"You proposed to Daisy over a year ago. She believes it was just a ruse, and with the recent information she has learned about Alina, she isn't even sure if you love her. It's quite sad actually." Abe felt sick to his stomach. Abe loved Daisy and truly had not been able to tell her that. The year apart had been crushing, and he could only imagine what learning about Alina would have done to Daisy.

"What are you thinking?"

"I want you to marry my sister. I will allow you some freedom to say as you please during the ceremony, and I will release her from her cage so she can be with you." Abe narrowed his eyes at Azalea. Something seemed amiss with this idea.

"How does this benefit you?"

"You must remain my pawn after the wedding, and you will work to convince Daisy to join our cause during your moments of freedom. Controlling as many minds as I do is exhausting, so I know you have moments of clarity. In those moments, you must persuade Daisy to stay with me. Here."

"And if I don't?"

"Then you will both die. If you can't convince her to stay and aid us, then neither of you are useful to me. I will destroy her and your family, and I will make you watch and suffer before finally killing you. Do I make myself clear?" The roots constricted tighter than they had been before.

Abe could barely breathe, but he managed to reply: "Yes, but I cannot do what you ask." Azalea flipped around. Her nostrils flared and her eyebrows were raised. Her face was nearly the same colour as her scarlet eye. She crossed her arms and stamped her foot like a child. If Abe could have laughed, he would have in response to this childish display.

"Why is that?"

"She does not trust me." Abe replied simply. Azalea stared at him, seeming to carefully consider his words. She closed her eyes and exhaled. Simultaneously, the root relaxed. Abe was able to take a deep breath and then continued: "How will she ever know if it is me or you she is talking to? She doesn't trust anything I do or say, and I don't even think she loves this version of me. If you want what you say, you must give me more freedom." Azalea paused and looked at Abe with squinted eyes.

"Give me your arm," Azalea finally said and Abe was forced to oblige.

The root untangled itself to allow Abe to extend his hand towards Azalea. She lifted her skirt and pulled out a small knife she kept strapped to her thigh. The blade was gold and decorated with four coloured stones. Abe immediately recognised the knife. It was an ancient relic that they used when first interacting with humans. The four stones were symbols of the four original forces; blue, green, red, and brown hues danced along the gold blade. The blade held powers beyond just the elemental forces. It was actual magic combined with the elemental forces, making it a terrifyingly powerful object. In the past, they used the knife to test a human's natural connection to the forces. As time went on, Azalea found other uses for the knife that Abe did not agree with.

Carelessly, she sliced away his sleeve to bare his forearm. In the process, she nicked his elbow causing a small trail of blood to stream down his arm. The small cut burned, but the pain was quickly overwhelmed as Azalea began carving into his forearm. She muttered some elder tongue as the knife cut through his skin. Each stroke of the blade felt like being burned with a hot iron. The skin sizzled and his blood boiled, but Abe couldn't pull away. Abe felt a different type of connection force its way into his body. Unlike the mind force, this connection was subtle, but significantly stronger. It ran through his entire body, filling his veins and his soul. It felt incredibly wrong and immensely dark. Once she finished, she pulled away and so, too, did the root that held Abe hostage. Abe collapsed on the ground. His whole body ached, and he felt weary to the bone.

"What did you just do?" Abe asked incredulously.

"You wanted freedom of your mind. I have given it to you," Azalea explained. With the last energy Abe possessed, he stood and ran at Azalea, aiming to take her down. As he neared Azalea, intense pain overcame his entire body. He smashed to the ground in a spasmed fit of agony. Eventually, the feeling subsided. Abe laid on the ground in the foetal position and softly cried from the pain. *What did she do to him?*

"I gave you the freedom of your mind," Azalea whispered as she bent down beside his head. "But I did not give you freedom of your body. I still *own* you. If you make any move against me, this is what you can expect. If you try to leave, it will hurt. If you tell someone of my plan, you will burn. If you try to hurt me, the pain you wished to inflict on me will be felt by you. The bigger the infraction, the more pain it will cause you. Now, get my sister to stay with us or expect a much worse punishment. Understand?"

Abe nodded his head and whimpered in pain. She stood and moved away from him. He listened as her heels clicked on the stone floor. As the sound faded, Abe could feel that his mind was mostly his own, but there was something lurking just beyond his consciousness. It was terrifying. He did not know what to expect or what this would entail, but it meant opportunity. It meant he could talk to Daisy as himself.

He could ensure that Daisy knew he loved her.

10

Ruin and Traditions

At some point in time, Daisy had crawled into the straw cot and fallen asleep. It was a fitful sleep full of nightmares. She dreamed of Rosie and the others being attacked in a wagon. She dreamed of painful brands being burned into her skin. She dreamed of endless trains being enveloped in darkness. No matter how hard she tried though, she could not wake herself from the dreams. She tumbled from one image to the next, each one slightly blending into the next.

When she did eventually wake, she felt groggy. It was like she had drunk too much wine. The room spun and her head felt fuzzy. She rubbed her eyes, trying to get them to focus. Daisy stretched to wake up her body, but everything felt heavy and tired. Somehow, she managed to get into a sitting position. As Daisy became more aware of her surroundings she noticed several trays of food by the door that were not there when she had gone to sleep. Perhaps, she had been asleep for longer than she thought. In addition to the trays, clothing hung from the bars of her cell. She slowly stood up and walked towards the outfit. A small note was attached to one of the garments. She expected it to be Azalea's writing, but found the familiar scribbles of Abe's penmanship.

Daisy,

I am eager to see you today and thought you might like a change of clothes. Azalea brought your trunk from your estate in hopes that you would arrive. I pulled some clothing from it for you. Hopefully, everything still meets your expectations.

Yours truest,

Abe

Daisy crumpled the paper and threw it to the ground. This felt like a game. It was as though her sister was using Abe to toy with her mind and her emotions which infuriated Daisy even more. She had missed Abe dearly over the past year, but this man was not Abe. He was but a shell. Nonetheless, Daisy did wish to change. Her clothes were tattered and dirty and the opportunity to change into something clean was overwhelmingly appealing.

Daisy pulled the clothes down from the cell door. While Abe had suggested in the note that the clothes were Daisy's, the outfit was a much more recent fashion preference. A pair of black trousers and a white blouse made up the majority of the outfit. The sleeves belled out from the elbows and had a frilled collar. A brown corset with black lacing was worn over the blouse. Her current carriage boots were a brown leather that matched the corset. To complete the outfit, Abe had provided one of his favourite brown jackets that Daisy had seen him wear while they were training. It seemed an unusual addition, but the coat was warm which was necessary in the draughty cell. Had her mother seen her in this outfit, Daisy would have been lashed and sent to her room. It surely wasn't hers from the estate, but Daisy liked the outfit nonetheless.

"Seems an unusual outfit for a lady," said Daisy's cellmate from across the hall, who Daisy now knew to be a red-headed man with olive skin. "He came by every day to check on you, but you kept sleeping. He left the outfit yesterday. He seemed concerned for you, but never really went into your cell. Just watched you sleep. He never even spoke."

"Are you speaking of Abe?" Daisy questioned, while turning her back to the hallway to change. She methodically stripped down, but left her undergarments on, so she did not expose herself to the stranger.

"If that is the man with the black hair, then yes, Abe checked on you often. It was endearing, how much he cared for you. I could only wish the same for my daughter, regardless of who she was partnered with. I'd just love for her to be with anyone that could love her now." There was a deep sadness to his voice that Daisy felt in her soul. Clearly, there was more to the story, but Daisy knew not to pry.

As she finally slid on the coat, she felt something heavy bump against her side. Daisy put her hand in the pocket and pulled out a hair comb. The comb was familiar and yet foreign. It had a wood base with several daisies carved into it, but additional blue and silver metal flowers were attached. Daisy recognised both parts of the comb. It was the comb Susan, her lady's maid and mother figure, had given her, but also the comb Abe had given her while courting.

She held the comb in her hands and felt a tear trickle down her cheek. It was an odd combination of both sides of her life merged into a simple yet beautiful piece. It was what existed before Abe combined with her current life. Daisy found it comforting and clutched the hair piece to her chest. Her hair had fallen into loose curls which she pulled back and tucked the hair comb into. It was like carrying a piece of the people she loved with her. It was welcomed and appreciated.

Having gotten dressed and refreshed, Daisy felt ready for whatever came next. At least mentally, she was prepared. Physically, her body felt exhausted. It was like all her energy was being drained away, while only leaving the bare minimum to survive. Daisy sat back on the bed and waited for whatever would come next. After only a few moments, Henry came to her cell.

"You have been summoned. I am here to collect you. Are you ready?" he asked, but it seemed more like a command. He opened the cell door and beckoned Daisy out.

"No chains this time?" Daisy inquired with a hint of sass.

"The Grand Master has decided you do not need chains. She also has a surprise for you apparently. Now, hurry up. I have places to be and things to do that do not involve escorting some stupid girl around."

Daisy stared at him for a moment. She wondered what exactly he knew about her. He didn't seem to care that she was the Grand Master's sister or that she created a new force. He seemed to think Daisy was a nuisance more than anything.

She exited the cell and followed Henry through the series of winding, stone carved halls. He did not speak, which Daisy did not mind. She considered trying to overtake him and run away, but she didn't know how to navigate the tunnels, and she assumed she would be quickly outnumbered anyways. Even if she could get away, Daisy imagined she would quickly be caught and refastened to the cell wall again. This option was not appealing to Daisy. The man stopped at a branch in the hall. He eyed Daisy before grunting and extending his arm.

"Third left. Second door. Don't dally," He dictated before turning down the other branch and leaving Daisy by herself. This was an opportunity to get out, but the place was a maze. There were too many hallways to keep straight, and she hadn't been here long enough to know any distinct markings. Surely trying to escape would lead to an even more unpleasant outcome. Instead, she followed the instructions. As she approached the door, she could hear voices on the other side.

"But she isn't from our world. She doesn't understand our customs at all. She's barely been exposed to anything Conductor at all," Abe exclaimed. He sounded more himself than he had the previous night. She found her heart getting jittery at the thought, but also worried what kind of condition this meant Abe was in. *Was Azalea just trying to make Abe sound better to Daisy?*

"This is a momentous occasion, and it should follow our practices," Azalea retorted, which immediately squashed Daisy's hope and excitement.

"I understand what you are saying, but I think we need to compromise. I think it should be a blend of both worlds. I don't think this is what Daisy would want."

"Well, let's ask her." The door Daisy was eavesdropping behind suddenly swung open. Daisy found herself exposed to everyone in the room. She stood still, frozen, uncomfortable and unsure of what to do. A bright smile crossed Abe's face before he bounded over to Daisy.

In one quick, fluid motion, Abe swooped Daisy off her feet and kissed her with a desperation she didn't fully understand. She resisted for only a moment before giving in and wrapping her arms around his neck. Her hands tangled in his soft, black hair causing hints of cedarwood and lavender to waft off him. His thin arms were strong and she could feel the muscles pulsing around her. It almost felt like their first kiss. There was the same passion, knowing, and love, but Daisy still felt apprehension sitting heavy in her chest. Shortly thereafter, Abe placed Daisy back on the ground and released her from the kiss. She studied his face looking for signs that it was him acting, and not Azalea through him. He carried a light in his eyes and his regular smirk, but something still felt off. This wasn't Abe. No matter how much Azalea tried to make it seem like Abe, this still wasn't her Abe. Daisy was sure he was in there somewhere, but everything about this felt off and uncomfortable.

"Be glad that her being ruined is not an issue in our society. Your behaviour is hardly appropriate in her society," Azalea remarked. Daisy had nearly forgotten Azalea was there. She was so focused on understanding Abe, that she forgot her sister was even present.

"Even if it did," Abe said while brushing a piece of hair behind Daisy's ear, "I would still marry her."

Abe interlocked his fingers into hers and guided Daisy into the room. Having been distracted earlier, Daisy had hardly taken notice of the room. Now, as she walked in, she noticed swathes and swathes of various fabrics. Blues, greens, silver, and gold dazzled the room. There were even different types of fabrics that Daisy just wanted to run her hands over. A few wood stools dotted the room, but they mostly held papers rather than people.

"We were just discussing your wedding," Azalea explained. "There are customs Conductors have for such events, but Abe thinks you would like to have some regular, human customs added."

"My wedding?" Daisy asked. Although she loved Abe and the idea of being with him forever, the thought of marrying Abe in his current state was appalling. Even as happy as he seemed, this was still not her Abe. She had to keep reminding herself of that. This was not Abe, no matter how much she wanted it.

"Our wedding, I suppose," Abe added and gently squeezed her hand in a reassuring and encouraging manner. He seemed overly happy and peppy for him. This overly positive demeanour felt odd to Daisy; he was typically more brooding and sorrowful, like the weight of the world sat on his shoulders. Daisy wasn't sure what to do with him like this. He was either a blank corpse being puppeted by Azalea or a happy, overly cheerful optimist that seemed completely unaware of their situation. At least the latter could speak to her and seemingly more freely. But this still wasn't Abe and he still reeked of Azalea's control.

"Yes, you are marrying Abe. You were engaged. You said you wanted to spend the rest of your life with him, but not in his current state. Remember?" Azalea asked.

"Yes, but I -"

"Good," Azalea interrupted. "I freed more of his brain for you, so he is mostly himself. Now we have to plan a wedding."

"More of his brain?" Daisy was confused. *So he was more Abe, but not completely Abe?* Daisy rubbed her face idly. Even if her sister wasn't lying and she had freed more of Abe's mind, he still wasn't Abe. His mind was still clouded and her sister still held some portion of it.

"My darling sister, if you can't keep up, then please shut up. You sound like an idiot with all these questions." Daisy tried to act like she wasn't slightly insulted. The whole situation was confusing, but Daisy didn't have many options. Daisy wanted to avoid being back in a cell and not enraging her sister seemed like the best way to avoid that. "Now, back to customs, shall we?"

"For Conductors, it is traditional for the couple to wear the colours of their partners' primaries," Abe explained. "For you, that would mean wearing green and blue. For me, it would be silver and gold."

"It is the human tradition to wear white now. When we were kids, you always said you thought the white was boring, so I thought the colours would be more exciting for you. However, I know you can be rather… traditionalist at times," Azalea added. Daisy was dazed for a moment at the mention of their childhood. Azalea was right about Daisy's childish desires, which was even more unusual. Perhaps Azalea did pay attention to Daisy growing up or perhaps she was just finding something to use against Daisy. Either way, Daisy wasn't sure what to think of her sister's motives. "So which would you rather?"

"Why can't we do both? Why can't I have the base as a white dress and add in the blue and green elements to appeal to both sides?" Daisy suggested. Azalea cocked her head to the side and eyed Daisy.

"That was Abe's idea as well," Azalea replied with a clenched jaw.

"Then I think we are in agreement then," Abe said definitively.

"Yes, I suppose we are," Azalea replied though she seemed rather displeased. Abe turned towards Daisy and smiled at her. He acted like a dog happy to see its owner. Daisy almost wanted to shoo him away. "I have a few other details I want to run by you as well. Shall we tour the potential rooms?"

"I think that is a great idea. What about you, Dais?" Abe added with a sickly sweet smile that felt entirely fake. Daisy didn't understand anything that was going on. Everything about the situation was uncomfortable and felt forced.

"Um. Yes. Okay. We can do that, but are we really planning a wedding right now?" Daisy appealed. *Weren't they in the middle of a war?*

"In times of hardship, it is best to find moments of joy where possible," Azalea added.

Azalea suddenly appeared by Daisy's side and grabbed her gently by the arm. They headed out of the room with Abe trailing behind them. After several twisting hallways and random turns, they arrived at a large hallway with several doors.

"I was thinking back to when we were children and I remember you saying you wanted to get married outside. You always loved the outdoors. I swear half of your lashings came from you being outside when you weren't supposed to be," Azalea laughed, but the sting of memories pained Daisy's heart in the moment. Her back ached from the years of scars and unwanted touch. It didn't start with a whip. It started with a hand and progressed from there. She hardly ever had a loving hand laid on her.

"I like the outdoors. Can we do the ceremony outside?" Abe asked with a painful flinch that Daisy didn't understand. Azalea scowled at him. "Never mind. Inside it is."

"I would certainly prefer outside as well, but I am surprised you remember any of my desires or dreams," Daisy added softly. She didn't wish to insult her sister, but these actions seemed unwarranted. *What was Azalea planning?*

"Of course I paid attention to you. I had never had a sibling before. I have never had someone that I actually cared about like I do with you. Daisy, you're the only one that matters to me anymore. However, outside is not safe, so I tried to bring the outside inside," Azalea offered and pushed open the first door. Behind it, was a dense, dark forest. It felt eerie and unnatural. The trees hung limp, almost seeming dead. "The trees haven't done well inside, but I know how much you like forests. You always said you found peace amongst the trees."

Daisy stared at Azalea. As Daisy learnt more about Azalea, she thought the soft moments of their childhood were a sham. Azalea tortured and killed their parents in addition to causing Daisy's abuse. It seemed like the happy moments were forged, fake, figments of Daisy's imagination at some points. And yet... Azalea remembered. She paid attention to small details and tried to do something that Daisy would like. She was actually trying to do something nice. It almost seemed like Azalea cared.

But why?

Why would Azalea care about Daisy? If Daisy had learned anything over the past two years, it was that Azalea only cared about herself. But Azalea was going beyond the normal acts of sibling love and seemed to be putting true effort into Daisy's happiness. It unnerved Daisy. Something had to be a foot. Her sister was never this kind.

"It feels too dark," Abe interjected, pulling Daisy back to the situation at hand, "and claustrophobic. Unless, of course, you love it?"

"No," Daisy stated with a head shake to clear her mind. "No, I don't see this being a place to get married. It makes me nervous."

"Well, that will not do. Onto the next room then," Azalea dictated and led the way out of the room.

They stopped at several other rooms each with different outdoor scenes. There was a prairie that looked harsh against the stone, a snow covered room too cold to stand in, and even a hillside that reminded Daisy of the hill leading to her old, family manor. None of them felt right to get married. They came to one last door. Azalea pushed open the room, and it was like walking into a dream.

At the back of the room, a small waterfall trickled into a clear pond. Moss hung to the walls with beautiful bioluminescent flowers sprouting from it. Tiny fireflies darted about the room, flashing colours of red, blue, green, purple, and bronze. They reminded Daisy of the solstice ball and Abe taking her to the gazebo. Something about this room felt right.

"This one..." Daisy indicated, "this is the right one."

"Really?" Azalea enquired. She paused and assessed the room before turning back to Daisy. "Do you remember that book I used to read to you through the door when the Duchess locked you up?"

"Do you mean the *Lady of the Falls*?" Daisy replied. "It was an old folktale that wasn't exactly a happy story. The main character got trapped behind a waterfall until her true love came and parted the water to free her. Wasn't her true love then stuck behind the falls?"

"Yes, he was. She had to decide between her freedom and her true love, but her true love wouldn't allow her to sacrifice herself again to the falls. So, she stayed with him and talked to him through the falls. I always read that story to you because I felt like you were trapped behind the falls. This is what I always imagined the falls would look like, but maybe it's suiting. Maybe Ambrose is the one that pulled you out of the falls."

"Maybe," Daisy added and looked at Abe. It was like he was behind the falls. Partially there, able to be spoken to, but still so far away. Maybe she could pull him from the falls. Abe turned his head to the side and stared back at Daisy curiously.

"May I steal away my bride for a while?" Abe asked Azalea, though his attention was completely on Daisy.

"I think we are done for the day. You can show her to her room. She need not stay in that cell any longer, but then I expect you back here to help finish this wedding planning," Azalea explained. Abe nodded his head.

Abe immediately led Daisy out of the room and began winding through the halls in various directions; Daisy started to feel dizzy. They eventually came to a wide hall with several ornate doors. Abe stopped in front of one and pulled out a heavy set of keys. He unlocked the door and pushed it open.

The room behind the door completely shocked Daisy. Like many of the areas Daisy had seen, this room also appeared carved out of stone. Unlike the other rooms though, this one had a small jewelled window. One could not actually see out of the window, but it cast dazzling shadows about the room. In the centre of the room stood a large, wooden, four-post bed. Cosy looking multi-coloured blankets and pillows covered the entire mattress. Daisy couldn't fathom anyone having an actual use for so many pillows. A large chest sat at the foot of the bed for storage while a matching armoire stood beside a secondary door. A large fireplace surrounded by terracotta tiles adorned with blue and white flower patterns nearly filled up the entirety of one wall. A blazing fire warmed the room and made the large wingback chairs that faced the fire seem even more welcoming.

What caught Daisy's eyes most was the one wall entirely covered in books. From floor to ceiling, thousands of books lined the wall. It was very similar to Abe's office in Grenich. Daisy immediately felt drawn to the wall of books and idly began running her hand along the spines. She felt comfortable and at home in this room. It made wanting to leave seem a bit more difficult. If this was her life with Abe, she could manage it. It was just the addition of Azalea that seemed unappealing.

"I thought you would like the books. I wanted to make sure you would like everything in the room when I made it," Abe breathed into her ear while sliding his hands around her waist from behind. Daisy found herself leaning back against his chest. It was a very intimate moment, one Daisy had longed for, but a small part of her felt as though it was wrong. However, she liked him being so close even if he wasn't entirely present.

"It reminds me of your office in Grenich. It brings me back to the simpler days when you were just training me and I didn't know about any of this other stuff," Daisy responded with her eyes closed. She listened to his breath which was soft against her cheek.

"Before we were engaged, as well."

"Also true, but were we really ever engaged?" Daisy pulled away and turned to face Abe. As she spoke a realisation dawned on Daisy and something inside her just snapped, opening the floodgates of things Daisy had been holding in. "You never did ask. You just gave me a ring as a part of a ruse. You've never even said you loved me. We spent months together as you trained me, but you never actually said you loved me. I thought maybe you found me interesting. You seemed intrigued. Honestly though, I wasn't even sure you liked me, but I was completely in love with you. I wanted to believe that you were more than interested in me and not just flirting or toying with me. Then that kiss....it felt so real, but now... everything is confusing. How do I know if this is you, *actually you*, or if this is Azalea? How can I trust anything you say or do?"

"Dais," Abe said with a hint of pain that Daisy felt wounded by. He was the only one that called her that and it made her heart ache with longing. "Dais, I know this is confusing and complicated. I can assure you this is not how I wanted this reunion to go. I had hoped I would have been completely free when we met again, but I will take what I can if it means being with you. You are right though, there were a lot of things I never said or did. When you became a Conductor, I knew we had time. I wanted you to have the choice of what you did, and I didn't want to push myself on you. You were young and inexperienced. I've had many lifetimes of experience. I was following your lead, but I suppose that is uncommon in your society. I just wanted you to make the decision rather than feel cornered into loving me."

He gently rubbed her arms in a soft and tender rhythm that eased the tension in Daisy's chest. She could feel the truth behind his words, but she still questioned if they were actually his words. She wanted so badly to trust him so she could love him, but Azalea's influence was all over him. *How could she ever get past that until they were free of her altogether?*

"Dais, I do love you, but I never expected to love you. I wasn't even sure what to do when I started to feel the way I did. I honestly hadn't loved anyone in such a long time that my feelings for you… were a surprise. I had to figure out what I was actually feeling. Now, though, I can just be honest with you and I know what I feel. I love you with every fibre of my being and soul. You are my light in the darkness and were the only reason I have kept going and fighting. I promised I would find you and I wanted to keep that promise. Just not in this way."

"But how do I know this is you?" Daisy said in a small voice.

"I don't know if there is anything I can do to prove to you my clarity. I will just keep trying to prove to you who I am. On that note, close your eyes for a moment." Daisy did as instructed. She felt wind moving about and felt the electricity of conduction being performed. Abe was clearly planning something.

"Now, open."

11

Chasing Trains

Rosie was thrown backwards as Alina released a massive fireball bigger than anything the other Conductors had cast. It was probably larger than the carriage they were in. The Conductors that had been pursuing them scattered to avoid the giant inferno. As much as Rosie had hoped the fire ball would be enough, it was only a brief moment before the pursuants recovered and began launching more attacks. Various unidentifiable objects flew around them. Rosie stayed tucked in the bottom of the carriage as the others sent counter attacks.

Alina, however, was concerning. She seemed to enjoy this attack just a bit too much. She launched fireball after fireball. Each one impressively large and full of immense power. Rosie had seen plenty of conduction over the past year, but nothing quite like the vigour and extremeness of Alina's attacks. Her immense power unnerved Rosie. *What if Alina was still mad? What if Daisy hadn't fixed Alina's mind, but only her powers?* There were too many questions and too few answers. Rosie tried to refocus on the moment.

Evander continued steering the horses. He pulled this way and that way as Storm and Lyla galloped on. They barely even seemed to flinch at the chaos surrounding them. At one point, the road split and Evander pulled a hard left. He briefly dropped the reins and did a strange motion with his hands. Suddenly, a dense, heavy fog appeared. Rosie could barely see the hand in front of her face. Rocks and fire balls still rang through the area, but further away. They were shot wide or completely missed. The fog gave Rosie and the others the needed cover to finally get away.

They had disappeared into the forest completely and rolled out of the fog. The air was silent as everyone listened for the sounds of their attackers, but nothing came. It appeared they had barely escaped. This time. Rosie was positive next time would not go as well.

Alina started squealing like a happy child. She had a huge smile on her face that Rosie thought was weird for Alina. In all the time Rosie had spent with Daisy and the Conductors, she could not remember seeing Alina… *happy?*

"Did you see that?" Alina marvelled. "Did you see my fireballs? Each one was so perfect and large and effective. Did you all see it?

"It was impressive," Arlo chimed in.

"It was amazing!" Brighid gushed. "I couldn't believe you cast such a big fireball."

"Nor could I," Alina added while slumping back into one of the seats. "To be honest, I wasn't sure what was going to happen. Since my… since my connection with the elemental forces broke, I haven't been able to cast anything without Abe's assistance, but, even with Abe's help, my conduction could be unpredictable. But that… that was incredible and felt so good. I didn't realise how freeing it was. I didn't realise how much… how much I missed being a Conductor."

Rosie watched the situation with complete amazement. Alina seemed like a completely different person, and Rosie wasn't sure what to make of it. Of course, Rosie never really understood the forces and she purposely tried to keep herself separated from them. She had to stay separate from the Conductors as much as possible. However, Rosie had gathered that a connection to the forces was essential to conduction. She imagined that conducting without the forces would be like riding a horse with no tack. Surely one can do it, but it is often more difficult to control and harder to correct. Not impossible, but certainly more difficult. The way Alina described it though almost made it seem impossible. Rosie sat back and listened as Alina explained how Abe would help her with her conduction. It was boring to Rosie, but her stories seemed fascinating to the others.

After several hours, Evander pulled off into a clearing just off the road. The horses devoured the grass; they were clearly grateful for the break. Everyone else seemed thankful for the opportunity to stretch their legs and relax. Arlo had ventured further into the forest and returned with apples and berries. Brighid had found some blue flowers that she was weaving into a crown. Evander leaned up against a tree and took a nap while Alina experimented with her reinvigorated powers. The calm, peacefulness in stark contrast to what they just went through unnerved Rosie.

In the past year, they had mostly been on the run. Anytime they came across another Conductor, they would pack up and move. Usually, they weren't in any place for longer than a month or so. Everyone had agreed that being nomadic was the best way to remain hidden. All the while, Daisy trained and became a stronger Conductor. Rosie supported Daisy where she could, but often found she was forced into cooking and mending and other womanly duties. Not that Rosie minded. She liked running a household in some capacity, but this whole experience was not what she expected.

What she had expected was some type of journey. She wanted it like the stories she read as a child. A journey like King Arthur and his Knights of the Round Table. Just something more than moving from place to place and cooking and cleaning. She expected more, but maybe more wouldn't be better.

All in all, a journey like the stories meant danger and peril. It meant fear and loss. Rosie wasn't sure if that was better. Perhaps more interesting, yes, but certainly not better. Generally, they had been safe, cared for, and provided for. Their needs were met, and Alina ensured they were safe. Alina was good about putting in the necessary precautions. It was the one thing Rosie was willing to commend Alina on. She was very cautious and able to protect those she cared about well.

"I must apologise to all of you," Alina started. Everyone looked towards Alina. "I should have told you about the mania earlier, but I was ashamed. I was barely even a Conductor, and I was dependent on Abe. I didn't realise how dependent I was, though. I should have told you that Abe was helping me. I thought I could manage the symptoms by myself, but I obviously couldn't. I shouldn't have tried to do this alone, and I put you all in danger. I am truly sorry for the risks I took for all of you. I am sorry for the decisions I made. I don't know if you will forgive me, but I do want you to all know I regret what has happened."

Brighid immediately hugged Alina. Tears streamed down Alina's face as she cradled Brighid in her arms. Alina had flushed cheeks and a creased brow. She seemed genuine and distraught. Rosie was perplexed by this level of emotion. From happiness to apologetic in a quick moment was weird for anyone, but even more unusual for Alina. It almost seemed suspicious.

"You're right," Evander said over his shoulder from the wagon as he was connecting the horses to the carriage. "You should have told us. You put us all at risk. While I am glad you have your conduction back, I just hope you use it well."

That was the end of the conversation. No one else spoke. They loaded into the wagon and took off. The remainder of the journey was a mixture of awkwardness, discomfort, and uncertainty. Arlo eventually dozed off and his light snores filled the silence, but otherwise not a single word was uttered.

When they reached the next town over, Rosie volunteered to scout the train station for any signs of other Conductors. Being common looking was the only thing she was good for. Unlike the others with their mismatched eyes, Rosie appeared mostly normal. Her hair was fiery and her skin was like honey which wasn't common, but she wasn't as obvious to other Conductors who were seeking out the common mark.

The train station at this town was even smaller than Grenich. They had arrived at Mullins which had a population of approximately three hundred people. The only reason Mullins had a train station at all was that it was conveniently located directly in the middle of two industrial towns. Had it not been for its location, Mullins would have been left off the map entirely. Since the station was small, it was easy to survey.

Rosie walked the platform and checked the schedule for the next train. Considering the next train was set to arrive in an hour, the platform seemed incredibly barren. Most people arrived before the trains as it was usually a mad rush to board. Rosie walked over to the ticket booth. An old gentleman with white hair and clouded eyes sat at the desk.

"Is the next train on time?" Rosie inquired.

"As far... as... I know," he spoke slowly with plenty of space between each word. It's how Rosie imagined a turtle would speak.

"Are tickets available for the train?"

"Yes... and no..."

"What do you mean?"

"It's a... roll-ing stop. The train will slow... but it will... not stop. You... would... have to catch it." He laughed at his joke which promptly turned into a choking coughing fit.

"Do I still buy tickets?"

"The man... on the train... will sell you them."

"Well, thank you for the information sir."

Rosie turned away from the ticket clerk and did one more quick walkthrough to ensure the platform was safe. As far as she knew, no one else was around. She returned to the others and explained the rolling stop and how they would have to chase the train. Since they really had no other option, they all agreed to it. Evander quickly took the horses and barouche to sell it for whatever coin they could get. Although Arlo and Evander could use the mind force for nearly anything, Alina, and therefore Brighid, insisted on being ethical and paying for things where possible. Rosie was curious if that trend would continue as there appeared to be a shift in power.

Evander returned a few moments later with a rather large sum of money. Alina attempted to interrogate him about how he obtained such a ridiculous sum, but one look from him and she immediately stopped. Rosie smirked; she was enjoying this new dynamic between the two of them.

They waited around the train station. Evander was concerned the train would be early and they would miss it if they wandered into town. As such, he refused to let anyone leave. Brighid and Arlo played some game in the dirt to pass the time while Evander paced anxiously beside the tracks. Alina seemed to be pouting in the corner which Rosie had very little interest in interrupting. Instead, she wandered over to Evander.

"Have you ever done this before?" Rosie asked in an attempt to open conversation. She really only spoke with Daisy. This was the first time she was without Daisy and not in crisis. *Did she have anything in common with these people?*

"Done what exactly?" Evander responded in a polite, but curious manner.

"Gotten on a moving train," Rosie replied. Evander chuckled to himself.

"Yeah. A time or two. We used to live in a train station. We did a lot of stupid stuff."

"Oh. That's fair, I suppose. " There was an awkward pause. "Any recommendations for getting on a moving train?"

"What kind of shoes are you wearing?" Evander enquired. Rosie lifted her skirt to show off a pair of riding boots. "Ah, those might be fun. Watch that your heel doesn't get caught. There's lots of little bars and nooks that your heels will stick in. Also, keep moving. Until you are in the aisle of the train, keep moving. When dealing with a large group like this, you don't want to cause a back-up. I will get on first, then Brighid followed by you, Alina, and Arlo last."

"Well, thank you for the information. These are probably things I needed to know."

"Absolutely, m'lady." Rosie found herself giggling; a response which seemed to insult Evander. "What? What's so funny?"

"M'lady?"

"Well, how else do you address one of your status?"

"Rosie is fine. My status is irrelevant." Evander cocked his head to the side and appeared ready to ask more questions when the quiet, tinny whistle of the train sounded nearby.

Immediately everyone got to their feet seeming ready to run. Oddly enough, Brighid held her shoes in her hand. The train rounded the corner and appeared to be slowing slightly. Right as the train reached the furthest edge of the platform everyone started to jog; Rosie followed their lead. The train was moving quicker than Rosie expected, but everyone else seemed so prepared.

The train reached the group. Evander quickly and gracefully swung himself up into the train. He leaned back out and extended his hand which Brighid accepted. In one smooth motion, Evander pulled Brighid up into the train. Rosie was next. She kept her pace to match the train. Evander reached his arm out to her. As she reached up to grab his hand, Rosie stumbled. She nearly fell to the ground, but the back of her dress was snatched and she was lifted off her feet and onto the train.

Her back smashed onto the train floor and the breath escaped her lungs. She laid on the ground trying to breathe as Alina and Arlo hopped on the train as if it was the easiest thing to do. They stepped over her like she was a bump in the rug they were used to tripping on. Eventually the air came back to her lungs and she was able to breathe. Rosie managed to get into a seated position.

"I told you to watch your heels," Evander joked while offering his hand to assist Rosie up. She rolled her eyes, but accepted the offer.

"I am guessing it was one of those nooks you warned me about," Rosie replied. Evander indicated she should pass him and enter the main cabin. Rosie smiled and passed through the door in front of him.

12

A Scar of Fire

Abe knew he had to do something special for Daisy. He needed to make up for all this confusion and loneliness he was sure she had been feeling over the past year. He watched as she closed her eyes, trusting him completely.

Quickly, he transformed the room into what he thought would be romantic. He placed lit candelabras and various flower arrangements around the room. He knew she loved flowers. When they were training, she would always stop to pick bluebells or smell a primrose. Abe thought her enjoyment of little things as endearing, and always wanted to allow her the simple pleasures of life. He knew though, he needed more than just flowers and candles. He needed something personal.

As a reminder of their first excursion, Abe created a plaid blanket on the ground with cushions and a picnic basket with Daisy's favourites. He ensured there were hazelnuts, treacle, and bread. He even included her favourite jasmine tea. He wished he could have added the sounds of the sea with the cool winter breeze, but without an actual body of water, he wouldn't be able to replicate the sounds. It was the best he could do, and he hoped it would be enough. For the final touch, he whisked the ring off of Daisy's finger with a gentle breeze and placed it in his pocket. She didn't seem to notice.

"Keep your eyes closed," Abe murmured into Daisy's ear as he guided her closer to the picnic. He released her hand and took a step back. "Now open!"

Daisy opened her eyes and immediately smiled. She took in the room and the picnic basket. She even grabbed a flower from one of the vases and inhaled its aroma. To Abe, she seemed genuinely thrilled. It eased some of the tension he had been feeling. After looking at all of the flowers and candles, she took a seat on the blanket and Abe followed her lead. He began handing Daisy various foods and treats. Unlike their last picnic, Daisy devoured the food she was handed. Abe must have looked concerned as Daisy immediately looked like a scolded child when she made eye contact with him.

"Sorry," Daisy muttered. "That's not very ladylike of me, but I haven't eaten anything since I arrived here. I didn't realise how hungry I was until you put food in front of me."

Abe's stomach churned with anger and guilt. He was so eager to have his mind back, he forgot that Daisy needed to be cared for. *What kind of a person did that make him?* Azalea assured him she was being fed in her cell, but he wasn't allowed to check on her. He so desperately wanted his freedom so he could be with Daisy, but completely forgot to ensure her basic needs were met. He could feel fear rising in him. Daisy made it almost impossible to think rationally. Instead, Abe defaulted to what he always did.

"Like I told you the first time, I don't want a lady," Abe remarked which earned him a slight chuckle and eye roll from Daisy.

"If you wanted this to be like last time, you would not be sitting," Daisy responded and slightly pushed his shoulder. Abe thought back to that early winter day on the beach, but couldn't quite remember what he was doing. He remembered trying to seem intrigued by Daisy but not desperate. She was fascinating to him, but he didn't want to scare her off. He needed to balance it all.

"No? What was I doing?"

"You were laying on your back and looking up at the sky. I remember how your eyelashes casted shadows on your cheeks and how you looked shorter laying down than standing up."

"How so?"

"Like this." Daisy pushed him and he fell onto his back. She moved beside him where he could feel the warmth radiating off her body. She grabbed a cushion and placed it under his head. She had a hand on either side of his face and was looking down at him with her toffee hair framing her face.

Her eyes sparkled, but with her this close, Abe could see the bags under her eyes. There were the slightest crinkles of worry lines on her brow which made her crescent scar above her golden eye stand out even more. Subconsciously, Abe reached up and ran his thumb gently over the scar. It had faded over their year apart. It was more white than pink now. She half smiled and dainty dimples appeared in her cheeks. She was simple in her looks, but absolutely stunning at the same time.

"Do you remember now?" she whispered.

"I think I would remember this," Abe responded lightly, "I don't think this is exactly what happened."

"You're right. I sat opposite to you and tried not to think about being alone with a man I barely knew. Shall I do that now?"

"No!" Abe said a little too quickly and forcefully. Daisy retracted slightly and sat in a more upright position beside him, her hands no longer on either side of his face. He sat up to face her more directly. "Sorry Dais. I just, I've missed you and having you close… having you here… it's just…"

Abe was at a complete loss for words. *How could he tell Daisy how much she meant to him without saying more that would push her away?* Mentioning Azalea and her hold on his brain was impossible because of the curse she placed on him. *Furthermore, what could he say that would reassure Daisy that it was him and not Azalea?* He needed Daisy to understand, but was bound by the curse. Speaking against Azalea would be painful, but losing Daisy would shatter him.

"Dais," Abe said softly. She looked towards him. "I can't pretend like there isn't a barrier between us. I can't act like what has been done hasn't occurred. I can't make you trust me or even love me, but I will do what I can to earn your trust back. I will show you in every way I can that I love you. I will never stop trying to be the man you deserve. I will always be there for you, no matter the circumstance, I will find a way to be with you. You have become my entire world and I will shatter without you."

Daisy rubbed her arm and turned her chin away from him. Abe could sense her nervousness and just wanted to take it away. *What more could he do?* Then a thought dawned on him.

The ring.

He took the ring from her with every intention of doing this properly. He moved to a kneeling position facing Daisy. He pulled out the ring and held it out to her. She looked surprised and glanced at her hand, noticing the ring was missing. When he made it originally it was a rushed job. The golden streaked stone was like Daisy's eye, but it was unrefined and rough. The silver band was bent and barely a circle, but still fit on her finger. Had he more time, he was sure he could have made something more beautiful, and yet, she seemed to love it.

"Daisy Mae Bloomsbury." Abe started. Daisy moved into a kneeling position fully facing him. Her hands laid on her lap. "I have spent the past year apart from you and now know I cannot live spending another day without you. You are the very soul to my being. I will spend the rest of my days proving to you that you are the love of my life. Even if my life is an eternity there will only be you. I will spend the rest of my days becoming the man you rightfully deserve. I will honour you and cherish you and ensure you know love for the rest of your life if you will allow me. Dais, will you do me the greatest honour of becoming my wife?"

Daisy wrinkled her nose up and sat in silence for a moment. Abe didn't want to rush her, but the anticipation of an answer was nearly killing him.

"Not as a part of a ruse to get me to run away with you?" Daisy questioned. Abe smirked, knowing where the remark came from.

"No. No ruse this time. Just actual, true love."

"No ulterior motives?"

"No. This is me in my own mind asking you to join me in marriage." Abe could start to feel nervous jitters building in him. He quickly rolled his shoulders back in an attempt to ease some of the tension. Perhaps he was wrong and she did not wish to marry him. Perhaps Azalea had so royally messed this up, that she could not see past what all had happened. Perhaps there was no recovering this and Abe had truly lost Daisy.

"How do I know this is you asking me and not Azalea just trying to reinforce the idea?" Daisy pleaded.

"Azalea is not one to re-do things. Once she gets what she wants she moves on rather quickly. She has already achieved her goal of setting up a marriage. There is no point in actually proposing," Abe replied.

"Then why are you proposing?" She cocked her head to the side and raised one eyebrow.

"To give you the choice. Just as I did when we started training and you weren't sure if you wanted to be a Conductor. I want you to be willing and aware. I don't wish to force anything upon you. I always want to give you the choice." Something seemed to spark in Daisy. Whether recognition, hope, or trust, Abe could not tell. She was about to speak when there was a loud knock on the door that distracted her.

They both sat still for a moment, staring at the door. Another loud knock confirmed it was their door that was being hammered on. Abe stood and indicated Daisy should remain seated. He opened the door to expose Kotravai. With Daisy behind him, he could now see how similar her gold eyes were to Daisy's. They were unnervingly similar..

"The Grand Master sent me to ensure that everything was alright," Kotravai explained. "By the looks of it, things seem fine. She had expected you to return sooner."

"We are busy. Does the Grand Master require something dire?" Abe retorted.

"Not to my understanding, but I believe you should come with me to her."

"No," Abe declared. Immediately, a fire started coursing through his arm. He winced in pain as the burning increased. "Not yet. I will be there shortly."

The pain lessened, but still tingled in his arm. He tried not to show the pain. He did not want Daisy to know. He worried she would ask questions, and the last thing he wanted to do was lie to her.

"I will inform the Grand Master immediately." Kotravai lowered her voice and moved closer to Abe so that Daisy could not hear. "She also wanted me to remind that she feels everything you do and can still sense your thoughts even though you've been released. Daisy is still an unwed woman. Don't ruin her anymore than she already is."

Kotravai turned on her heel and trudged down the hallway. When she rounded the corner, Abe slammed the door shut. He pinched the bridge of his nose in frustration and clenched the ring in his other hand. This whole situation was rightfully messed up and he didn't know how to resolve any of it. Suddenly, a warm and soft hand wrapped around his tight fist holding the ring. He released the bridge of his nose and opened his eyes. Daisy stared at him with big eyes, drawn eyebrows, and a look of pure concern.

Gingerly, she turned over his arm and began rolling up the sleeve of his shirt. Despite his efforts, she must have seen him wince and was now investigating. As she slowly rolled up the shirt, the large pattern exposed itself. A heavy black drawing with various circles and lines etched into his skin. Some sections bled from the recent infraction against Azalea. Abe wanted to pull his arm away from Daisy, but instead he watched as she gently traced the pattern.

"What happened Abe?" Daisy quivered. Abe's heart broke with each wavering syllable. He knew he couldn't tell her the truth and that hurt even more.

"I accidentally burned myself," Abe responded. He felt no pain meaning this line of lies was satisfactory to Azalea. In his heart, however, he felt pure agony for lying to Daisy. "It's a long story, but I am okay now. It's healing."

Daisy looked at him. Abe tried to portray the real story through his eyes. He wanted her to know there was more to this, but he couldn't tell her. She searched his eyes intently before rolling his sleeve back over the blackened scar.

"I understand," she said. She walked over and sat on the chest at the end of the bed. She placed her hands on her lap and seemed to assess them intently. Abe was not sure what to do. He slid the ring into his pocket and waited for some signal from Daisy. Eventually, she looked up at him with tears in her eyes. She was sobbing silently. Abe immediately moved to kneel in front of her. He grabbed her hands and kissed them gently.

"Dais, what's wrong?" Abe pleaded. She shook her head. "Please talk to me."

"You lie… you're not free of her. This is all a ruse again and I am a fool," she cried. Abe reached his hand to cup her cheek but she swatted it away.

"I am not completely free of her, you're right." Abe could feel his arm burn. There was even a slight glow through his shirt that Daisy also seemed to notice. She rolled up his sleeve again and saw the black scar that was now glowing red. If she learned on her own, there was nothing Azalea could do. He just had to give her the pieces. "I cannot say much else, but know that my actions and my words are my own. I can do what I please within reason."

His arm flared even more. He clenched his hand to fight the pain and bit his lip so hard that he could taste the metal tang of blood. As he hunched his shoulders to bear the pain, he found his head resting in Daisy's lap. Her hands were suddenly tangled in his hair. He looked up towards her, trying to hide his pain, but seeing the fear in Daisy's eyes brought a new sorrow to his soul.

"I am so sorry, Daisy," Abe begged. He had nothing else to say. He couldn't explain anything more without inflicting physical pain on himself and emotional torment on Daisy. A sudden resolve came across Daisy's face. Her tears stopped and she now stared at Abe even more intently.

"Then yes," Daisy said firmly. Abe wasn't exactly sure what she was agreeing to.

"Yes to what?" Abe inquired.

"Then yes, I will marry you."

Abe felt his whole face light up. His smile was so big it hurt his face. He reached into his pocket and pulled out the ring to slide on her finger. He looked back at her face. She was also smiling and her cheeks were flushed.

She brushed a piece of hair behind her ear. Without thinking, Abe leaned in and kissed her.

There was a tension in Daisy at first, before her arms wrapped around his neck and she relaxed. There was a desperation to Abe that he didn't fully understand as he delved deeper and deeper into her kiss. He grabbed her hips and lifted her off the trunk. She gasped against his mouth which only made him want her more. Gently and slowly, he laid her down on the blanket on the floor while continuing to kiss her. Her one hand extended above her head which Abe ran his hand up and interlocked their fingers. With each kiss, he felt a piece of himself come back to life. It was like she was knitting his soul back together. Abe found it difficult to stop.

He brushed her hair aside and began kissing her neck and collarbone. Daisy let out a small, pleasant moan. He ran his hands down her side feeling every curve of her body. As he trailed his hand back up her body, her body suddenly went rigid.

"Abe, stop," Daisy stated and slightly pushed him off of her. He held on for a second unsure if he was hearing her correctly. "Abe, please stop."

It took Abe a moment to register what was going on, but he slowly moved away from Daisy. He left like he was coming off a high and feeling a bit dazed and confused. His breath was heavy and rapid. His palms were sweaty and his body was ready, but something was wrong. Daisy moved into an upright sitting position and hugged her knees. Her hands were so tightly closed that her knuckles were turning white. A single, silent tear trickled down her cheek. Abe must have done something horribly wrong.

"This is wrong. I think it's best you go now," Daisy said without looking at him. Abe sat facing Daisy completely dumbfounded. "I need you to leave, Abe. Now."

"Oh - um- yes, okay," Abe stumbled, uncertain of what had changed. He stood up and began walking towards the door. "Did I do something wrong?"

"Please just leave. I can't do this right now. I cannot do this!" Daisy snapped with an anger Abe had never seen before. She stood up and raced past him to open the door. She pointed out the door. "Now. Leave now. Please!"

"Yes, of course," Abe said as he walked through the door. The door slammed behind him, almost hitting him on the way out. He leaned his ear back against the door and listened as Daisy let out huge sobs. *What had he done?*

13

Pained Memories

Daisy collapsed against the door as heavy sobs overcame her body. She couldn't help it. She felt possessed by fear and disgust, her whole body vibrated. Her eyes blurred. She tried to breathe but it was like her lungs couldn't expand. She couldn't escape from the memory corrupting her mind.

Lord Corinthian.

When it happened, it didn't seem so bad, but everything that came after corrupted Daisy's peace. The way her mother acted, being locked in her room, being sent away to Dame Agatha's finishing school, losing her sister. It was like everything overwhelmed her at once, but Lord Corinthian was at the forefront of her mind. Daisy couldn't shake the lingering feeling of the painful memories. A subtle motion, a soft touch, and Daisy found herself reliving every ounce of pain she had experienced in the hands of her parents, Lord Corinthian, and Dame Agatha.

It wasn't Abe's fault. Daisy doubted he even knew, but the memories came back fresh to her mind. The simple brush of her hip destroyed the peace and joy of the moment as Lord Corinthian intruded in her mind. The pungent odour of brandy filling her nostrils as he whispered demands in her ear. His hand clutching her wrist and trapping her to the wall. The breeze harassing her skin as he ripped her dress away from her body. It was like a trigger that released everything. All of her memories just came out with one simple thought.

The endless whippings.

Being locked in a room for days.

Being constantly criticised and ostracised.

Never being good enough for anyone.

And Abe had fallen victim to it all.

Everything hidden deep in Daisy's mind suddenly came to the forefront and overwhelmed her entirely. Her breath was shallow and quick. Her heart drummed in her ears. Sweat dripped down her back. She grabbed the closest bucket-like object and promptly emptied what little food she had eaten. Her insides felt rotten and her soul felt hollow. She cried and cried and cried. She needed to rid herself of the memory, of the pain, of the horror that plagued her mind.

A bottle of wine sat beside the basket that Abe had set up. Daisy managed to crawl over to the nearly untouched bottle and devoured its entire contents. After a few minutes, her brain felt numb, but the memory still crept around the edges. She dug around in the basket and found another bottle of wine. She drank the whole bottle though a bit slower this time, enjoying the flavour and losing herself a bit more with each swallow.

By the bottom of the bottle, Daisy found herself rather giddy. She rummaged in the basket looking for another bottle of booze, but came up empty handed.

Displeased with this outcome, Daisy attempted to stand. She stumbled, but managed to make her way to the door. She half expected the door to be locked, but was pleasantly surprised to find it open.

She fell out into the hallway and caught herself on the opposite wall. She felt dizzy and the floor seemed slanted. The hallway appeared the same both ways and Daisy couldn't remember which way she had come from. Everything was dark and gloomy and rocky. *Why was everything rock?* The hallways, the roof, the floor. It was all the same rock. It was unwelcoming and Daisy hated it.

Daisy hiccupped and found herself following the slant of the floor. Down and down and down she went until the hallways widened, but she still felt incredibly lost. There were several hallways that branched off this one area and Daisy wasn't sure which way to go. *Where was she even trying to go?*

Abe!

She had to find Abe. She needed to apologise. She wanted him to understand that it wasn't him. When she kicked him out, he looked like a beaten dog, all sad eyes and droopy lips. Daisy liked dogs. She hoped one day she could own one with Abe.

Right - Abe!

Daisy glanced around at the various stone corridors, trying to pick one to go down. The labyrinthian style of this place was confusing and unpleasant. Instead of picking any particular direction, Daisy fell to the floor.

"Abe!" Daisy called and listened to her voice echo around her. It sounded funny which made her giggle and hiccup. "Abe!"

Nothing. *Where could he be?*

"AMBROSE!" She yelled as loud as she could and promptly fell over from the force of her own voice. She found herself giggling on her back as her voice bounced all around her. She could hear slow, methodical footsteps coming down one of the hallways. She rolled her head to look at the person coming. Daisy hoped it was Abe, but was completely disappointed when Azalea came walking into the room.

"Ugh! Not you!" Daisy groaned and rolled on her side facing away from Azalea. Azalea scoffed loudly behind Daisy. .

"Who were you looking for?" Azalea questioned.

"My betr - bethro - betroth-ed. Gosh, that is a hard word to say. The one I am marrying, which is not you. You're my undead sister."

"Undead sister?"

"You died, but then didn't die. Undead." Daisy laid on her back with an exasperated throw. She was annoyed with questions and her sister's general presence. "Which was not acceptable I might add. I cried over losing you. For no reason! You didn't even die. But you killed my parents which was also not acceptable, you hornswoggler."

"Daisy. Are you drunk?"

"No." Daisy hiccupped and then giggled at the sound. "Maybe."

"Dear Lord, what did he do to you?"

"Lord Corinthian corrupted my mind and body." Daisy punched the ground in a fit before sitting upright and looking directly at Azalea. "He ruined me and I was sent away because Mama couldn't see what happened."

"What are you blabbering about?"

"You were asleep. At the party. At *your* party. In the room of naked people. And I left you to sleep but when I left, *he* attacked *me*. My beautiful dress he ripped and the air tickled my skin. But Mama - Mama didn't see it that way. She hit me and sent me away. But she sent me to Abe. What if Abe doesn't want to marry me because I am ruined? Oh, my lovely Ambrose. Where is he? Do you know where he is? I have to apologise. I have to tell him the truth."

"I think you need to go to bed. You are being a church bell, my dear."

"I can't sleep until I find Abe." At that moment, another set of footprints sounded down one of the hallways. Daisy shakily stood and started running down the corridor towards the sound. Azalea called after her, but Daisy didn't acknowledge her. Eventually, Daisy could hear Azalea's steps following her, chasing her. Having very little balance and coordination, Daisy found herself tripping and running and smacking against the walls, but still Azalea couldn't catch her. It reminded Daisy of when they were children playing games together. Daisy giggled as they ran, but clearly Azalea did not find it as humorous.

"Daisy!" Azalea called after her. "Daisy stop running."

"No. You can't catch me," Daisy chimed and continued down the hallway forgetting what she was trying to do in the first place.

The hallway opened into a large foyer with several heavy tapestries hanging around the room. Fluffy rugs covered the floor and seemed like a comfortable place to lay. She tumbled into the rugs and cuddled one like a blanket. Azalea came huffing into the room, short of breath.

"Daisy!" Azalea yelled.

"What?" Daisy snapped back.

"You can't just go running off like that. You shouldn't even be out of your room unattended!"

"Why not? I can't find anything here. It's all a big maze, so it's not like I can leave."

"The hallways change everyday so they can't be mapped, but it's dangerous. The rooms can change vastly from one moment to the next," Azalea explained while slowly moving towards Daisy with her hands out. Daisy dismissed Azalea with a wave and a laugh. Then, it came back to Daisy what she was trying to do.

"I was looking for Abe," Daisy recalled. "I must find him as soon as possible. Where is Abe?"

"I don't know where he is!"

"Well, go find him then." Daisy thought this was an obvious answer, but Azalea seemed more irritated than anything. She was almost within arms reach of Daisy.

"I don't have time to go chasing down people."

"Don't you control his mind? Can't you just call him here?" Daisy rolled away from her sister and further wrapped herself up in the rugs.

"No. I don't control his mind anymore, but he is bound to me."

"So he wasn't lying?"

"I don't know what he told you, but his mind and his actions are mostly his own."

"So he loves me then?"

"From what I can tell, yes. That is quite true." Daisy laid on her back and stared at the ceiling. The floor beneath her rocked as the ceiling spun in circles. She rolled on her side and vomited on one of the rugs. She wiped the back of her sleeve across her mouth to remove the excess. "Dear Gods Daisy. We need to get you to bed."

"Abe first."

"Daisy, let's go to bed." Azalea gently touched Daisy's knee. Daisy swatted Azalea's hand away and curled her knees closer to her chest.

"No!" Daisy sat up and began screaming, again. "ABE! ABE! AMBROSE, WHERE ARE YOU?"

Seemingly out of nowhere, Abe appeared from behind a tapestry. His hair was like liquorice, but Daisy knew it wasn't sticky. It was soft and luscious and smelled fantastic. He always smelled great. Like lavender and cedarwood. He had a small scar above his lip that Daisy found herself longing to bite. His sapphire and emerald eyes jumped off his snow white face, but Daisy noticed the slight redness around them like he had been crying. He was tall and slender and very handsome. Daisy felt like he was often too handsome for her. She was often confused why such a dashing gentleman would pick such a plain and ugly partner. Daisy seemed so far from what Abe should be with.

"Abe!" Daisy exclaimed and started crawling towards him.

"What is going on?" Abe asked Azalea which Daisy didn't appreciate.

"I have been looking for you," Daisy explained before Azalea could answer.

"Yes, I gathered that, but what happened to you?"

"I found her in the hallway like this," Azalea stated. "She has been looking for you, so I think she is your responsibility now. I have many things to attend to which don't include my drunken sister."

Azalea turned and left through one of the many hallways attached to the room. Daisy finally reached Abe and pulled on his hands until he sat.

"Daisy, are you drunk?" Abe asked with a furrowed brow.

"No - well, maybe. I drank two bottles of wine. I think. Maybe there was more. I don't remember honestly," Daisy said matter-of-factly. "But that's not important. I needed to talk to you. I have to apologise and tell you the truth."

"How about we get you to bed and we can talk in the morning?"

"Why is everyone trying to put me in bed?" Daisy threw herself back on the cushioned floor. "I just came from my room with a bed. I am not sleepy."

"We don't think you're sleepy. We think you are drunk."

"But I don't want to."

"How about I carry you back to your room and you can tell me whatever it is you need to tell me?" Daisy contemplated his offer for a moment before nodding in acceptance. He scooped her up with her knees slung over his one arm and his other arm supporting her upper body. She wrapped her arms around his neck and rested her head against his shoulder. For being as skinny as he was, he was certainly strong.

As they walked, Daisy recounted her experience with Lord Corinthian and her mother. She reviewed the whipping and endless torture her mother put her through. She explained what Lord Corinthian did to her and how she became the villain. She explained why she was sent to finishing school and how she finally met Abe. She explained how tonight, when he brushed her hip and held her wrist all of those memories came rushing back and overwhelmed her. She apologised profusely and rambled on about the confusing hallways and trying to find him.

By the time they reached her door, Abe appeared very solemn and quiet. He opened the door without putting her down. Slowly, he moved over to the bed and placed Daisy down. He sat on the edge looking away from her. He supported his head with hands braced against his knees. He seemed pained and uncomfortable. In most cases, Daisy would give him time to process and space to feel, but this was not like most situations. Daisy's head felt full of wool and processing any information was difficult let alone strong emotions of others.

"I apologised. Are you still upset with me?" Daisy remarked rather unsympathetically.

"I was never upset with you, Dais," Abe responded. He dropped his hands and moved one leg onto the bed to better face Daisy. "I was confused because I didn't understand what I did wrong. Now that I do… I am sorry."

"For what? I needed to apologise to you. You shouldn't be apologising to me."

"I should have asked more questions to know what had happened. This whole thing could have been avoided if I had known. I often forget myself with you and give in to my feelings rather than maintaining my logic."

"You're being ridiculous. I never told you. How would you even know to ask?" Daisy threw herself against the pillows. She was starting to feel sleepy now. The room shifted before her. She had to close her eyes to stop the world from moving.

"I don't know, but I understand now and wish I knew about it before. Dais, I love you and I want to be able to understand you."

"Then look in my mind. I give you permission to view all my memories."

"Daisy, you are drunk. I am not going to do that right now. We can discuss this after you sleep it off." Daisy could hear him saying more words, but everything was getting muffled. With her eyes closed and her body cushioned, sleep didn't seem like such a bad idea. Before she was fully asleep, she felt Abe run his hand across her forehead to push her hair back and plant a small, soft kiss on her head. She fell into a deep sleep.

Abe stood in front of a waterfall inside a cave. There were lights hanging all around him casting shadows on the water that almost seemed to dance. The lights danced across the silver suit he wore which was adorned with intricate gold designs. He had attempted to tame his mess of midnight hair, but it's usual unruliness poked through. Music started to play and Daisy walked forward towards Abe. He beamed at her the closer she approached. She reached out her hand to grab his, but was torn away.

Suddenly, she stood on a black, slate cliffside. She had been here before, but things were slightly different. There was the dead tree that Abe stood under. He was still wearing the same silver pants, but his white shirt was unbuttoned with the sleeves rolled up, exposing the angry black mark on his forearm.

"You could have prevented this," Abe said. Daisy expected blood to start pouring from his chest as it always happened, but this time, the mark flared and Abe winced in pain. He let out an excruciating scream as blood began weeping from the mark.

"How do I prevent this?" Daisy yelled over his pained cries.

"You are the connection past this realm. You are the bridge. You just have to choose to remove it. Your power and love can drive out this evil."

Daisy sat up in bed quickly. Her head throbbed and the room spun. She puked over the side of the bed before righting herself. She collapsed back against the pillows and fell back into a dreamless sleep.

14

The Black Hole

The train slowed in a small town called Northern which Rosie thought was rather humorous since it was nearly as south as it could possibly be. The town consisted of one main street. There was a barber, a general store, a bank, a church, a bakery, a saloon with modest accommodations, and the town hall which had a small park in front of it. There were a few horses tied outside of the saloon but otherwise the street was deserted. The emptiness unsettled Rosie.

"Are you sure we're in the right place? There is nothing here." Rosie questioned Alina.

"This is the last place I knew they were. I don't know if they are still here, but I am hoping they are," Alina explained and started walking with determination. "This is a small farming town. Most of the residents live nearby, but not actually in town. When I last spoke to Gideon, he said they were living in a cave just outside of town."

"Gideon? Do you mean Gideon Grey?" Arlo asked. Evander snapped his head towards Alina, also seeming quite surprised.

"Yes. Gideon Grey," Alina replied.

"Not *the* Gideon Grey?" Evander pushed.

"Yes, *the Gideon Grey,*" Alina exaggerated.

"Who is Gideon Grey?" Brighid inquired. Rosie was glad she wasn't the only one confused, but she didn't want to say anything. She already felt like an outsider and didn't want to add to it even more. She often thought the less she knew, the better. If she only knew small pieces… there was only so much information she could possibly disclose.

"Gideon Grey is a legend of Conductor history. He was a sort of General during the war, but Abe would never talk about him. I found a copy of our old history books that talk about his victories, but I thought he was just a legend," Evander elaborated. Arlo nodded eagerly. Based on both of the men's excitement, this Gideon character was obviously important.

"And Alina knows him?" Brighid asked.

"Yes. Quite well." Alina replied. "He was one of the few people Abe would speak to after he lost Isabetta. It was just me, Ambrose, and Gideon for a while. Eventually, Gideon left and started training his own Conductors."

"Who is Isabetta?" Brighid inquired as she cocked her head to the side and scrunched up her nose. Alina smiled and placed her hand on Brighid's shoulder.

"That is a story for another day. We must get moving or we will draw too much attention."

Alina started walking and everyone followed. They quickly exited the other side of town. Alina walked with a confidence that Rosie couldn't emulate. The flat farm land gave way to rolling hills and dense forest. After a while, they seemed to be aimlessly wandering through a forest, but Alina held her resolve. They delved deeper and deeper into the forest until they came to a river. Alina started following the river upstream.

"Alina!" Rosie called. "Do you know where we are going?"

Evander shot Rosie a warning look. Rosie glared back encouraging him to challenge her. He shook his head and went back to focusing on his steps.

"Mostly. Gideon gave ambiguous clues and mapping in various letters, but never all in one. He was worried they would get intercepted," Alina explained.

"He was against the Grand Master then? The history books never mentioned that," Evander added.

"The Grand Master controlled the narrative in every single history book. Of course she would say the biggest war hero was on her side. That's why he has become a legend that no one believes still exists. He disappeared. He's been in hiding just as Ames has been. They were never really free from her though they did temporarily delay her. It's taken the Grand Master quite a while to make a move again. Longer than I think any of us expected."

Eventually, the river opened up into a basin with a waterfall pouring into one side. It was quite beautiful. The water was the bluest blue Rosie had ever seen. There were trees all around the water, and colourful flowers peeking through the dense green foliage. It felt tropical and warm. The intensity of the colours almost seemed unnatural. Alina began stripping down to her undergarments. Rosie was taken aback by the sudden disrobing. It was as far as possible from being a lady. No one else, however, seemed to bat an eye.

"We will have to swim, so make yourselves lighter. Can everyone swim?" Alina said over her shoulder. No one protested, and continued to follow Alina's lead. Evander and Arlo took off their shoes, shirts and jackets. Brighid stripped down to her undergarments. Rosie blushed and took off her ring skirt, outer skirt, petticoats, and shoes. She did not nearly match the rest of them in their levels of nakedness, but she felt uncomfortable taking off more in front of men. With everyone mostly bared, they started wading into the crystal clear water. They reached the halfway point between the shore and waterfall. Alina took a deep breath and dove under the water. Rosie shook her head but followed anyway. She didn't have much choice.

Under the water was even more beautiful than above. The water was crystal clear. Small, colourful fish swam around them. Vibrant coral of orange, red, and purple painted the floor. The beauty of the water quickly diminished as Rosie noticed an unnatural feature. Just below the churning water of where the waterfall entered the basin sat a large, black hole that seemed to suck all the light around it. Alina began swimming towards it. Rosie reluctantly followed. The black hole of nothingness was not inviting. The closer they got, the darker it became. Rosie's lungs began to burn. She wasn't sure how much longer she could hold her breath, but she kept swimming.

Eventually, everything became black. It was like walking on a moonless night. There was no indication of where they were going, but Rosie could hear the swishing of the others swimming and just kept following it. Rosie's lungs felt like they were going to burst. She could taste metal in her mouth and was starting to panic. She breathed in water, making her lungs burn even more. She just had to keep swimming. Just keep swimming. Her arms started to slow and distant sounds of the others swimming started to get further and further away. She was falling behind, losing breath, and her consciousness was starting to falter. She kept trying to push forward, but she was struggling. A hand grabbed her wrist and started to pull her along. They moved significantly faster than Rosie ever thought she could by herself.

A faint light started to appear in the distance, but blackness was edging her vision. She wasn't sure she could make it. Suddenly, a bubble of air stuck to her face. Rosie inhaled desperately, but the bubble did not seem enough. The light got bigger and another air bubble came to Rosie's aid. Finally, they all emerged from the water. Rosie gasped for air and spat water out of her mouth. Everyone else seemed completely fine. They crawled out of the water like it was a bathtub and began ringing out the water of their clothes and hair.

"How - are - you - not - out - of - breath?" Rosie muttered between large heaving breaths.

"What do you mean? You just held your breath?" Brighid asked. Rosie flopped out of the hole in the ground onto the cave floor trying to regulate her breathing.

"For most of it, yes."

"We can just move the air and make, like, a pocket of air around our heads," Evander explained.

"Is that what was happening at the end? Who helped me?" Everyone looked sheepishly around, clearly trying to avoid eye contact with Rosie. They did not seem to want to admit helping Rosie. She did not understand their apprehension.

"Shh," Alina hissed. "We are not alone."

At that moment, several balls of light shone in the depths of the cave. There were blue, red, green, and brown orbs of light hovering above the ground. Rosie froze in fear, uncertain of what to do.

"Gideon Grey," Alina called. "Gideon, show yourself, you big meater."

"If it was anyone else," a man spoke while stepping forward in the light. "I would have killed you."

Gideon, presumably, was a large man that radiated military prowess. He carried himself in a mature and seasoned manner that made Rosie instantly respect him. He had silver hair that was fitting of his last name. One of his eyes was a light ice blue while the other was a deep brown, almost black in colour. He had stubble across his chin and a thin moustache that matched his hair. He would be the definition of attractive, except for a large scar that ran from his forehead over his brown eye and ended just above his lip. It added a ruggedness to his appearance. Rosie was rather impressed, attracted, and fearful of him all at the same time.

Alina squealed with glee and ran towards the man. She wrapped her arms around him in a large hug. He lifted her off of her feet and spun her in a circle before setting her back on the ground. Rosie saw Alina's cheeks flush bright pink and a strange smile cross Alina's face. Several other people also stepped out of the dark. Rosie suddenly felt very out of place and extremely unnumbered. *How many more people did Gideon have down here?*

"Alina, what are you doing here?" Gideon asked while gently pushing Alina's hair back. "Not that I am not happy to see you, but I wasn't expecting you."

"Ah, yes. Perhaps we should discuss in private the intricacies of the situation."

"I see Ambrose is not with you. Shall I assume this is not good tidings or a simple visit?" Alina smiled sadly at Gideon and rubbed his arm tenderly. Rosie had only seen this level of care and affection from Alina for Brighid. Seeing it for someone else was unusual.

"This is not a casual visit. But please, let's go somewhere private to discuss the situation," Alina pleaded. Gideon extended his arm to invite her in. She linked through his elbow and followed him into the darkness.

"Help the others get dried off, please, and get them some proper clothing." Gideon called from the dark. The other people began moving about the group. One girl came over and helped Rosie to her feet. Rosie smiled appreciatively, but the other person suddenly seemed very concerned.

"You're not a Conductor," the girl announced. Other heads turned towards Rosie. She suddenly left like she was standing on stage, naked, in front of a large, judgemental audience. She knew however, she couldn't let this phase her.

"Quite right," Rosie replied while brushing off her clothes.

"How did you get through the tunnel?"

"We gave her a bubble," Evander interjected and immediately came to Rosie's aid. He slid his hand around her waist and pulled her to his side. Rosie tried not to act shocked or repulsed. The girl assessed Rosie and Evander before scoffing and turning away. Evander turned to face Rosie making a barrier with his back between them and the others.

"Not everyone will take kindly to you. Being smitten with me may help ease some of their concerns. Also, saying you are in the processing of becoming a Conductor is probably better than just saying you aren't one. Understand?" Evander dictated.

"I am used to being isolated. And besides, you're not exactly my type," Rosie said rather snidely. Evander looked suddenly insulted.

"Clever, dashing, and devilishly handsome is not your type?" Evander puffed out his chest with overconfidence. Rosie rolled her eyes.

"More like men aren't my *type*. And, even if they were, I couldn't be with you if I wanted to." Evander seemed confused by Rosie's remark. She had never really outright said she was a sapphist to anyone, but she was annoyed enough with the situation to ignore social cues. She groaned and put her hands on her hips. "Yes. Fine. I understand what you are saying and will play my part."

"Very well." Evander nodded and turned back towards the group. The others were mostly collected and making their way through the darkness. Rosie and Evander followed with the others.

15

Useless Memories

Abe sat on the edge of Daisy's bed for a long time. She looked peaceful in her sleep. Her breathing was deep and slow. She hardly moved at all. Occasionally, her nose would scrunch up like something was annoying her, but otherwise, she slept soundly. Watching her sleep was relaxing to him. With each breath, Abe wished for her innocence to remain. However, that innocence was already tainted.

He really knew so little about her, but loved her with every fibre of his being. He wanted to know more about her so he could understand her and love her fully. It pained him to see Daisy fighting her own demons and brought out the fear that maybe Daisy wouldn't like his demons. Abe had lived a long time meaning he had seen, and done, a great many things.

His past was not clean. There was blood painted across many of his memories, but when you've existed since the beginning of time and lived for the majority of human history, it would be almost impossible to keep your hands clean. Abe was not proud of all he had done, but all he could do was make the next right choice. The past could not be changed, but the future was unwritten. Abe wanted to ensure that the future was positive and bright. He mostly wanted that because of Daisy now.

Surely, he had loves in the past. Alina was something of an old flame. He even had Isabetta, who died bearing his child. He also had his studies which were more like family than loves per se. There were others that he held dearly in his existence, but for some reason, none could quite hold a light to Daisy. She was pure and genuine. She was beautiful and confident. She was bold and independent. She was everything that Abe wasn't and all that he needed. Daisy had quickly become his balancing partner without even realising she was doing anything. Abe didn't think she knew even half of the power she held over him. He would do anything for her and he didn't know how to explain that to her.

She made a small whimper and readjusted in the bed. Abe stood and brushed her hair back so he could gently kiss her on the head. He looked over his shoulder as he walked towards the door. While closing the door, Abe watched to the very last moment he could, cherishing Daisy's essence. The door clicked shut. Abe stood for a moment, his forehead resting against the door. It was taking everything in him to leave her, but he had other things to attend to.

He began walking down the hallway to find Azalea. Abe had much to discuss with her. Mostly, he wanted to discuss Daisy. Surely, Azalea knew of Daisy's past, and yet, she never said anything in the past year. She played in his mind and knew his desires, but never thought anything about Daisy was worth sharing. Abe was furious with

Azalea, and he wasn't even sure she deserved it. Nonetheless, he had words to say to her. None of which were kind.

There were a few places that Abe had grown accustomed to finding Azalea. Firstly, there was the war room. Not that she called it that, but it was essentially where Azalea and her followers met to discuss movement of various allies and enemies. Abe was often excluded from those meetings or deafened so he could not hear anything. Alternatively, Azalea was in her quarters, the library, or, the most recent addition, the wedding room. She did not often stray from these locations, but the locations often moved.

Whether to confuse him or potential insurgents, it seemed like the floor plan always changed. Hallways would randomly appear and disappear. Sometimes, a hallway would dead-end where the day before it continued on. Abe found it frustrating, but he did admire her cleverness. There appeared no logic to the set-up or any pattern to follow. For anyone to get in, they would have to understand the changes. Even being here for a year, Abe still struggled to figure it out.

After several wrong turns and nearly falling off a newly appeared cliff, he managed to find his way to Azalea's chambers. He knocked on the door and waited for permission to enter. The door opened on its own exposing the room behind it. Azalea was always one for grandeur. Even when they first existed, Azalea always wanted to create more. She created mountains so vast that no human could climb them. She created pits so deep that no light existed. She always wanted things bigger, better, and bolder. Her room now was no exception.

Abe walked into a sitting room. Unlike most rooms in these caves, it did not feel like it was underground. The floors were wood and the walls were a deep green with a gold flowering pattern. A roaring colour-changing fire floated in the middle of the room. Heavy, mahogany chairs with plush cushions and gem encrusted detailing sat around the fire. The colours on the cushions were deep, rich tones that even royalty would have a tough time affording. Branching off of the sitting room were four carved wood doors with various images of Azalea. Abe couldn't place any of the scenes, but Azalea seemed victorious in all of them. Around the one door were stained glass windows that threw beautiful rainbows around the room. Abe considered himself more humble and found these loud displays rather unsavoury.

He sat in one of the chairs and waited for one of the other doors to open. Whatever door opened usually indicated which room Azalea was in or which room Abe was allowed to enter. The doors were not able to be opened manually and instead required Azalea to release them to open.

He tapped his fingers on his knee. He was bored and anxious and had no interest in waiting. He stood up and began pacing around the chairs. He hoped that pacing would make waiting less annoying, but it did not help. Eventually a door opened, and Azalea entered the sitting room. She sat down on one of the chairs and gestured that Abe should do the same. Abe did as told. She snapped her fingers and a tray of tea and cookies appeared beside her. She picked up a cup of tea and took a small slip.

"Would you like a cup?" Azalea offered.

"Not really," Abe stated.

"Hm." Azalea set the cup down and turned back to Abe. "What do you want then, Ambrose?"

"Firstly, don't call me Ambrose. I hate it. Secondly, I have some things to discuss with you."

"I am not exactly trying to make you happy, so I can only imagine what issue you have fixated on now." Abe was surprised for a moment. *Wasn't Azalea always trying to make him fall in love with her? Had something changed?*

"Do you no longer desire my affection?" Abe questioned with a head tilt. Azalea stared at him with a flat face. Abe could not read her emotions at all and that flustered him even more.

"There has been a shift in our balance. The addition of Daisy has changed things. I find I do not love you in the same way I used to, but I do love my sister and will do anything to make her happy, even if that means losing you. We are no longer meant to be together. There is a new person that has restored the balance. Perhaps it was the unbalanced nature that drew me to you. I don't feel that anymore."

Abe felt a tidal wave of relief wash over him. He did not realise how much he had been anticipating some type of explosion or destruction from Azalea that Daisy would get caught in the middle of. Although he had no reason to, Abe trusted every word that Azalea said. Maybe it was because he wanted it to be true more than anything. Or, maybe it was the simple nature of Azalea's statement. Either way, Abe was grateful for the release.

"I understand," Abe responded, trying not to give anything away regarding his emotions. "Things have certainly changed."

"I assume though, my affections are not what has brought you here," Azalea retorted while looking over her teacup at him.

"Well, yes actually, but not your affection for me. I am concerned about Daisy." Azalea sat upright like an alert dog indicating to something. Abe was taken aback by the sudden display of concern. Earlier, Azalea seemed like Daisy was a nuisance. Now, it appeared like Daisy was the only thing that mattered.

"What about Daisy? Is she okay?"

"Well, you saw she was drunk."

"Yes, I've never seen that before."

"Based on her chatter as I brought her back to her room, she drank to forget Lord Corinthian."

"Oh." A sadness overcame Azalea which quickly passed and changed into indifference. All of her earlier emotion completely faded and she returned back to the stoic Azalea Abe was used to. It was like Azalea did not want to show she cared about Daisy.

"You never told me or showed me what happened to her. You had my brain for a whole year and you never gave me anything useful. If Daisy is your focus, why didn't you give me the information to help her? To not hurt her? To properly love her?" Abe rambled. Azalea seemed surprised at Abe's outburst, but her face quickly stilled. She picked at her nails in contemplation of what to say next.

"Honestly… I never thought I would see her again," Azalea said in a small voice that Abe barely heard her.

"What?"

"I never thought I would see Daisy again in a way that she wasn't fighting me. I surely never expected her to be here or planning her wedding. I thought you or her would be dead and not reunited. I thought she would try to stop me and I would have to kill her or you would get in the way of me killing her and you would die. This is not what I expected in my wildest dreams, so it never occurred to me to help you in any way. I didn't think it would come to the point where you would need help. I was just waiting for the inevitable."

Abe sat for a moment in silence to absorb Azalea's words. She had expected Daisy to be dead. This was not Azalea's plan. Abe was still supposed to be her pawn.

"Oh," Abe finally managed to say. "I - uh… I am glad that isn't what happened."

"Quite agreed," Azalea stated with a nod of her head. "Hence why I am focusing on this wedding. I need her to understand I do care and make this valuable and memorable for her. You make her happy, so I will do what I can to make her happy and change how she sees me."

"Yes. The wedding."

"Tomorrow."

"What?"

"Everything is ready so you are getting married tomorrow."

"Tomorrow?"

"Yes. Tomorrow."

"Does Daisy know?"

"Probably not."

"But tomorrow?"

"Yes."

"Dear Gods. I am getting married tomorrow."

16

Forgotten Feelings

Alina followed Gideon down a long, dark hallway to his office. Gideon's office was nothing like Abe's last office. There was stuff everywhere. Globes, trunks, sculptures, and art were all scattered purposefully about the room. Rugs of various colours and fabrics covered the entire floor. The space was filled with mismatched furniture that seemed to defy any conventional sense of style or design. It was clear Gideon was well-travelled as pieces of memorabilia and treasures from every corner of the globe could be seen. Perhaps, eclectic was the only way to describe it.

After taking the room in, Alina's eyes were drawn to a small box with a crane carved into it; she instantly recognized it. Before Gideon had left Alina and Abe, they journeyed to a small island in the Pacific Ocean. Alina had bought the box as a parting gift for Gideon. She was surprised he still kept such a trinket as well as his other treasures. Most Conductors moved regularly in order to avoid unwanted questions and attention due to their delayed ageing process, so they often retained very few personal possessions.

"Do you remember the little market where you bought this box?" Gideon asked.

"Yes, I remember Abe drunkenly walking behind us as we shopped at the stalls. It was one of the last happy memories I had for a while. It took a long time to get Abe off the bottle after that. He didn't do well with you gone," Alina replied.

"I am sorry you had to go through that, but I had to leave."

"Had to leave? Why?"

Gideon immediately turned his back and walked away from Alina to clear off two chairs in the middle of the room. He lounged in one chair while Alina delicately sat in the other. He truly hadn't changed much since she saw him last. With pride, he adorned his victories, and with wisdom, he embraced his defeats. Gideon always presented as mature and regal, but he had a tendency to loosen up when Ames was around. He was years and years older than Alina, but she had always found him intriguing. Handsome even.

"So, what brings you here?" Gideon asked. His voice was deep and husky. It was almost like a growl that sent pleasant shivers all over Alina's body. Alina tried to suppress the tempting thoughts playing at the edges of her mind.

"How up to date are you on Conductor politics?" Alina responded. Gideon raised an eyebrow which Alina knew to mean he was cautious and suspicious.

"I have heard rumours of turmoil but nothing concrete enough to make decisions. I am assuming you are more aware of the current situation?"

"Quite, actually. The Grand Master is active and has Ambrose under her control."

Gideon sat up straight and stared at Alina. "What do you mean?"

Alina quickly reviewed the last two years. She explained how Ambrose met Daisy and how Daisy became a Conductor. Then, how the Grand Master found out their location and attacked them. Alina explained going back to Daisy's house, the emergence of a new force, and Ames's sacrifice. Finally, Alina went over more recent events like losing Daisy to the Grand Master. By the end of Alina's explanation, Gideon sat with his elbows on his knees and his fingers tented in front of his face in deep concentration.

"Now, I have come to ask for your help," Alina finished. Gideon stood up and began pacing the room.

"I heard the Grand Master had returned," Gideon said. "But based on what you've said, she is doing things very differently."

"With the emergence of a new force and the presence of all three creators in one area, things are unpredictable. She has never had such power in her hands. And I honestly don't know where Daisy's allegiance lies. Azalea is her sister; she has known her and loved her entire life. Ames, she knew for a few months and maybe fell in love with him in that time, but he's been gone for the past year, and she has kept mostly to herself and Rosette. I don't know how much I can trust her. I worry that she will change sides and that her loyalty does not lie solely with Ames." Alina could hear the fear in her voice and could only imagine what Gideon thought. His expression gave nothing away.

"What is your plan?"

"I am not a militant, Gideon. You know that. All I know is that we need to get Ames out of the Grand Master's grasp and potentially Daisy, as well. If the opportunity arises, I suppose. We cannot allow the Grand Master to retain such power."

"Do you know anything else? Like where the Grand Master is? Or how many people have sided with her?"

"I have told you all I know."

"You are asking me to put up a great deal."

"What choice do we have? We fight, or we are enslaved, or we die. None of the options are ideal." Gideon stopped pacing and faced Alina. There was a sadness to his expression that sent a sharp pain through Alina's stomach. He sat down and reached his hands out to Alina. She graciously accepted.

"Alina, darling. I want to help, but I must discuss this with my studies and decide what is best for all of us. I cannot make the decision for us all. I will need your support and you will need to fill in the details of the story that I cannot provide them. This includes who Ambrose really is. Most of them have met Ames or have heard of him, so it will help convince them. If I can recruit some of them, I will assist you, but I must support my studies. That is where my allegiance lies."

"I understand your position, but your preference may not be a long-term solution. I didn't see the war like you did. I saw the aftermath of it, so you understand better than I do what she is capable of."

"I cannot make the decision for them, but I will help guide them on the correct path as much as I can."

"Shall we handle this now?"

"Perhaps, but first…there is something I must say… something I must do…" Gideon leaned over and gently kissed Alina on the cheek. Alina felt heat rush to her cheeks. Her heart fluttered and her eyebrows raised. He pulled back and stared into Alina's eyes. Gideon hadn't been around in a long time, so she honestly wasn't sure what to think of this. "I… uh, you had always been with Ambrose, but I … I never understood it. I just…"

Alina sat in silence, considering what he was implying. She had been so fixated on the past that she often forgot to live in the present. Perhaps it was because she never had anyone else to focus on, but here with Gideon… Alina felt breathless. Alina and Gideon had kept in contact ever since he left to start his own studies over seventy years ago, and even though they had been apart everything felt so easy with him. It didn't feel like work or like she had to convince him of anything. He was his own person. He wasn't broken; he hadn't lost in his memories. He was present and interested and so very handsome. Ames has moved on, so *why couldn't she?*

"I know- I… uh - I'm not him. I could never be, but you - I… you are-"

Alina gently placed her hand on his cheek. He stopped babbling and closed his eyes for a moment. His body relaxed ever-so-slightly. When he opened his eyes, a new seriousness had come over him. He rolled back his shoulders and lifted his head. He held Alina's gaze. Alina kept a soft expression and a light smile trying to encourage him to keep going. He swallowed so hard that Alina could see his throat move.

"I thought my feelings had passed," Gideon whispered. "Even with your letters, I felt connected to you, but not the same as when I was with you. All those years ago, you were with Ambrose, so I never acted. I loved Ames like a brother, and I cared for you immensely. I would never want to inflict additional pain on you. That's why I left. I couldn't keep pretending. When I saw you today, all those emotions came flooding back, and those feelings are still raw. I didn't expect it at all, but you are here and my heart feels full. With the letters, I never had to actually face any of my emotions. Now you say we are faced with impending doom and I have to say something, Alina. I have to tell you how I feel. I understand if you don't feel the same, but I felt I needed to say something."

Alina smiled softly and kissed him. It was quick and sweet. She pulled back and looked at him through her lashes. She wasn't sure if that was where he was going, but it felt right. He grabbed her waist and pulled her on top of his lap. She kissed him deeper and longer. He was tense for a moment under her before relaxing. His breath was short and his kisses were desperate. His hands ran across her corset slowly loosening each strand. He briefly stopped kissing her to pull off her corset and shirt. His pupils were dilated and a bead of sweat ran down his temple. Alina bit her lower lip in anticipation of what would come next.

His hands explored her bare chest slowly and purposefully. Alina let her head drop back and relish in the sensation. He kissed her collarbone. Alina started undoing his shirt and promptly threw it on the floor.

"Alina," Gideon moaned against her lips.

"Gideon," Alina replied while tracing the waistline of his trousers.

"Alina!" He threw Alina onto the rug-covered floor and shortly followed her into a mess of rugs and fabric.

17

A Circus Meeting

Rosie and the others walked into a large room that hardly seemed underground. Large windows portrayed different landscapes that Rosie was certain were pictures until they started to move. One was a snowy area with pine trees and a lake. Another was the exact opposite, displaying a dry desert, sand dunes, and a hot sun. A third window had a dense rain forest while the fourth had an open prairie. In the middle of the four windows was a large double door with various animals carved into each of the eight panels. Several chairs and couches were scattered about the room in various seating positions. Heavy bookcases overstuffed with books lined the walls without the windows. One wall also had a large fireplace that seemed to light and heat the whole space. It was cosy and welcoming.

A door slammed behind them which made Rosie and the others jump. Some of Gideon's students chuckled at their reactions which Rosie did not appreciate. Evander gently patted her arm before untangling himself from her and proceeding towards one of the other students. They spoke in hushed voices that Rosie could not hear. She wanted to be able to hear, but they purposefully seemed to be avoiding her. Eventually, Evander returned to Rosie as several of the new Conductors disappeared behind the large, carved doors.

"They are getting us some dry clothes and blankets to warm up," Evander explained to Rosie and the others. Arlo and Brighid nodded politely.

"Can you not just dry yourselves off? You can control air so can't you just use air to dry the clothes?" Rosie enquired. Evander stepped closer and lowered his voice.

"I wouldn't recommend asking such questions until we fully assess the extent of our welcome. The old war divided many conductors on one side or the other. Not all Conductors are friendly to other conductors, let alone outsiders. We are dependent on Alina to get us through this. Try to keep questions regarding conduction to a minimum. Understand?" Rosie nodded. "Good. However, to answer your questions, it's generally quicker to just change. Drying clothes can take quite a while and it feels weird against your skin. It gets rougher somehow."

At that moment, the heavy doors reopened and two people came walking in carrying a trunk between them. They set the trunk down on the ground and opened the lid. The trunk was full of all sorts of clothes. It was swathes of fabrics that Rosie had never seen the likes of. Loud patterns and bold colours that conflicted with each other. Rosie was unsure if she would find anything that matched in the box.

Brighid immediately began digging through the box and managed to pull some clothes she was willing to wear. She dawned a pink shirt with a silver and gold paisley pattern. Her pants were brown with a fine striping on them.

Arlo pulled a random shirt and pants with loud green, orange, purple, and yellow patterns. Evander gestured to Rosie to go next.

Ideally, she wanted a different frock or dress to cover her current undergarments, but everything that was being pulled out seemed to lack any sort of structure. As she dug through the box, she came to realise there were no dresses at all. Every garment was either a shirt or a pair of pants. Rosie had never worn anything but dresses. Pants had always been out of the question. It would not be ladylike at all to wear something so form fitting. She had seen Daisy create clothes, but that didn't seem like much of an option here. She looked to Evander, who stared back at her.

"There are no dresses," Rosie indicated. Evander moved closer to Rosie.

"Most female Conductors don't wear skirts or dresses," Evander whispered. "They can easily get caught up in conduction and cause more risks to the wearer. They wear pants, so they can move easier. I would not recommend asking for a skirt or dress either."

Rosie nodded her head and continued digging through the box. She eventually pulled out a pair of deep purple pants that felt fuzzy, and a royal blue coat with a frilled collar shirt. There were several partitions around the room. Rosie selected one and disappeared behind it.

She peeled her clothes off her skin. She was wet and clammy, and the various articles of clothing were stuck to her. It was a struggle to get each piece off, but she eventually managed. As she slid into the new clothes, while she was fully covered, she felt exposed. The outfit clung to each and every curve of her body in a way dresses never could or should.

When she rounded the screen, everyone else was already dressed. They looked like circus performers with the number of colours and patterns. Nothing quite matched, but somehow it all came together. Rosie felt ridiculous, but no one seemed to care. She approached Evander who smiled at her presence.

"You look good in pants," Evander joked. Rosie rolled her eyes.

"What do we do next?" Rosie asked in an attempt to redirect the conversation.

"We wait. Alina will discuss the situation with Gideon, then we will be directed what to do next."

"Are we sure that Alina is the one who should be discussing it? She doesn't exactly like Daisy and her mind hasn't been completely… clear."

"She has a relationship with Gideon which none of us do. I think she is the only one that can actually do it. As much as I would love to discuss many things with Gideon, I don't think I would be able to convince him of anything."

"So we just sit here and wait?"

"Correct!" Evander threw himself down on a chair and titled his head back. He closed his eyes and almost seemed to drift off into sleep. Rosie sat on the floor beside the fireplace and poked the fire with an iron. The hours passed slowly. It seemed like time barely moved. Rosie was bored, tired, and hungry. She desperately wanted to move on or do something, but she was bound by other people's wishes.

Finally, a door creaked open, and Alina strode out. The door closed behind her and everyone crowded around her eager for news and information. Brighid hugged Alina and looked up at her expectantly. Alina kissed her lightly on the head before looking at the others. Rosie noticed her hair was slightly askew and her cheeks were rather flushed. The clothes she wore were significantly too large and distinctly a male's. Obviously, Gideon and Alina were *quite* familiar.

"What happened?" Evander demanded. He was obviously eager to find out.

"Gideon is collecting his studies. We will present the information and they will decide. Gideon believes his studies have to make the informed decision on their own rather than dictating their actions. It also tests where his studies' alliances lie. They will be joining us shortly."

Shortly was hardly any time at all. As Alina finished her sentence, a door opened and several of the studies entered the room. They varied in age, size, and race. Rosie compared Abe's studies to Gideon's and noticed that Abe was more patterned. They were all white with varying shades of brown and blonde hair. Brighid was the only exception with Red hair that was deepening to a reddish-brown. Gideon's studies, however, were from every walk of life. He also appeared to have a great multitude more. Rosie had only ever seen three with Abe. Gideon appeared to have nearly twelve. It would require many more Conductors to eliminate Gideon's group. The last person to enter the room was Gideon whose hair also appeared quite tousled and clothes slightly crinkled. Rosie knowingly smirked.

"Thank you everyone for joining us. I would like to introduce our guests which I have not yet had the opportunity to welcome to our home. This is Alina, who is

Ambrose's assistant teacher." Gideon stated which corresponded to several hushed whispers. Clearly, Abe's name was also something of a story and myth. "Hush now. We have much to discuss and her associations will be further explored momentarily."

More murmurs rang through the crowd. Gideon's attempt to placate them only seemed to excite them more. Gideon gave them a moment to mutter before tapping a cane on the floor and silencing the crowd. Rosie hadn't even noticed he was carrying a cane. *Perhaps he conjured it?* Conduction was an enigma to Rosie, but she couldn't learn it. She wasn't allowed to learn it. She avoided learning about conduction at all costs. It was safer that way.

"If you will all remain silent, I will allow Alina to introduce her studies. Shall you choose not to, there will be unpleasant consequences," Gideon stated with a thundering voice. His threat obviously held weight as the crowd nearly froze.

"Thank you, Gideon." Alina said. She smiled softly at him. Her cheeks flushed further when Gideon grinned back. Rosie rolled her eyes. Discretion was not their strongest skill set. "These are my studies: Evander, Arlo, and Brighid as well as... a potential recruit, Rosette."

"Lovely. We are all very glad to have you joining us. Now, we have much to discuss." Gideon began. He started explaining the current situation including who Abe and Daisy were as well as their current predicament. He explained the potential threats and what could happen. Alina often interjected some important detail or fact about the last two years to provide further information, but otherwise, no one interrupted. The crowd listened with tense anticipation and uncertainty.

"Now, we ask you all if you will join us in going against the Grand Master," Gideon said. The room was silent. Rosie was certain you could hear a pin drop. "I know this is not an easy situation. Deciding to go to war is not something to take lightly, but I want each of you to make your own decision. I cannot make it for you."

"Isn't the Grand Master supposed to be our leader?" One girl with bright orange hair asked. "You are asking us to go against our leader."

"The Grand Master is a self-appointed leader that has earned the title through fear and pain. Little of our history has been shared as the books are not the truth. I lived through the war. I watched Ambrose lose everything and the Grand Master laugh in his face. She is not our ally. She is not a leader that listens to our people. Her reign needs to end for good, but we cannot do it alone."

"Didn't you fight for her in the last war?" A man with greying hair shouted. "Weren't you her greatest militant captain?"

"No. It is not something I like to speak of, but history is written by the victors. Ambrose and I were brutally defeated and barely survived, but the Grand Master knew we were loved and viewed as heroes. She corrupted the stories to support her narrative, maintain her grasp on her followers, and expand her influence to other Conductors."

Several whispers waved through the room. People talked amongst themselves to determine the validity of their statements. Rosie could hear the fear in their voices. She could hear the questions of reality versus fiction, of story versus myth. As Gideon opened his mouth to speak, a loud bang rang from the opposite wall. All the books fell from the wall and covered the floor.

Gideon immediately moved through the crowd towards the wall. Another loud explosion sounded from the wall and the shelves crashed to the ground. People began moving away from the sound and the collapsing wall. Gideon lit a fireball preparing for a fight. Rosie was unsure what to do as everyone else appeared to conjure some force to protect themselves. Evander appeared beside her and grabbed her wrist with a blue orb ready in the other hand.

"Stay with me," Evander whispered. "Do not lose sight of me."

Rosie nodded her head. Another loud bang rang through the room, and a crack scattered across the wall. Rosie assumed that alliances wouldn't matter when they were being attacked. All that mattered was surviving. One more crash and the wall dissolved into rubble. Bright light shone through the hole causing Rosie to squint and lift her hand to cover her face from the light. When she lowered her hand, a mass of people came running through the hole, ready to fight.

18

Sapphires and Emeralds

Daisy awoke the next morning with a pounding ache in her skull. She groaned as she rolled over to bury her head in the next pillow. The idea of getting out of bed was unpleasant. A hand caressed her back. Daisy tensed at the gentle gesture. She was unaware of who else was in the room. Slowly, she peeled the pillow back from her face and saw Abe with a light smile on his face. She covered her face back up. She was certain she looked like death, for she felt like she had died.

"How are you feeling?" Abe asked sympathetically.

"Like I was hit by a train," Daisy mumbled from beneath the pillow.

"I am sure. You were certainly… out of it. You've been asleep for quite some time." Daisy moaned in embarrassment. She did not remember much of the previous night. Perhaps small glimpses of endless hallways and soft rugs, but otherwise, her memory was blank.

"How long have I been asleep?" Daisy hoped it was long enough that Abe had also forgotten her behaviour. She was certain it was unsavoury at best.

"About a day." It was certainly not long enough. Daisy hugged the pillow tighter around her head.

"I don't remember much."

"I am sure you don't. However, you need to get up." Daisy removed the pillow from her face and managed to sit up despite her splitting headache. She winced and rubbed her temple gingerly.

"Why do I need to get up?" Daisy very much wanted to crawl back into bed and sleep it off, but Abe made it sound like that wasn't an option.

"Azalea has finished preparations and plans to marry us in about..." Abe glanced at his pocket watch, "six hours."

"Say that again?" Daisy was befuddled. She said she wanted to be with Abe, and she was willing to marry him, but she did not think it would be a mere matter of days before it came to fruition. It had been a dream of Daisy's to marry Abe, but she barely planned anything. She didn't even know what her dress looked like.

"We are getting married in six hours. That is... if you still want to. After last night, I wasn't sure if you would still want to marry me," Abe murmured. Daisy thought back to what caused her excessive drinking, and didn't think any less of Abe for it. It was not his fault in any way.

"I want to marry you, but I... I didn't plan anything. We didn't plan anything. I don't know what is going on and I don't know what to do..." Daisy looked at her hands. She could feel the tears building behind her eyes. "Abe. I don't understand why my sister is doing this, and I feel so completely alone. I don't know what I am doing here."

"I cannot begin to imagine how you are feeling." Abe grabbed her hands. His eyes were soft and understanding. She noticed some tiny wrinkles around his eyes, and an idea suddenly dawned on Daisy.

"You're immortal. Correct?"

"Sort of. I can still be killed and lose this form. I am not sure if I am killed, if I can reform or if I am lost, but I do not age and I do not appear to die from old age. What does this have to do with marrying me?"

"What if I am not like you? What if I die in fifty years time? Or what if I am like you and I am ageless? Will you still love me in one hundred years? One thousand years?" Abe brushed Daisy's hair back and stroked her cheek gently. He smiled softly and looked deeply into her eyes.

"Dais, none of us know what tomorrow holds. All that we can know is this moment. Right now, I know I want to spend every moment with you. You are my everything, and I have never felt like this with anyone before. My love will not diminish. My soul is yours if you want it. I give myself willingly to you for as long as we both shall live." Daisy paused and surveyed Abe's face for any indication of deceit, but found none. He seemed genuine and heartfelt. Although Daisy was still concerned, she didn't know what else to do.

"Then I suppose I should get ready. As should you."

Abe's whole face lit up like fireworks in the night sky. He seemed genuinely thrilled that Daisy was still willing to marry him. There wasn't a doubt in her mind that she loved Abe, but that didn't necessarily mean marrying him was the best option. Nonetheless, she was going to go through with it.

Abe stood from the bed and extended his hand to aid Daisy to her feet. She certainly felt woozy and lightheaded but managed to stay upright. Abe's eyes darted down Daisy's body before locking back on her face. His cheeks were flushed, and he was very purposely avoiding looking down. Daisy also looked down to see that she was wearing the sheerest nightgown possible. Hardly anything was left to the imagination. She did not remember when she put this on, but she knew that right now she felt exposed and incredibly uncomfortable.

"That – uh – was not what you were wearing when I put you to sleep last night," Abe said while trying to sound polite. Daisy quickly moved to the wardrobe and grabbed out a frock to slide over the sheer fabric.

"I don't remember putting it on. I don't even think it is mine. It's not exactly something I would wear," Daisy stumbled over her words in an attempt to explain away the situation, but it just made everything more uncomfortable. She stared at her feet and rubbed the back of her neck, uncertain what to do or say next.

"Well, um, I shall leave you to get ready then." Abe turned on his heel and quickly exited the room.

Shortly after he left, there was a knock on the door. One of Azalea's servants stood behind the door. She was a small thing, even smaller and simpler than Daisy. Nothing about her was extraordinary. Her features were plain. Her eyes were brown and blue, but not bright or dark. Daisy found it unusual. Most of the people Daisy had seen around Azalea were the definition of beauty. Having someone ordinary and simple was surprising.

"The Grand Master has asked me to escort you to her chambers to get ready for the wedding," the lady explained with a lilting accent that Daisy found intoxicating. Perhaps her voice was what captured Azalea's attention for it was amazing.

"Lead the way, miss," Daisy said and closed the door behind her. The lady scuttled away down the halls seemingly uninterested in whether Daisy was following or not. As such, Daisy followed closely behind, concerned about losing her escort in the twisting hallways.

After several turns and twists, Daisy started to feel dizzy. In her current condition, it felt like she was rolling down a hill. She was positive they were descending at some point, but even when she wasn't walking, the whole room seemed to move. After several minutes, Daisy was finally led to a plain, unassuming door. The girl opened the door and pushed Daisy through. Azalea sat in a chair casually sipping tea. She looked up at Daisy and smiled. The smile seemed genuine and made Daisy feel quite anxious. Daisy walked cautiously into the room.

"I see your adventures last night have carried into today. Here, drink this," Azalea stated and handed Daisy a cup of purple liquid with blue flecks in it. Daisy stared at the liquid.

"What is it?" Daisy asked prudently.

"An old cure that should refresh you." Azalea pushed the liquid towards her.

"Not mind control?" Daisy questioned quietly. Azalea laughed at her comment.

"I haven't found any ways to control one's mind through food, yet. Besides, that isn't quite how conduction works." Daisy sipped the liquid. It felt like liquid honey on her throat and immediately re-invigorated her. She felt like she had just awoken from the most amazing sleep of her life. Daisy craved more. Before she could take another sip, Azalea pulled the cup out of her hands. "It can also be quite addictive. That is all you need. I wouldn't want to become dependent. Besides, I need you to have your wits about you."

"Well, that's rude."

"Agreed. Now, to the task of the day!" Azalea clapped her hands excitedly. "Your wedding."

"Apparently. I didn't realise it would be so soon."

"I have got everything done," she shrugged. "I didn't feel like waiting. I have other things I need to attend to. I do promise you though, it will be perfect. I have thought of everything."

"You have something more important than your own sister's wedding?" A smile spread across Azalea's face that brought Daisy back to their childhood. Those few moments of stolen bliss and happiness that made Daisy's youth less miserable. Her sister was everything to her growing up. Just as quickly as the memories came, they were crushed by the reality of who her sister was and what she had done. Azalea must have felt the switch in Daisy's attitude for she also seemed suddenly uncomfortable.

"Perchance. There are a great many things going on that you know very little about, but I do want you here. I would love to have you by my side and teach you the ways of the Conductors. We could be so good together..." Azalea trailed off and fell silent. Daisy wasn't sure what to do, so she waited on some sign from her sister. "Now, would you like to see your dress?"

Daisy nodded eagerly. Azalea opened an armoire standing on one side of the room. Hidden within was a gorgeous dress like nothing Daisy had seen before. The dress was a brilliant white with a pleated bodice that gave way to a long, elegant skirt that filled the entire wardrobe. The skirt was layers upon layers of delicate, sheer fabric that sparkled like stars in the night sky. Upon closer inspection, Daisy noticed tiny gemstones of sapphire and emerald were attached to the fabric giving the dress small pops of colour. Large, flowy sleeves hung loosely off the shoulder exposing the collarbone. The sweetheart neckline was also decorated with sapphires and emeralds. As Azalea pulled the dress from the closet, Daisy noticed layers of blue and green fabric hiding deeper within the skirt. It was never something Daisy would pick out for herself, but it was truly gorgeous.

"What do you think? You should have had the base layer delivered to you this morning," Azalea stated. It clicked in Daisy's head as to what she was wearing under the frock. The sheer nightgown was for her wedding dress; however, she didn't remember receiving it or putting it on for that matter.

"I am currently wearing the base layer."

"It just protects your skin from some of the boning for structure. Whale bones can be exceedingly sharp. I'd rather you not die by being stabbed to death from your wedding dress." Daisy nodded to act like she knew what Azalea was talking about. "But what do you think of the dress? I made it for you. I've spent the last three days focusing on every single detail. I even hand stitched some of these gemstones on your neckline. It was difficult, but I had to make sure it was perfect for you, Daisy. You deserve only the best and I made sure you had it this time."

"It's stunning, but I could never see myself wearing it. This is so much more than what I am."

"Well, let's put it on and then we will see."

Getting the dress on proved more difficult than expected. The layers were difficult to navigate, and the corset was challenging to tie. After several minutes of struggling and cursing, Daisy was finally fastened into the dress. Although there were so many layers and jewels, the dress barely felt like it was on Daisy's body. It was light and moved in smooth motions around her. Before Azalea would allow Daisy to look at herself in the mirror, Azalea insisted on doing Daisy's hair and make-up to complete the full bridal look. Azalea created victory curls with a cascading drop running down her neck and over her shoulder. Her lips were painted a deep red like currants and rouge was added to her cheeks.

"One final touch," Azalea stated and held up two hair combs to Daisy to choose from. Although Abe had combined them, Azalea had separated them somehow and Daisy knew both combs well. One was a small silver comb with blue flowers. The other was a hand-crafted, wooden comb with daisies carved into it. Both combs were incredibly important to Daisy. One was given to her by Susan, her lady's maid who had cared for her since she was a baby and the other was given to her by Abe. Picking either was almost impossible.

"I can't choose," Daisy muttered. Azalea huffed and placed her hands on her hips like an irritated mother.

"Well, you are going to have to."

"I want both. Lay one over the other then press them into my hair together."

Azalea rolled her eyes but did as requested. When completed, Azalea guided Daisy to a mirror. As soon as

Daisy looked in the mirror it was almost impossible to believe it was herself staring back.

"What do you think?" Azalea enquired while scrutinising hems and various minute details of the dress.

"The dress is stunning. It's incredibly detailed," Daisy said in complete awe. She reached out and touched the mirror, trying to convince herself that what she was seeing was real. "I can't believe it's me."

"You look quite amazing, but you were always amazing Daisy."

"Hardly." Daisy giggled. "I was nothing compared to you."

"Daisy." Azalea moved to stand between Daisy and the mirror. She caressed Daisy's arm and then grabbed both of Daisy's hands. The gesture was tender, loving. She stared deeply into Daisy's eyes: "Daisy, you are truly incredible. As we grew up, I was doing so many things, and I never had the time to really see how amazing you are. I've appreciated these last few weeks and have gotten to know you even better. Seeing how Abe views you and loves you and the memories you have shared, it shows me how amazing you truly are."

Daisy stood quietly. Her sister was never this kind or open. Daisy honestly wasn't sure what to do or how to react. If anything, this declaration made Daisy more uncomfortable. *Was this some cruel joke? What was her sister trying to achieve?* Daisy took her hands back and stepped back from her sister. The soft and warm expression on Azalea's face immediately dissipated. Azalea rolled her shoulder's back and cleared her throat.

"Anyway," Azalea said, breaking the silence. "Are you ready?"

"Ready for what?"

"To get married."

Azalea extended her arm to invite Daisy to follow her. Daisy linked elbows and followed her out of the room. They walked down a short hallway. With every step, Daisy felt her heart speeding up. She could hear her heart thumping in her ears. Her feet and hands tingled. She felt like she was going to pass out. Her breathing was short and sharp. She had to remind herself to breathe, to take each step, to keep moving forward.

Azalea stopped at a large door. She gestured to Daisy to wait here. She entered the door leaving Daisy in the hallway. Daisy began pacing through the hallway, trying to remain calm. She took several deep breaths to slow her heart.

A single string instrument began humming behind the door in a slow and melodic beat. Daisy rested her ear against the door to hear better, but the door swung open to an audience standing and staring at Daisy.

19

Everlasting Matrimony

Daisy began to walk slowly down the aisle to the hum of a string quartet. The room was just like Azalea had shown her earlier. The waterfall thundered ahead and thousands of fireflies flitted about. The only difference was the large crowd. There were hundreds of people staring at Daisy, none of which she recognised. Everyone's eyes on Daisy made every attempt to slow her heart beat futile. She felt uneasy, like they were very expectant of her. She wasn't entirely sure what she was doing until she saw a mess of black hair standing at the front of the audience.

Abe slowly turned towards Daisy and immediately smiled like nothing she had seen before. He seemed truly ecstatic to see Daisy, but she was just relieved to see him. He wore a dark five piece suit with silver and gold embellishments that made his eyes shine like bonfires lit on the darkest of nights. He nervously fidgeted with each step Daisy took towards him, but each step calmed Daisy as got closer to him.

When she neared the front, Abe extended his arm which Daisy eagerly accepted. Any worry she had melted away with his touch. The weight of the audience disappeared and it suddenly felt like her and Abe were the only two in the room.

"We are gathered together on this momentous day to unify two beings in lifetime bond," Azalea's voice resonated around them, but it barely pulled Daisy from her illusion. All she could see was Abe. "A Conductor wedding is rather rare as we don't often travel together once graduated. Because we live long lives, our relationships are different. When true love that is unequal to any other is discovered, however, it is something to be truly celebrated. A bond of this magnitude, a joining of two creators, has not been recorded in our history.

"Today, we merge two worlds into one. We join a new Conductor and a new era of conduction with one that is as ancient as the universe. To do so, will we merge traditions and understandings to support the longevity and fruitfulness of this beautiful union. From spoken words to blood vows, these two souls shall unite.

"Daisy Mae Bloomsbury, I call on you to repeat after me. I, Daisy Mae Bloomsbury, do solemnly declare no reason why I cannot be married to Ambrose. In doing so, I declare that I wish to be bonded to this soul in union until death do us part. I vow to love and to honour you in all life's forms. I vow to stand by you in your victories, support you in your downfalls, and be your guide in your darkest days."

Daisy slowly repeated the phrase while staring deeply into Abe's eyes. With each word, his eyes watered a little more until a silent tear fell down his cheek. Without thinking, Daisy reached up and gently wiped the tear away.

He closed his eyes, turned his head towards her hand, and gently kissed her palm.

Abe repeated the same vows with strength and determination. He stared at Daisy with such attention and focus that Daisy felt compelled to look away, to avert her eyes, but this was the man she planned to spend the rest of her life with. She needed to be able to face him. For even with this heavy stare, there was no judgement or anger. There was no ridicule or hate. It was pure love, support, and encouragement. She longed for someone to act in such a way that Abe staring at her and confessing its deepest affections was nearly impossible to believe. But this was Abe and he was here with her. Everything about this was real.

And yet...

Doubt sat heavy in Daisy's heart. She wanted this to be real. She wanted to feel like this was actually their wedding, but it felt like a dream. It felt like Daisy was watching this full event through someone else's eyes. Daisy repeated the words and followed the steps, but Daisy still didn't feel like she existed at all in the moment. It was a strange sensation and Daisy didn't know what else to do but continue on. One way or another, Daisy wanted to be with Abe and this was a step towards that. Daisy would eventually figure out how to free Abe from Azalea so they could be together properly.

"Your declaration and vows of mundane have been completed. We now turn to the world of Conductors to complete this union," Azalea announced and pulled out a large gold blade and handed it to Abe. Four stones were embedded along the blade each symbolising one of the original four forces. "This dagger was a gift from the celestials that was a foundation in our early creation. We bring it forth today to create an unbreakable blood vow blessed by the highest of powers. Ambrose, take this blade of power and create a small incision on your left ring finger. Do the same to your bride."

Abe held out his left hand and skilfully created a small cut on his finger. Deep, red liquid oozed from the wound. Daisy willingly held out her left hand. There was a quick flicker of pain as Abe dug the blade into her finger, and, from the blade, a few sparks flew. Daisy quickly looked around, but only Abe seemed to notice. When she looked back to the cut on her finger, Daisy was surprised to see gold liquid seeping from the cut. The gold colour lasted only a second before turning red and running down her hand. A look flashed across Abe's face that told Daisy not to react or say a word. Instead, he quickly pocketed the knife and covered Daisy's bleeding hand with his own. As the knife slid into his pocket, Daisy noticed him flinch slightly.

"An opened wound can weaken a person, but when cared for and tended to, it can heal and leave no trace. In marriage, you open your heart to pain, but also to love and care. Allowing yourself to be open to another will allow you to be stronger individually and together. Allow this blood that runs from your hands to mix together and join your souls. Allow your partner's pain to be yours and share in agony so that you may rise stronger together. Allow your minds to be shared so that you can understand each other's greatest sorrows and greatest triumphs. Allow this blood to join two into one. "

Azalea placed her hand over Daisy and Abe's clenched hands. She began muttering something in elder tongue that Daisy did not completely understand. Images began flashing through Daisy's mind that were not her own, but she recognised as being Abe's memories. She saw Abe's greatest victories and sorrows. She watched Abe fall in love with the woman that birthed the fifth force and Daisy watched her die. Daisy saw past wars that he fought and the friends he lost. She saw his past studies brutally murdered and the revenge he took. She saw him happy when he thought he defeated the Grand Master last time. She saw him saving and teaching his current studies. She saw how Abe viewed her and those first moments that sparked his love for her. He was completely exposed to her and she imagined she was the same to him. However, Daisy had not lived all of history. Her life was short in comparison and she couldn't imagine there was much to share. She understood so much more of him that had previously been so shrouded and guarded.

Azalea's hand pulled away from theirs. A dark brand now marked each of their left fingers like a tattoo. Daisy felt dizzy for a moment before regaining her bearings and refocusing on Abe. Although he was still happy, some sadness had tainted his overall glow.

"With the sharing of your souls, you have become bonded to each other like no other. This bond can only be broken in death. You have made your intentions clear and shared your greatest sorrows and victories. You are now bonded in everlasting matrimony. As the Grand Master, I grant you marriage and wish you happiness. Ambrose, the bride is yours to be kissed."

Abe slid his arm around Daisy's waist and pulled her close against his body. His other hand slid behind her neck and pulled her lips up and towards his. She closed her eyes as he gently kissed her. It felt soft and delicate at first, but quickly dived into a desperation that Daisy felt in her soul. She gently pushed him off, aware that other people were around them. As he pulled back, he looked slightly drunk and uncertain before shaking his head and turning towards the crowd.

The crowd erupted in cheers and hollers. Abe lifted their hands above their heads and began walking down the aisle. The doors opened and Abe kept moving. He turned down several hallways and eventually came back to Daisy's room. He opened the door and scooped Daisy up into his arms. She giggled as he carried her over the threshold and gently placed her on the bed. She grinned from ear to ear and couldn't stop smiling. Abe leaned over her, also beaming with happiness.

"My wife," he said tenderly and gently ran his thumb across her cheek. Daisy closed her eyes and enjoyed the simple gesture.

"Abe," Daisy whispered.

"Yes?"

"I know… I know there is, well, more, but I don't know what comes next." Abe laughed softly and sweetly. He seemed to laugh more at himself than at Daisy's comment.

"I never expected you to know anything, Dais. If you will allow me… I will show you…"

"Please."

Abe got up from the bed and locked the door to the room. Daisy sat up on the bed and watched him cross the room. He slipped off his jacket and dropped it to the ground. He undid his vest and stood in front of Daisy. He looked down at her through long lashes. There was a fire in his eyes that Daisy had never seen before.

"If at any point you wish me to stop, you need only say so," Abe whispered in a husky, low voice that Daisy very much liked. She nodded her head in agreement, unable to speak. He placed his hand on her cheek. "Are you certain you want to continue?"

"Yes," Daisy croaked. Before Daisy could say anything else, his lips were upon hers. He kissed her with such desperation and desire that her whole body felt it. Slowly, he laid her back down on the bed and braced himself over top of her. He took off his vest and threw it across the room while continuing to kiss her. While he said she could ask him to stop, he seemed unable to fully contain himself. He moaned against her lips.

His hands explored the outline of her body with purposeful grazes eventually finding the fasteners to her dress. Skilfully, his fingers loosened each button and string releasing the dress from Daisy's body. He pulled away from her momentarily. Keeping his eyes on hers, almost expecting Daisy to say stop, he pulled the top layers of her dress off leaving her in the translucent slip she had on that morning. This time, however, Daisy didn't feel uncomfortable or exposed. This time, she felt wanted and loved.

A hunger filled Abe's eyes as he surveyed Daisy's body. He bit his lower lip and ran his hand along her side. Goosebumps covered every inch of her as his gaze graced her bare skin. A nearly inhumane groan escaped Abe as he pulled himself back into a standing position and turned away from Daisy. Confused, Daisy sat up and watched him.

He was sweating and breathing hard. He rubbed the back of his neck like he was anxious or uncertain. Daisy stood and slid her hands around his waist from behind him. She rested her head on his shoulder blade and listened to the loud thumping of his heart.

"What is wrong?" Daisy asked softly.

"I am not pure. I do not want to taint you with my sin. I am struggling to contain myself and fear we will not return from where I wish to take you," Abe explained. His hands ran idly over Daisy's arms that were wrapped around his waist.

"I am your wife now as you are my husband. We are joined by our souls. I know your greatest victories and your greatest sorrows. I know what makes you feel impure and yet… I love you. I have loved you from that moment on the beach and I will continue to love you regardless of your past or future sins. I love you, not in spite of your mistakes, but because of your growth from them. Your soul is mine just as mine is yours." Abe turned to face Daisy and gazed into her eyes. He smiled sadly and Daisy wished to bring back his joy.

"I have dreamt of this moment for months and worry I will not meet your expectations."

"I have no expectations," Daisy stated. Abe laughed under his breath and gently pushed a piece of hair behind Daisy's ear.

"Are you certain you want this? There is no returning from this. I will try to stop, should you ask, but I have desired this for so long and I do not know if I will be able to."

Daisy slid her hands down and started undoing the buttons on his shirt. She could feel Abe's eyes on her, heavy and starved, begging for more. With his shirt undone, Daisy ran her hands across his bare chest and abdomen. She could feel each muscle tense as her hands grazed his skin. She had seen him shirtless before, but never touched his skin like this. She could feel every ridge of muscle, every scar of the past, every bump of anticipation. He closed his eyes and tilted his head back. She gently kissed his collarbone which caused Abe to inhale sharply. Her hands ran across his shoulders and pulled the shirt down which fell to the ground. He opened his eyes and he lowered his gaze with Daisy.

"Abe," Daisy whispered.

"Dais," Abe breathed.

"I want you."

Abe paused for a moment and searched her face for any signs of doubt. Although unsure of what was next, Daisy was determined and held strong. He lifted her up and wrapped her legs around his waist. He kissed her passionately, deeply, feverishly, as he carried her back to the bed and laid her down. He crawled over top of her. His weight against her body was foreign, but welcomed. She arched under him, wishing to be as close as possible to him which seemed to entice him further. His hands explored every inch of her body. His hand cupped her breasts as he kissed her neck. He then grazed the inside of her thigh which sent pleasant shivers up and down her entire body. He slid the slip up and over her head leaving her completely naked.

He stood up for a moment and removed his trousers while analysing every part of Daisy's exposed body. Daisy was doing much the same as he de-robed. She had never seen a naked man before, but she believed Abe was an extraordinary specimen. He came back to lay over top of Daisy and gently lifted her leg. He levelled his eyes with Daisy as if asking for permission one more time. Daisy nodded slightly. He explained that there may be pain, but Daisy urged him on. He grinned brightly and kissed Daisy again. There was an intense pressure as Abe slid in-between her legs. There was a sudden click and a strong connection forged inside Daisy's mind. It was a brief moment before Abe suddenly pulled away and fell to the ground screaming in pain as his arm erupted with golden flames.

20

Pulling Blood from a Stone

Rosie grabbed onto Evander as he began running towards the assailants. Boulders and fireballs flew in every direction. Rosie tried to stay out of Evander's way while staying as close to him as possible. He navigated the outer edges ensuring that Rosie was protected from the most intense parts of the battle, but he seemed to want to press further in. Staying out of conflict seemed unnatural and uncomfortable to Evander, but Rosie appreciated it. Eventually, they came across Arlo and Brighid. While Brighid appeared to fight bravely, Arlo was doing everything to protect her. Had they not been fighting for their life, Rosie was sure this moment would have been sweet and brotherly, but right now, it was just terrifying.

"Who are these people?" Arlo shouted towards Evander as he threw a large water tornado sweeping up several people; Rosie only hoped none of them were Gideon's studies.

"Your guess is as good as mine. However, we are severely outnumbered!" Evander yelled back. Rosie looked back towards the hole in the wall. More people continued to stream through the gap. There were maybe ten or fifteen people between them and Gideon's group. It was significantly more than Rosie would have ever expected.

"We need to find the others. We need to retreat. We cannot beat them."

"Yes, but where are they?"

"I saw Alina and Gideon by the big doors," Brighid offered.

Evander nodded and immediately began moving towards the doors. They dodged and ducked various obstacles. At one point, Evander nearly threw Rosie over a large boulder. She fell on the other side, dazed for a moment, before hands pushed her back up and kept her moving forward. She stumbled and grabbed her side as Evander continued pulling her towards their mark.

As they neared the doors, a huge fireball caused a massive explosion. People were launched backwards and slammed into the ground. This cleared an area leading to Gideon and Alina, the only two standing. Evander used this opportunity to close the remaining gap. Alina quickly smiled before returning back to the battle at hand. Brighid grabbed Alina's unoccupied hand.

"Gideon, where can we go?" Alina shouted.

"If we can get through the doors to my office, there is a secret exit that should kick us out two towns over," Gideon replied.

"Let's move then," Evander shouted.

"Have you seen any of my studies?" Gideon cried.

"No," Several of them answered at the same time. Rosie wasn't even sure she could identify any of his studies. They really hadn't had the opportunity to get to know any of Gideon's group.

"Very well." As Gideon started to make his way towards the doors to his office, two other people joined them. Gideon seemed relieved to see them which Rosie assumed to mean they were his studies.

They eventually got to the door. Evander immediately started building a wall of stone to buy them time. The wall fully encased them and slightly dampened the thundering blasts. Gideon unlocked the door and directed everyone through it. Once closed, Gideon sealed the door. He led everyone towards the back of his office. Evander continued building walls as quickly as he could to further delay their pursuants. Anything to buy them some time.

Gideon moved a heavy looking bookcase from the wall revealing a hatch in the floor. There were several complex designs on the hatch that Gideon began moving around. There was a loud crash that meant their chasers had either broken through the door or the walls. Rosie wasn't sure which and didn't care to find out.

"Got it!" Gideon said and the hatch sprung open. Everyone began climbing down the ladder on the other side. When the last person was through, Gideon closed the hatch and reset all the security measures. Rosie could even hear the bookcase dragging across the floor; Gideon's ability to move it back over the hatch was baffling to her.

They stopped for a moment to catch their breath. It seemed like everyone plus three or four of Gideon's studies got through safely. Rosie felt immense relief followed by an intense dizziness, but she managed to stay on her feet.

"We need to keep moving," Evander stated. Gideon nodded his head in agreement.

"Yes. We do. There is a mix of tunnels along the way that should confuse other people. For us, just keep left. As long as we keep on the left tunnel, we should get to the exit," Gideon explained.

Everyone began moving down the tunnel. While they did not run, everyone certainly moved at a quickened pace. It was obvious that everyone was exhausted and terrified, but they kept going. The silence was tense as everyone listened for any sign they were being pursued again. Rosie kept one hand on the wall to help her balance.

They came to several y- and t-intersections which they always took the left-hand path from. The tunnels got darker and smaller the further they went. At one point, Rosie couldn't even see her hand directly in front of her face. Someone suggested lighting a torch which Gideon strongly discouraged as light would give away their position.

After several hours of stumbling through pitch blackness, they eventually came to a dead end. Gideon felt around for a ladder and directed the rest of the group to climb. It was a long climb. Rosie slipped and nearly fell. A sharp pain stabbed her in the ribs as she caught herself on the ladder. Evander helped Rosie resituate herself on the ladder and pushed her onward. When they finally reached the top, the hatch opened into a cellar. With everyone out of the tunnels, they rested for a moment. Gideon handed out food and water which was greatly appreciated.

"The owners of this home are under my employ," Gideon informed the room although no one asked. "I pay them to watch the house and ensure no one, besides those I have authorised them to allow, enter the home. We should be safe here for a while. At the very least, we should be able to rest and take care of our injuries."

Rosie looked around at the battered and bruised crowd. Everyone was coated in dirt which made their condition look worse than it really was. So far, the worst of the injuries appeared to be a broken arm. Evander immediately took to healing injuries where possible and aiding those that could not be healed. His talent for medicine surprised Rosie. Eventually, Evander came to her. Rosie had not taken inventory of her own injuries. She did not think she was injured at all, however, as Evander pointed out, there was a good amount of blood on her clothes.

Rosie looked down at her outfit and noticed a large splotch of blood on her abdomen. Gingerly, she touched the area and nearly fainted from the pain. Evander caught her and sat her down gently on the floor.

"I believe there is something quite wrong," Rosie muttered. Evander then laid her down on the ground and began systematically removing clothes around her abdomen to get a better look at the wound. When the corset was removed, Rosie noticed a rather large rock embedded in her side with blood trickling out around it. Before she could say or do anything, blackness overcame her, and the dirt welcomed her.

21

Gods' Blade

Daisy screamed as Abe writhed in pain on the ground. Golden flames blazed from his arm. Inhuman sounds echoed through the room as he spasmed. Daisy did not know what to do. She reached out her hand and felt no heat from the flames. Feeling like she wouldn't be burned, she moved to pin him to the ground so he could not hurt himself. However, he was much stronger than her and simply tossed her aside.

"Abe!" She shouted, trying to break through to him. "Abe! Please!"

She again tried to pin him, but his flailing arms caught her across the face with a stinging smack. Daisy felt useless. She held her face and watched helplessly as he writhed in pain. All her attempts to help him were futile. The only thing she could do was move away anything that he might hit or that could inflict further injury.

After several minutes, the flames died down and so, too, did his rapid movements. His breathing slowed and the horrible sounds stopped. He seemed almost asleep, but Daisy was still petrified. To ensure his dignity, Daisy covered him in a blanket. She dressed herself in his shirt and anxiously sat beside him, chewing her fingernails, waiting for any sign that he was okay. He eventually stopped moving all together aside from the shallow, rhythmic rise and fall of his chest. Minutes felt like hours as time dragged on. Eventually, his eyes fluttered open. He stared at the ceiling for a few minutes before directing his gaze to Daisy. She crawled over to him and laid down beside him.

"Dais," he croaked. "Daisy… what happened?"

"There was a click in my head, and golden flames started coming out of your arm," Daisy whispered. Abe shot up; it was like a switch flicked in his brain. He seemed disgusted, ashamed, and afraid all at the same time. Daisy had a tough time piecing together his furrowed brows, frown, and scowl. She pushed back slightly from him, uncertain if she had done something wrong.

"Dear God. We're *married*," he said while glaring at the mark branding his finger. He did not sound pleased, and Daisy wasn't sure what to think. She slid back even further. Her heart pounded. *Did he regret marrying her?* He glanced away from his finger towards his forearm "It's gone!"

He stood up and stared at his arm in complete disbelief.

"It's gone. I am no longer bound!" Abe shouted and began dancing around. Under normal circumstances, Daisy would have found this humorous, but Abe was completely naked which left Daisy feeling confused and uncomfortable. She averted her eyes and tried to hide her blushing cheeks.

"What are you talking about?" Daisy asked while trying to keep her eyes on his face.

"The mark that bound me to Azalea is gone. I can speak freely about how terrible she is and all that she is doing, but more importantly." Abe kneeled on the ground in front of Daisy and held her hands. He seemed truly happy. "More importantly, I can get you out of here. I know how to stop Azalea, and you're the only one that can do it."

"Abe, you need to start making sense."

"Of course. Sorry, let me explain." He took a deep breath. "Azalea branded me with a magical mark that bound me to her. I had my mind, but I could not do anything that went against her or would threaten her plans. I was still her pawn, but a bit freer. My emotions were guided by her desires and my thoughts were limited to those that benefitted her, but I did have some choice."

"So, the black mark was binding you to Azalea?"

"Correct."

"And you couldn't go against what she wanted?"

"Yes, correct again." Daisy paused for a moment and stared at Abe. Some things made more sense, but there was one thing that Daisy couldn't shake. She had to know the truth.

"Did you want to marry me then… or was that her plan as well?" Abe's joy faltered, and a solemnness came over him.

"Yes. I did. I wanted to marry you. It was me that proposed to you to give you the option. I did truly want to marry you… Just not like this." He reached up and brushed a piece of hair behind her ear, before cupping her cheek in a loving manner. Daisy's pounding heart slowed. "I do love you Daisy, and I am happy to be married to you, but I did not want it like this. Nor do I think you did."

"Maybe not. I just don't want you to regret this." He leaned forward and pulled her face towards him. He kissed her softly at first. He pulled back for a moment, seemingly out of breath, then kissed her again. Deeply and passionately this time which melted away all her fears. He desired her without Azalea's influence.

"I will never regret being with you, but Dais. There are more things I need to tell you. Our marriage is not my most pressing concern."

"I'm listening, but -uh…. could you put some pants on?" Abe looked down and realised he was completely naked. He then looked at Daisy with flushed cheeks as he surveyed her apparel. Daisy wrapped the shirt tighter around her.

"Did we…?" He cleared his throat and raised his eyebrows. He appeared to not want to finish the sentence.

"Nearly. I think. You started burning before much happened."

"Oh! Well then…" he stood and picked up a pair of pants from the floor. He slid into them as Daisy crawled onto the bed and waited for Abe expectantly. Standing at the edge of the bed, Abe bit his lip as his eyes travelled Daisy's barely covered body. With just his shirt on, her thighs were bare, and she hadn't done up most of the buttons. His gaze felt heavy and starved, like Daisy was the only thing that could ease his hunger; however, he shook his head and sat just out of arm's reach from her.

"Azalea is planning to take over the world by completing mass genocide of all non-Conductors. She has already infiltrated some governments and completed several assassinations. She has started to infiltrate and dismantle large entities. She has no interest in peace and every interest in destroying all that has wronged her. Usually, I wouldn't be overly concerned, but she has more power and commitment this time. She has recruited celestials to her efforts. She is gaining momentum, but I have learned how to stop her," Abe started.

"Celestials?" Daisy asked.

"Gods. Deities. Spiritual beings. They have many names, so whichever you choose to call them will work. But essentially, they are the beings that run the universe. We created the earth, but they created the people. They govern everything and have immense powers. They could choose to wipe out all of mankind in a blink of an eye. "

"I understand… I think." Daisy tilted her head to the side in confusion. Abe offered a reassuring smile.

"They are immortal beings that control how the people side of the world operates. We made the rock so they could make the people. They are stronger than Conductors, including both me and Azalea, and typically play their own games. For some reason though, they have found our war intriguing. Celestials are joining Azalea, and she is gaining more momentum and power than she has ever had."

"So, celestials are the reason we are losing the war now."

"Yes, but celestials are also our key to getting out of this. Celestials are the only thing more powerful than Azalea and me. One of them should be able to tell us how to get rid of Azalea. I have tried to allow her to remain and be on her own, but… it's no longer an option."

"What do you mean get rid of her?" Daisy narrowed her eyes. Abe got quiet and started picking lint off of his pants. "Abe? What do you mean by getting rid of her?"

"I am not sure exactly, but a celestial will tell you how to get rid of her. I would never wish harm upon any being, but I fear what she will achieve if we do nothing." Daisy did not like the sound of his suggestion. She hated the idea of her being involved even more.

"What does this have to do with me? Why am I the only one that can do this?"

"You saw your gold blood before it turned red during our ceremony?"

"Yes, but I thought it was a trick of the light or something."

"Golden blood, when cut by a celestial blade, can be a sign of a godly parent. It's very rare and I have only seen it one other time. I did a lot of research after that, and I believe you have celestial blood, but I don't know how much. Mortals cannot pass into the celestial realm. They will perish painfully, but if you have celestial blood, you can go to their realm. You can ask for their assistance and learn how to turn this war back in our favour." Daisy sat dumbfounded at Abe's idea. This plan seemed half thought out and risky.

"It could still be a trick of the light. There is no guarantee as to what we saw."

"Shall we test it then?" Abe retrieved the large golden blade from their wedding ceremony off the floor. She saw him sneak it into his pocket while Azalea was distracted. She also saw him flinch, which Daisy now knew to mean the action went against Azalea.

As Abe turned the blade in his hands, Daisy saw flickers of images in the flashing surface. The jewels held something in them that Daisy could feel but did not understand. She wanted to touch the blade, but she also feared it. It was something powerful and wrong. Daisy fidgeted with her hands to keep herself from grabbing the blade.

"It is said that celestials and their immediate offspring can only be hurt by the blades forged in the sun. Only celestials can get close to the sun; therefore, only celestials can create blades to harm themselves. They wage war amongst each other just like humans do so weapons are often forged. This particular blade was gifted to Azalea and me to show gratitude for our creation. It was the first created blade and holds great power when wielded," Abe explained. Daisy nodded as she listened intently.

"What test are you wanting to conduct?" Daisy finally managed to ask after a long period of silence.

"I want to draw your blood and see what colour you bleed." Abe tried to deliver the request gently. "Nothing large. Just big enough that we can see if you bleed gold. I do not want to lose you, so I fear sending you to the celestial realm could kill you if I am incorrect. I cannot live without you Daisy." He paused and looked down at his hands. "But I know that you may be our only chance."

He looked back at Daisy with pleading and desperate eyes. Despite all of Azalea's wrongdoings and sinister plans, Daisy still viewed Azalea as her sister. However, something about the way Abe acted told Daisy there really wasn't an alternative. She had never seen him quite this way, but she also felt like she didn't have enough information. She still had so many unanswered questions.

Abe had been Azalea's captive for the past year and was sure to know more than Daisy, but Daisy still wanted to know the truth from her own eyes. This was Abe's story and there was still Azalea's side.

"What are you thinking, Daisy?" Abe questioned.

"How do I know what the truth is?" Daisy cried. "Everything since I got here has been a lie or manipulation. How do I even know if you are truly free or if Azalea still holds you? I am uncertain of everything and fearful of reality. I don't know what to do or what to believe."

Abe looked at her sadly. He gently raised his hand and placed it against her temple.

"May I?" Abe enquired. Daisy nodded.

In a quick moment, images flooded Daisy's mind revealing Abe's captivity. She watched as his mind was taken from him, as he suffered in silence, as he was forced to do things we would never do normally. She watched his memories and felt his pain. She watched as the mark was etched into his skin and how different Abe felt. She understood his limitations and his freedoms. She understood his pain and his fear. She understood his position, but she still didn't necessarily agree with it.

When they were married, Daisy saw Abe's greatest triumphs and losses. She had seen the memories that changed Abe's perception and love for Azalea. While justified and understandable, Daisy still couldn't shake the feeling that something was amiss. She trusted and loved Abe, but she still couldn't silence her mind.

"This is all too much," Daisy exclaimed and pushed his hand away. She stood up and paced the room. She rubbed her arms to comfort herself, but pure terror was building in her soul.

"I know it is Daisy," Abe sympathised. "War does not make decisions easy, but we unfortunately do not have much time. Azalea will eventually notice our severed connection, so I have limited time to help you."

"What exactly is your plan?"

"We have to get out of here first. With the bond broken Azalea will come here soon to figure out what is different. I want you to carve the symbol back into my arm so at least we have the opportunity to escape if we come across Azalea. Once we are out, we will go to Grenich. I will teach you to connect to the celestial realm and you should be able to cross into the celestial realm, but I cannot go with you into the realm. From there, it's up to you. You have to get the information and you will still be able to make the decision."

He raised the golden blade in offer to Daisy. While he said this was still her decision, Daisy knew that picking up that blade meant going against Azalea. She would lose her sister again if she picked up that blade. Abe was asking her to choose between himself and Azalea.

Abe moved the blade closer to her and asked, "What do you choose?"

22

Doctor Evander

Evander walked laps around the bed watching for any signs of life. He kept thinking of what more he should have done or could do. He flipped through books of medicine and care practices. He read reams and reams on Conductor healing forces; however, the issue seemed to be that Rosie wasn't a Conductor. Typical healing strategies and techniques that worked on Conductors did not seem to be working on Rosie.

Usually, the opposite force would heal a wound. She had a rock embedded in her side, but no air force could seem to remove the rock. Eventually, when conduction proved futile, and after much consultation with books, Evander removed the stone manually. He and Arlo pressed bandages to her side, but the bleeding wouldn't stop, and their options were running low. The blood loss would surely kill her if Evander didn't act immediately.

Quickly, Evander grabbed a metal poker and threw it into the fire while Arlo continued applying pressure on the gash. Evander removed the poker and, without hesitation, pressed the hot metal to the wound causing a sizzling of flesh just long enough to stop the bleeding. The smell was unlike anything he had ever experienced, nearly causing him to vomit. Arlo was less fortunate and quickly excused himself from the room.

Now, since her wound had been tended to as best, he could, Evander could do nothing else but hope that Rosie would be okay. Her skin was pale. Her breathing was shallow. It looked as though every breath was painful. She looked so fragile and vulnerable. Evander regularly checked her temperature and changed her bandages. At the very least, there did not appear to be signs of infection. He seemed to have successfully prevented that.

Once Rosie's immediate peril had been dealt with, Evander and Arlo knew they needed to keep moving; it wouldn't be safe for them to linger longer than necessary. Unfortunately, Rosie was in no condition to move under her own power, so Evander and Arlo created a make-shift stretcher to move her from location to location. It was cumbersome, but it worked well enough and didn't seem to slow them down too much. After the third day and the fourth move, the group finally agreed to rest for a while. They were close to the sea now, and Evander found that calming. He had spent most of his life by the sea and always found it homey. It was not enough, however, to ease his tension. They were staying at the Greenway Inn. Gideon managed to buy the inn which ensured that they had the entire place to themselves. Rosie was placed in a room on the main floor just off of the bar. Evander picked that room for Rosie because he could see the ocean from its window. Being able to see the ocean as he paced about the room kept him calmer.

Three days after Evander completed the impromptu surgery, Rosie still showed no clear signs of regaining consciousness. She had occasionally stirred or made sounds, so they knew she was alive, but Evander desperately wanted her to wake up. Perhaps, he was not skilled enough. Perhaps, his efforts were useless. Perhaps, the books didn't provide enough information. Perhaps, they were carrying around a nearly dead body this entire time. Evander needed a sign, anything, to show him that she was alive.

He finally sat on a low, wooden stool beside the bed. He glanced out the window and took a deep breath. He then gently grabbed Rosie's hand and felt for her pulse. It was low and slow, but still beating. He let out a heavy sigh that indicated a mix of relief, disappointment, and exhaustion. Over the past year, Evander had grown to care for Rosie, and the weight of her injury was nearly crushing him. He also felt responsible for her in Abe and Daisy's absence. The responsibility was weighing on him; he could only imagine how Abe felt taking care of him, Arlo, and Brighid. It was a feeling that Evander couldn't quite explain which nearly drove him mad. This whole situation challenged his intelligence and abilities. It was exhausting and infuriating.

The door creaked open, and Brighid snuck in. Her bright smile loosened some of the tautness in his chest. Although Arlo and Alina were much closer with Brighid than he was, she was still like family to Evander. She always brought joy to their solemn group.

"How is she?" Brighid whispered.

"No change," Evander responded.

"I brought someone with me to help," Brighid stated. Evander raised his eyebrows. He had made it clear not to bring any unnecessary attention to them.

"Who and why?"

"Our forces don't work on her. She needs someone who does regular human medicine, so I got a doctor."

"You did what?!" Evander spoke louder than he meant to and instantly regretted it when Brighid flinched. "Sorry. I shouldn't have raised my voice. I'm just surprised."

"I know you told us not to interact with people in town, but Rosie needs help. More help than what I think you can provide." In most cases, this would have sent Evander over the edge. Not only was she challenging his ability, but she was saying someone else was better. He looked down at Rosie and knew Brighid was right. This was beyond his expertise. He sighed in defeat and threw his hands up in the air.

"Bring in the doctor then. Let's get this taken care of immediately."

The doctor was a small man with white hair and dark skin. He had kind, brown eyes that softened Evander's distrust. He carried a large, heavy, leather bag adorned with a red cross. He seemed very frail as he hunched over a black cane and hobbled across the room. Slowly, he placed his doctor's bag on the stool beside the bed and pulled out a set of glasses. He precariously perched the glasses on the bridge of his nose.

"Pray tell, what happened?" his voice shook as he spoke, but he still seemed confident.

"She fell down a hillside and got a large rock stuck in her side. We removed the rock, but when the bleeding wouldn't stop, we had to cauterise the wound. We cleaned it and stitched up what we could."

The doctor peeled back the thick bandages. The wound looked angry. It was red and black, but there still didn't appear to be any signs of infection. Evander held his breath as the doctor began inspecting the wound. He pressed on different parts of Rosie's abdomen and listened with a stethoscope.

"You've kept it clean, and it appears the injury missed all her vital organs," the doctor stated. "Her pulse is weak, however. Have you been keeping her hydrated? Tried to get any sustenance in her?"

"She has been unconscious. We weren't sure how to do that and books can only tell you so much," Evander admitted. Brighid shot him a surprised look. He shrugged.

"I can do some additional care to the wound and provide a transfusion to help her along. Afterwards, you will need to feed her broth and water to ensure she is receiving sustenance until she comes to. Understand?"

"Yes, Sir."

"Now, I ask that the girl stays to help, but I will need you to leave. Less people the better, and I can feel the stress coming off of you sir."

"Sorry? You want me to leave?"

"Yes. Miss, help him out." Brighid gently grabbed Evander's arm and guided him towards the door. Evander attempted to back pedal, but Brighid was quite adamant.

"I will come get you as soon as the doctor is done. I promise," Brighid said in a kind, but forceful manner. Evander looked down at her. She suddenly seemed so much older and mature. "Go eat, try to get some rest, and please, dear Gods, please wash up. You smell like a barn."

With that, she closed the door behind him. There was a loud click as a lock slid into place. He paced outside the door for a while until Arlo appeared with a plate of food. Now that he wasn't staring at Rosie, he realised how hungry he actually was.

"I was just coming to give you some food. Alina said you haven't eaten since we left Gideon's," Arlo explained while showing the plate of food. He handed the plate to Evander whose stomach audibly growled.

"Thank you," Evander replied. He tried to eat slowly but found himself quickly devouring it.

"Also, Gideon and Alina wanted to see you."

"What for?" Evander spoke through mouthfuls of food.

"Not sure. They had been discussing recruiting more Conductors, but I don't know what they actually want you for. They seem to be planning something, but I haven't been included exactly."

"Oh?"

"They sent a few pairs off when we got here yesterday to some groups that Gideon knew were in the area. I don't know what they are planning, but one group returned today with at least six new Conductors. The rooms upstairs are getting crowded. I've barely been able to find a decent spot to nap." Evander laughed which caused him to choke on some food leading to a coughing fit.

"Warn me before you make jokes next time."

"I hardly make jokes. They often take too much effort and energy," Arlo smirked. Evander rolled his eyes. If anything, Arlo was quick to make jokes if it meant making other people happy. This time was no exception.

"Where are they anyway?"

"Who? The new arrivals?"

"No, Alina and Gideon."

"Ah. Yes. Keep going up." Evander pointed towards the ceiling and shrugged. He turned and walked back toward the bar leaving Evander alone with his plate.

He contemplated staying and waiting until the doctor was done. However, *what good would waiting do?* It was quite clear Evander did not have the skills to fix this situation and waiting would only make this worse. He quickly conjured up some paper and ink and wrote a note for Brighid which he stuck to the door. Evander looked towards the stairs at the end of the hall.

"Just keep going up," he said to himself and headed for the stairs. Evander climbed up three flights of stairs and finally came to a small ladder leading to a turret at the very top of the small inn. He could hear Alina's voice just above him.

He climbed the ladder and poked his head into the room. Alina and Gideon stood around a circular table. She was frantically pointing to something, but immediately noticed Evander as his head peeked out of the floor.

"Evander!" Alina called. "Come here. We've found something exciting!"

"I guessed as much by the shrill shrieks I've heard while climbing this ladder," Evander muttered and pulled himself out of the hole in the floor. As he stood up, he noticed a large map sprawled across the table. There were nails, thimbles, corks, and other miscellaneous things spread across the map, but each piece seemed purposefully placed.

"We found them, Evander." Alina said as she eagerly grabbed his arm and pulled him closer to the map. "We actually found them!"

"Found who?" Evander looked at the map of random items trying to piece it together.

"Ames and Daisy and the Grand Master. We found them all."

Evander stood there for a moment in complete awe. They had been looking for Ambrose for over a year and now… they had finally found him. Their work had actually paid off. They had, against all odds, potentially succeeded. It was a moment of release and relief immediately followed by pure fear. If they had found them, that meant Alina and Gideon had a plan. If Gideon was involved, that likely meant a fight.

"You've been recruiting more Conductors. You're planning to fight your way in there," Evander stated. Alina looked at Gideon. Her one eyebrow was raised, and she smirked. Evander knew what this expression meant. Evander's guess was right, and it was likely Alina's idea. He felt like he had just been hit in the stomach with a bag of rocks.

"We have an opportunity now," Alina stated flatly as though this was the obvious answer and Evander should not seem so apprehensive. "We've been looking for Ames for over a year and we finally found him. We can save him, Evander. I thought you would be excited."

"We barely made it out from the last assault," Evander shouted, completely overcome by the stupidity of the suggestion. "The Grand Master out-powers and outnumbers us. The probability of this succeeding is next to nil. As much as I want Ames home, I would never risk the lives of those I am responsible for to save the life of one."

"If we don't fight, we die, and the last assault proved that. We have the upper hand. We know where they are, and this is the opportunity to strike before we are attacked again."

"How do you know where they are? How are you certain?"

"They got sloppy on their return. I assume they had an informant in our ranks and either captured, injured, or killed the spy during their attack. In not knowing where Conductor groups were, they started storming train stations. Not the Grand Master's best idea, but based on the lack of coordination and elegance, we can assume these individuals were acting on their own accord. Regardless, we followed the reports of destruction and pinpointed a sort of starting point. We sent a scout to the area yesterday. They just got back and confirmed our suspicions. They've been hiding underground in some type of fortress." Before Evander could retort, Gideon jumped in to support Alina.

"We want to send out more scouts to the area and slowly build our numbers so as to not draw attention," Gideon explained in an authoritative, no room for negotiation kind of way. "Ideally, I want to send small units into the fortress to identify exits and weak points. From their intel, we can stage an attack to free Ambrose and Daisy. We know that the Grand Master with Ambrose in her possession is significantly more dangerous. If we can separate them, we stand a better chance."

"Exactly, we are not planning a full-scale invasion yet," Alina added.

"Yet," Evander scoffed. He ran a hand through his hair in exasperation. The plan had merit, but it still seemed risky. "And who are you planning on sending? To do your recon and to spring Ames?"

They looked at each other; a knowing glance passed between them. It was like they were speaking without saying anything. They had obviously had discussions and meetings without him present. Evander did not like feeling on the outside. He slammed his fist against the table.

"I will not be pushed to the outside again. You will not cut me out of these decisions. Ames put me in charge of the studies. Not you, Alina!" Evander yelled.

Alina placed a hand on her chest and raised her eyebrows. Her mouth gaped open. Of course, there were more things Evander wanted to say about Alina being unfit and unsound to lead, but somehow, he managed to hold his tongue.

"We were thinking… you would lead the charge actually," Alina stated. Evander immediately felt guilty. "You've proven yourself a competent leader, and we think you would be a good fit for the job. We hadn't discussed this with you, as you've been caring for the sick and wounded. We thought your skills were better used elsewhere than analysing random data and recruiting Conductors. You needed to be with the ranks and actually doing work, rather than sitting in the background. Your purpose was elsewhere, and it was more important."

"Also, I had connections with various Conductor groups. We were using my network for information and to gather groups. I didn't feel you were necessary for me to instruct my own studies," Gideon challenged. He held his nose high, and his chest puffed out. Evander tried not to shy away, knowing that showing any wavering would only lessen their view of him.

"I appreciate your trust in me," Evander tried to recover while still remaining confident. "I have felt isolated, and this situation seemed to push me further outside your circle. I understand now, but I do not think I can leave with Rosie in her current condition."

Alina sighed and threw her hands up in the air. It seemed his reaction had been the topic of much discussion, and Alina had expected the opposite.

"You are being a child," Alina cried.

"You talk about not risking the lives of many for the life of one. Staying for Rosie and leaving Ambrose in the Grand Master's hands risks the lives of us all. You would be foolish to stay," Gideon dictated. Evander swallowed hard. This suddenly didn't seem like an offer as much as it was a command. Evander rolled his shoulders back and stood tall.

"I will leave with a crew tomorrow evening at dusk. I will bring Arlo with me and two of your studies. Brighid will remain and care for Rosie in my stead. I expect you two will continue to recruit troops, so when I inform you that Ambrose is free, you will be ready to storm the fortress. I expect to be included in any major decisions from this point on. Understand?"

"Maybe not a child after all," Gideon sneered.

Evander turned on his heel and jumped down the hole in the floor. He wanted to be as far away from them as possible. He had made a fool of himself and wished beyond all reason to disappear. A heavy weight had just been set upon his shoulders, and all he wanted to do was run away.

It's what he did the last time. He always ran away when things got rough. It's why he became a Conductor. It

231

was easier than facing the truth of what he was leaving behind.

23

Adventure Awaits

Evander walked down the stairs and towards Rosie's room. Alina called after him, but he refused to go back. It was the last place he wanted to be. As Evander approached Rosie's room, he noticed Arlo leaned up against the wall. He was supposed to be standing guard although he looked more asleep than anything else. He even had a hat tipped over his face, but he immediately stood alert when he heard Evander approaching.

"Are you sleeping or watching?" Evander enquired.

"A bit of both," Arlo yawned and stretched out his back. Evander could hear his spine crack.

"I can't imagine that is good for you."

"Well, read a book on it," Arlo winked teasingly.

"I may just do that," Evander replied. Arlo shrugged and proceeded to lean back against the wall. "Any updates?"

"No… Nothing." The humour suddenly vanished from Arlo, and a heaviness set in.

"We are leaving tomorrow night at dusk."

"Who is?"

"Me, you and two of Gideon's choosing. We've been sent on a mission. They found Ames and the Grand Master." Arlo looked dumbstruck with his mouth gaping open and his eyes wide. "Close your mouth before you catch flies."

"How do you know where they are?"

"Alina and Gideon have been doing extra recon and found their location. We are to be the scouts and determine the exact entrance. Hopefully, we find a way in." Arlo let out a slow, low whistle and removed his hat to fan himself.

"We aren't even graduated yet, and Rosie's condition is so fragile. Are you sure we should be going?" Arlo asked.

"We haven't been given much choice," Evander remarked contemptuously. Arlo raised an eyebrow in question. "It doesn't matter. We are set to leave, and we must go."

"Very well. I shall go pack then." Arlo turned and started walking down the hall.

"Only the essentials!"

"Yeah. Yeah." Arlo dismissed with a wave as he turned around the corner and out of sight.

Evander was now alone. He pressed his ear to Rosie's door but couldn't hear much through it. Pacing seemed to alleviate some of the anxiety, but not nearly enough. At some point, he stopped walking and sat against the wall. His head fell back, and he looked up at the ceiling. It consisted of exposed beams and the floorboards of the second story. Every once in a while, someone would walk over him, casting shadows through the cracks and holes. The ceiling creaked with each step. Evander found the distraction helpful, but the condition of the second story floor was concerning. The amount of spiderwebs alone was frightening. Evander didn't even want to think about the general condition of the beams, but it at least kept his mind busy while he waited.

The sun began to set, and Evander grew tired. He just wanted to know what was happening. He wanted to know Rosie was okay before leaving. He couldn't bear to relive his past any more than he already had with Rosie. The past was painful, and he had spent a long time running from it.

He didn't want to run anymore.

Evander grew up in a large family. He was the fourth child in a family of seven children. His mom died during childbirth, leaving his dad, his sister and himself to care for the three younger children. His two oldest siblings married and had families of their own to care for. Evander tried his hardest to care for the family. He tended the garden and cared for the animals. He picked up a part-time job mucking stalls at a local stable to bring in some extra income. He did what he could, but he was only ten.

The turning point was when his older sister got smallpox a few years later. She was wasting away so quickly. Then his other siblings got sick. And his father. His family was quickly overrun and dying. They couldn't afford the care of a doctor or medicine. He was only a child, and suddenly the only one capable of caring for five other people. Eventually, Evander couldn't handle the pressure, or the pain, of watching his entire family slowly die. His heart ached, but he needed to free himself.

So, he left.

In the middle of the night, as his entire family rested, he packed a small bag of essentials and ran away.

He got on a train and headed for the border. When he crossed the border, he went to the closest town and found work. He continued as a stable hand for several years, and eventually became a blacksmith. He spent most of his spare time at the local tavern drowning his thoughts and feelings. That is where he met Alice.

Alice was beautiful. She had short curly hair that hung in tight ringlets around her face. Her eyes were like bronze and sparkled in the light. She was so short and small that Evander could easily wrap her entire body in his arms. She was playful and happy. She complained about her tooth being chipped, her big dimples, and her freckles, but Evander found each flaw even more endearing. To him, she was perfect.

They became close very quickly, and he valued her above all else. She taught him to read and sparked his interest in learning. They would discuss ancient philosophers, plants and herbs, mathematics, and even current events. He became who he was because of Alice. He worked hard and eventually bought a house with the intent to ask her to wed. However, the day he went to ask for her hand had become a thing of nightmares to him.

She opened the door and beamed brilliantly at him, but Evander quickly noticed the signs. Red splotches on her collar. She had flushed cheeks and a stifled cough; she grasped a handkerchief in her fist. She even appeared to slim down from not eating. All of the signs of consumption were there, and Evander wasn't sure he could handle watching more people he loved die. He spoke with her for a while and watched her cough up blood. He tried to act unaffected, but his stomach turned. She was going to die, and he was going to have to watch her.

He turned to books and tried to find a cure or a solution. He stopped going to visit her or care for her. He became so focused on finding a solution that he stopped focusing on loving her. He eventually came across the story of the Conductors and their magical abilities. Grenich wasn't that far from his little town, and he was certain he would find more information there.

He went to Alice's house to tell her of the plan, but when he knocked on the door, her mother answered wearing all black. Instantly, it hit him. By being consumer in finding a solution, he ran away from his problem rather than facing it. He couldn't watch Alice fade away and stop being the woman he loved, so he lost himself in books and stories to escape. Alice's mother swore at him for abandoning her daughter and slammed the door in his face. Evander didn't stay to fight or mourn. He ran away one last time and vowed to himself he would never do it again.

This brought him to the Conductors and the war and caring for Rosie. She was facing death, and Evander wasn't going to run away from it this time. He wanted to stay and care for her. He wanted to prove to himself that he could stay when things got tough. He tried to stay and yet… he was being sent away and not by his own choosing. He was at war with himself. Between proving he could be more than a coward or being loyal to the man that saved him, Evander was stuck.

At that moment, the door opened, and the doctor stepped out, followed by Brighid, snapping Evander out of his self-pity. The doctor carried a bag of soiled linens and garbage that Evander was sure were covered in blood. Brighid thanked the doctor who smiled and hobbled down the hallway towards the exit.

"So? What news do you have? Did she make it? Will she live?" Evander pestered while trying to look behind Brighid into the room.

"She is going to be alright," Brighid reassured and placed a hand on Evander's arm. "Your quick thinking and cauterising the wound saved her life. The doctor cleaned up the wound and got some fluids and blood back into her. She is stable and will likely wake up in a few days. She will need to rest and limit her movement until the wound is healed. Otherwise, she will live."

Evander felt like the room was spinning as relief flooded over him. He had not realised how much tension and anxiety he was holding until it was released by someone else. Rosie was going to live, but Evander still had to leave.

"Can… can I…?" Evander stammered.

"She is resting, but yes you can see her," Brighid stated. She gave his arm a reassuring squeeze before leaving down the hall. Evander stood outside the door, uncertain of how to proceed. He wanted to enter, but something was telling him to run. Shaking his head to clear the thoughts, he twisted the knob and entered the room.

Rosie laid on her back with her hands by her side. Her fiery curls blanketed the pillow, almost completely hiding its white cover. She had a thin sheet over her body which clung to every curve and highlighted the bulk of bandages on her side. Blushing cheeks and pink lips reassured Evander that she was on the mend. She looked better than she had in days. Slowly, Evander made his way around the bed and sat on the small stool. He picked up her hand and noticed it was warm again. Even more important was that Rosie's hand slightly tensed in his grasp.

Each sign reassured Evander. She was alive, and she was safe. He had a few more hours to stay with her before he had to leave. Her breaths were deep and slow. Evander braced his head with his arm on his knee and watched her breaths. It was calming in a way.

"Evander?" croaked a voice through Evander's haze. He strained to open his eyes. Apparently, he had fallen asleep at some point. "Wake up sleepy head."

Rosie was awake and watching him intently. Evander jumped up, feeling overwhelmed that Rosie was conscious. He ran to the door and yelled for Brighid and Arlo. Brighid came running around the corner. After seeing the excitement on Evander's face, Brighid beamed and began sprinting down the hallway. She pushed past Evander and into the room. She launched herself onto the bed and wrapped her little arms around Rosie. Rosie winced and whimpered, which caused Brighid to pull back sheepishly.

"Sorry. We are just excited to see you are alright," Brighid explained.

"It's okay. I am glad to see you care," Rosie replied. Her voice was raw and raspy. Usually, Evander found her a joy to listen to, but this sound was unpleasant. He moved over to the windowsill where a jug sat with a glass and poured some water.

"Here," Evander offered while handing her the glass. She graciously accepted and painfully pushed herself upright. In doing so, the sheet slid down, exposing her torso and the many layers of thick bandages covering her entire abdomen.

"Oh my!" Rosie exclaimed as she analysed her stomach. "I didn't think the injury was that bad."

"It was difficult to care for, but you are on the mend now," Brighid said.

"We've got you mostly cleaned up. We had a doctor finish your care today. You've been unconscious for a few days, so we are glad to see you awake," Evander added.

"A few days?" Rosie asked with palpable concern. "How many days exactly?"

"I am not sure exactly. Maybe three or four?" Evander offered. Rosie's face paled. She swallowed hard enough that Evander could see her throat move.

"I need to get out of bed. Right now. I need to get up." She started throwing the covers off of her and struggling to sit up. Evander moved to her side, but she winced and clutched her side. She stopped moving and leaned back against the headboard.

"You need to rest, Rosie," Evander pleaded and gently picked up her hand. She smiled softly at him, but concern still plagued her face.

"I've been useless," Rosie whispered. "I haven't been able to help and worry that this will burden us all."

"Rosie, you've been injured. We didn't expect anything of you." She squeezed his hand and opened her mouth to speak when a knock on the door interrupted the moment. Evander sighed but opened the door to Arlo carrying a heavy sack. "Can I assist you?"

"I believe I am assisting you?" Arlo retorted jokingly, but the humour quickly dissipated as Arlo noticed Evander's displeased expression. "We are supposed to be leaving in about fifteen minutes. I was just coming to collect you."

Evander looked at the window and noticed the evening tones painting the sky. In his unexpected sleep, all his time to get ready had passed. He needed to get packed and leave. He looked back at Rosie who innocently watched.

"I am leaving tonight, and I don't know when, or if honestly, I will be back," Evander called from the door. He wasn't sure he could move closer and still convince himself to leave.

"Oh. Where are you going? I feel so lost and helpless. I don't even know where we are."

"Currently we are at the Greenway Inn in Smollton. Gideon bought it as a temporary headquarters. Arlo and I have been given a special assignment to scout out a potential camp of the Grand Master."

"Sounds very important."

"It may be. Alternatively, it may be a complete waste. Either way, I must leave."

"I understand." Rosie gave a small nod. Evander started to leave when Rosie called his name. He stuck his head back in the room. "Thank you for caring for me," she said shyly.

Her smile was weak, but it warmed his heart. He gave a slight nod in recognition before disappearing into the hallway. Arlo handed him a bag that was on the floor outside the room.

"What's this?" Evander questioned.

"My stuff," Arlo stated simply. Evander raised his eyebrows in protest. Arlo shrugged. "I couldn't fit it all in one bag."

"You better be joking."

"Of course!" Arlo laughed which earned him one of Evander's rare grins. "I saw you sleeping and packed your bag. Although, the mead and peanuts in the bottom are mine. I couldn't actually fit everything in my bag."

"What on earth do you need peanuts and mead for? You were supposed to pack the necessities."

"It happens to be my favourite mead and I find conjured peanuts don't taste as good. They always taste slightly fishy, and I find it revolting."

Evander lightly punched Arlo in the shoulder. They slung the heavy bags over their shoulders and headed for the meeting point. When they arrived, Gideon and Alina were there with two other people.

"Evander and Arlo, this is Charlotte and Edward. They are recent graduate Conductors and have been studying under me for several decades. They are my best and brightest," Gideon beamed. Evander tried not to seem irritated. It was infuriating that Gideon would pair them with graduates when they hadn't had the chance to be tested in Ames's absence.

"Pleasure to meet you," Arlo replied and tipped his hat towards them. Evander noticed that Arlo's hat brim was missing a large chunk. It was very much Arlo's character and lessened some of Evander tension.

"Yes. Quite the pleasure," Evander added through slightly clenched teeth.

"Evander here has been briefed on the details of your journey. He is the head of this excursion and will give you the information as you head to your final destination," Gideon explained. Evander nodded his head curtly.

"Shall we depart then?" Charlotte asked with a forced grin.

"Yes, immediately," Evander replied and started off. They left the inn and grabbed a carriage that they would take them two towns over. From there, Evander planned to walk or, ideally, use the forces to accelerate their transportation. Before Ames had left, Evander and Arlo were learning how to fly with the air force. It was difficult and required a great deal of concentration, but both were proficient the last time they tried. It was significantly faster than walking.

As they travelled in the carriage, he explained the information Gideon and Alina had provided as well as his general plan for when they got to the area. The location they were provided was still relatively large. They would have to do significant recon. Charlotte and Edward both seemed annoyed and disinterested in Evander but did not complain. They sat in awkward silence for a long time before Charlotte finally spoke.

"So," she started. "When did you complete your second test?"

"Technically, we haven't," Evander replied.

"You aren't a graduate Conductor?" Charlotte said with evident disdain. Evander did not appreciate her reaction. He had hoped that Gideon might have provided more information to his studies, but it appeared that everything was a surprise.

"No," Arlo stated simply. "Our instructor was kidnapped, and we've been on the run for the past year trying to avoid being murdered and protecting the one person that might be actually able to stop the war. So no, we haven't done our second test. We've been preparing for war."

Charlotte sat in silence while assessing the both of them. Evander wasn't sure if she was irritated or impressed. In contrast, Edward seemed completely unphased and appeared to be in his own world. The silence remained for a long time. Evander preferred it that way. He tried to pay as little attention as possible to his counterparts. He didn't want to focus on them as he would only see all the ways they were better than him. Evander needed to keep his confidence and focus. Ignoring them allowed Evander to do this.

Eventually, the carriage stopped. They had been going for several hours and finally got to a town with a train station. After surveying the station for other Conductors and finding nothing, they hopped on the next train out of town. Trying to gain energy, everyone took turns sleeping on the train. Conversation was minimal which Evander appreciated. At least while they slept, they weren't judging him and Arlo.

When the train stopped, they were about a four-day hike from their target area. They walked to the outskirts of town. Evander checked his compass against a map to verify their location. Charlotte idly watched Evander. He tried to ignore her critical gaze.

"I am assuming since you are both graduated that you can fly," Evander stated while rolling up the map and slotting it into his backpack. "Otherwise, we have a four-day walk."

"Yes, we can fly." Edward replied and tightened his backpack straps around his body.

"You both can fly?" Charlotte enquired.

"Yes," Arlo and Evander announced at the same time. Rather than arguing with Charlotte, Arlo took to the air.

"Shall we then?" Evander remarked while indicating Charlotte should take off. She scoffed at him then took to the sky, quickly followed by Edward. Evander joined the group. "We fly west. We should start to see the forest in a couple hours. I want to get most of the way there but walk the last leg to make sure we don't draw too much attention."

Everyone nodded then took off to the west. The sun was setting on their second day of travel when they finally touched down. The flight was relatively uneventful, but Arlo did manage to lose his hat, forgetting it was on his head. They stayed high above the ground, so they weren't easily identified. So far, their journey has been going well.

"We will rest during the day. I think it is best we get where we need to go tonight. We have about a six-hour hike to the area," Evander dictated. Charlotte looked like she was going to protest, but Edward immediately started walking, pulling Charlotte's attention away from Evander.

Charlotte and Edward walked ahead of Arlo and Evander, speaking to each other in hushed tones and occasionally looking back at them. Evander tried to seem undeterred. He couldn't let them get under his skin. Arlo was focused on losing his last hat and complaining about it, he barely even seemed to notice the other two. Evander was glad for the distraction.

Night had fully set in when they came to a small clearing in the woods. The moon was a sliver in the sky, but the stars were bright. Evander quickly checked his map by the light of a tiny fireball balanced on his pinkie finger. This was the clearing that Alina and Gideon had suggested setting up camp in.

Evander put away the map. He cleared his throat and closed his eyes. He began moving his hands in an intricate pattern to move the grass and branches and vines into a shelter of sorts. He wanted it to look natural so they could be hidden, but big enough to sustain four people.

When he opened his eyes, an odd-looking bush sat in front of him. It was a bit squarer than he intended and had vines hanging off one section, but it looked natural otherwise. Evander moved the vines aside and crawled inside the bush shelter. There were two sets of bunk beds and a couple log stools. It was minimal and quickly made, but it would work for their purposes. The rest entered the shelter quickly after Evander and unloaded their various bags. Charlotte moved to the corner furthest away from Evander. Edward joined her for a while before coming over to Evander.

"Nicely done," he whispered to Evander. "I couldn't have done this well as quickly as you did."

Evander wasn't sure what to say. He was rarely complimented on anything, and Charlotte and Edward seemed hard to please. Instead of saying the wrong thing, Evander nodded in acceptance. Edward half smiled and walked away. Evander crawled into a bunk bed and stared at the foliage ceiling.

At least, he hadn't screwed up.

Yet.

24

Ligamen Marcam

AAbe tried to keep the blade steady in his hand as he offered it to Daisy. He knew he couldn't show doubt or fear. He needed to be strong for her. Her whole world was being brought into question and Abe was the one forcing it. Of course, over the past few weeks, Daisy didn't know what was true or who to trust. All she knew was that nothing was completely true. She searched his face. Abe was sure she was looking for signs that he was in full control of his own mind. He understood her apprehension. He could only imagine what she was feeling.

"What will this binding ritual do exactly?" She asked.

"I will not be able to do anything that goes against you or that could harm you," Abe explained. She nodded her head.

"Will you be able to lie to me then?" Abe was slightly taken aback by the question but could see where she was coming from.

"Technically, no."

"I will follow-through with your plan on one condition."

"Which is?"

"If you are bound to me, then I wish to be bound to you."

"No, Daisy." Abe was forceful, but Daisy didn't flinch. In fact, she placed her hands on her hips which Abe knew to mean she was not willing to negotiate. "I do not want that."

"Nor do I want you bound to me, but I am going to make incredibly difficult decisions and I need an open connection between us. I need to know that no harm will come to you when I decide on the future of literally everything. We are already bound in matrimony. Why not be bound by magic?"

"Daisy. There is much more to this than -" Daisy held up her hand to stop him.

"You have made it clear this is urgent. We are both bound or neither of us are bound which will impede our ability to leave. Make your decision." Daisy extended her arm and pushed her sleeve up to bare her forearm. Abe bit his lip. He was backed into a corner with two unsavoury options. Gently, he grabbed her wrist and pulled her closer to him.

"This will hurt."

He plunged the blade into her skin and gold blood poured out. Relief overwhelmed Abe. At least his hunch about Daisy's blood was right. With some of his stress gone, he began carving the symbol into her arm while muttering elder tongue. She flinched and turned her face away. The skin sizzled with each dragging movement. Abe could feel the connection opening, but he did not like it.

With the last flick of his wrist the mark was complete. She looked pale, but otherwise fine, and smiled softly back at him. He turned the blade back to Daisy. She gingerly grabbed the knife.

"Will you help me?" Daisy inquired softly.

"Of course," Abe stated.

He grabbed her hand and guided it over his own foreman where Azalea's mark used to be. There was still a faint line on his arm that Daisy could partially trace. She muttered the same words though not as quickly or clearly. Abe worried the spell wouldn't work, but the pain pulsing through his arm suggested it was working fine. It was excruciating, and Abe fought his instincts to pull away. He needed to complete the mark. Once complete, he could get them out of here and away from Azalea. He could get her to safety. Hopefully, at least. With the last flick, the mark was done, and Abe could breathe easier. The first part of the plan was done. Now, the hard part. They needed to escape.

"How do you feel?" Daisy questioned.

"Fine. And you?" Abe responded.

"No different honestly. I expected to feel differently. Like you were controlling me or that I had control of you, but I feel the same."

"Perhaps now you will understand more of what I was feeling these past couple days since the mark was placed. You're still yourself, but there's just certain things you can't say or do. It's weird when the feeling overcomes you."

"Yes, I can see that now. What is next?"

"Well, firstly, I think we need to get dressed." He looked down at Daisy who wore only his shirt. It was incredibly attractive, and he wished to take it off of her. In contrast, Abe only wore pants. Together, they made an outfit, but separate, neither was acceptable.

"How much of a rush are we in?" Daisy inquired. Abe rubbed the back of his neck. He felt like they needed to leave as quickly as possible, but in reality, he knew there wasn't really any reason to rush, yet. With the fake mark in place, Azalea wouldn't be able to physically tell their connection was broken if she came to investigate. Furthermore, Azalea would likely still be tied up with the wedding. After most Conductor weddings, the couple immediately left, but guests had to dance the night away in a drunken fit. They weren't allowed to retire until noon the next day or, as many elders would say, the couple's marriage would fail. He glanced at a clock which showed it was the wee hours of the morning. They still had several hours before people would start heading to their rooms and Azalea would be relieved of her hostess duties. They had time.

"Maybe a few hours before we really need to leave, but the sooner the better." She stepped closer to him and grabbed his hands. Cinnamon and vanilla wafted off of her which Abe found intoxicating. Her hair was messy and loose and beautiful. She looked up at him through long lashes, her silver and gold eyes shining bright in the dim light of the room. Abe longed to kiss her, to disappear into her love. He was struggling to contain himself. His mind was completely his own now, and he wanted nothing more than to act on his own desires, unimpeded.

She walked backwards towards the bed, tugging on Abe's hands. Abe followed her lead, unsure of what she was exactly planning. She was innocent and naïve. Her understanding of intimate activities was limited while his was extensive. His heart sped up with nerves and anticipation. The back of her knees hit the bed. She ran her hands up his arms before linking her hands behind his neck. He grabbed her waist and pulled her close against him.

She was skinnier than he remembered. Through the thin shirt, he could feel her rib cage slightly. Clearly the past year of training, being on the run, and living in constant fear had worn on her.

His concern immediately vanished as her lips pressed against his. He parted her lips and gently ran his tongue along her lower lip. She gasped which allowed Abe to move further into the kiss. He ran one hand down her back and pressed her body tighter against his. He moaned against her mouth, which caused her to smile. He struggled to breath, and even more so, to control his instincts. Suddenly, Daisy fell back on the bed, pulling Abe down with her. Her one leg was bent and touched the side of his bare torso. Abe gently ran his hand up her thigh, feeling as goosebumps dotted her skin.

"Do we have time?" Daisy whispered.

"I will make time," Abe murmured breathlessly.

Abe leaned down and feverishly kissed Daisy. Her heart hammered against her chest which Abe could feel against his. Her hands explored his body. Abe finally abandoned reason and gave into his desires. Daisy hardly seemed to mind. She followed his lead, returning each gesture with a curious naivety. Eventually, her shirt hit the floor quickly followed by his pants.

"Ambrose," Daisy mumbled.

"Daisy?" Abe replied and gently kissed her thighs.

"Tell me you love me." Abe moved to look Daisy in the eyes. Her hair was spread out against the bed like a halo. She smiled, but her eyes were sad.

"I love you, Daisy." A spark of joy came to her face. "I love you with every fibre of my being. There is no other being that I have loved or will love like you. You are my heart's deepest desire. You complete me in every way. So yes Daisy, I love you, but it is so much more than just love."

Abe stopped and watched her for a moment. She seemed lost in thought before pulling Abe down on top of her. Her lips pressed against his over and over again. They pulled back for a moment, breathless and sweaty. Daisy nodded and Abe understood. She gasped and briefly tensed before relaxing into Abe's movements. Her fingers dug into his back and Abe relished in the pain. He kissed her neck and nibbled on her ear as Daisy shook with pure pleasure. Abe followed his instincts, but listened to Daisy's body, seeing what brought her more euphoria and what she seemed to like. He allowed her to explore his own body as well. She was curious and adventurous, and Abe allowed her to do as she desired. Everything with her felt like fire in his veins. His mind became focused on only one thing.

Daisy.

Time passed and Abe ensured Daisy experienced all that she could before her body decided it needed rest. Now, Abe laid beside Daisy and ran his finger along her bare spine. She slept soundly and peacefully. Abe watched with adoration and love. She was stunning and, in this moment, Abe was certain he had never felt so much love for another person. He loved everything about her. He wanted nothing more than for this moment to go on forever.

A loud knock on the door caused Daisy to stir and pulled Abe out of his serene moment. He kissed her head which seemed to calm her slightly.

"Shhh. Stay asleep," Abe whispered.

Carefully, ensuring not to disrupt Daisy, Abe got out of bed. He grabbed a blanket from the end of the bed and wrapped it around his waist. He would have preferred clothes, but he honestly wasn't sure where his pants or shirt got thrown. Besides, he was sure he could get rid of the disturbance quickly.

Abe threw open the door to find an infuriated, and slightly drunk, looking Azalea standing behind it. Her anger quickly dissolved into surprise. He had opened the door enough so that the bed and a sleeping, naked Daisy could be seen.

"Oh!" Azalea muttered. "I did not expect you to succeed with her."

Abe stepped into the hallway and softly closed the door behind him. Azalea looked impressed, but the flames of fury still burned in her eyes.

"Is there something I can help you with?" Abe asked politely though he felt like punching her in the face. Although he was free to do as he pleased now, he knew he had to maintain the illusion. At least until they could escape. Abe hoped that this interaction would buy them some more time by diffusing some of Azalea's suspicions.

"I felt a change in our bond, and I needed to identify what changed. However, I think I understand now. You actually love her and somehow managed to consummate your marriage. I assume you are feeling intense love which can impact celestial magic and therefore change the bond. Yes?" It finally made sense as to what had occurred. Abe was sure that had Azalea not been drinking she would not have disclosed such information. Abe appreciated the clarity, nonetheless. "But did it break? Are you freed? It shouldn't be possible... and yet..."

"You tell me. You were the one who caused this!" Abe flipped over his arm and pointed to the mark. It had previously been a sign of control and hate where now, Abe found a tenderness in it. He tried not to show the change in his attachment to the black scar. Something seemed to flip in Azalea at seeing the mark. She relaxed and appeared more assured of the situation.

"Nothing. It is nothing," Azalea said with scrunched lips and furrowed eyebrows. Abe leaned back against the door frame and stared at Azalea who swayed slightly in her stance. "I should be returning to the ball. I am the host responsible for honouring your love and vows."

"How is the party?" Abe enquired, knowing he had to seem somewhat interested. A smirk crossed Azalea's face. He felt the blanket slide down an inch or so but didn't really care. He was sure it would encourage Azalea to speed things up.

"A great time I assure you. It's been a long time since a Conductor wedding and people seem to enjoy letting loose. I have a feeling tomorrow will be quiet, but it speaks a great honour to your matrimony and a sign of a long, happy marriage.

"I would hope so. Now, may I return to my wife? The night is still young."

"Quite right. I expect you to report to me at dinner tomorrow. We have much to discuss about moving forward, but your *wife* shall not be permitted. Understand?"

"Yes. Go enjoy the party. I shall see you tomorrow."

Abe re-entered his bedroom. He now had a more concrete timeline to escape. He knew the party was still raging with no end in sight and that tomorrow would be quiet until dinner. He locked the door and walked back to the bed. He watched Daisy sleep for a moment, so peaceful and young. He brushed a piece of hair out of her face. He desired nothing more than to crawl back into bed with her but knew this was the best time to move.

"Dais," Abe called softly and lightly shook her shoulder. She groaned and turned her head away from him. "Daisy. You need to wake up. We need to get moving."

She grabbed a pillow and covered her head. She clearly was not ready to wake up. He tried once more to wake her, but she did not seem to budge on wanting more sleep. However, Abe knew it was now or never.

He started digging about the room to find clothes and such to pack for Daisy. He purposely was not quiet. He slammed cupboards and scraped chairs across the floor. She slowly began stirring with the more ruckus he made. Finally, a loud groan meant success.

"You can be such an ass," she spat beneath the pillows.

"I tried to wake you nicely," he retorted. She sat up in bed holding the covers to her chest. Her hair was a complete mayhem, but Abe found it endearing. He longed to run his hands through it one more time, feeling the silky strands run between his fingers.

"I am guessing it's time to leave?"

"I've been given the exact window of opportunity and we need to get out of here now."

"Must we leave right now?"

"Yes, we really must be going."

Daisy shrugged, seeming displeased with his answer. Abe wasn't sure what else to say though. She stood up from the bed, leaving the blanket behind. Abe couldn't help but stare at her exposed body, reliving the moments of the night before. She walked towards the wardrobe and opened it. With her back turned to him, Abe noticed how scared her back was. Each lashing from her parents etched into her skin. Suddenly he found himself behind her, tracing the lines that marked her back; he couldn't help himself. Daisy froze and looked over her shoulder at him. He wasn't sure if she was insulted, uncomfortable, or fearful.

"I… I didn't realise… I had only seen the ones on your neck. I didn't even notice last night… I didn't know… it's so extensive," Abe whispered. His fingers lightly traced each stroke and imagined how much pain this must have caused.

"They are old now. It is in my past, and we needn't dwell on the past. We need to move forward," Daisy stated. She sounded irritated. Abe took a step back and gave her space. She quickly dressed. She slid into pants and a blouse with a matching jacket and carriage boots. Like magic, she spun her hair up into a bun and pinned it with the wooden comb he had given her nearly two years ago now.

"You look beautiful," Abe breathed. She nearly took his breath away. There was nothing extravagant about what she wore or how she looked, but she was still stunning. Perhaps it was that she was willing to be different. She was comfortable wearing pants and abnormal clothes. She was willing to be dirty and do the hard work even though she was technically a duchess. She was a walking contradiction to the society that surrounded her, and Abe loved everything about it.

"Hardly." She laughed lightly, causing Abe's heart to jump. She eyed him suspiciously with a strange smirk that Abe wasn't sure what to think of. "Are you going to get dressed?"

"Yes." Abe blushed as he looked down and realised, he was essentially naked. "I suppose that would help."

He surveyed the room until he found clothes and quickly donned them. Fully clothed, he was ready to leave. Now, they only had to escape.

25

A Choice's Price

"Ready?" Abe said and offered his hand to Daisy. She graciously accepted although she felt incredibly nervous. Her stomach felt like a fire burned within and she was trying everything to remain calm. "Just follow my lead and I will get you through this. I promise."

He smiled, but Daisy could see the fear behind his eyes. She knew exactly what he was feeling because she was also feeling those same emotions. Fear. Worry. Anticipation. The only difference was that he was better at hiding it. He was generally better at everything than her, but Daisy didn't mind. She hadn't experienced much yet; he had experienced the whole world. He was bound to be better at most things than her.

They stepped out into the hallway and walked as quietly as possible. Abe stopped at every corner and listened for people coming toward them. The hallways started to narrow. As they neared the centre, however, different pathways converged into larger channels. Daisy could start to hear the sounds of a party. Abe kept trying to go the opposite direction of the music and ruckus, but every turn seemed to lead to different sounds.

They rounded one corner and unexpectedly ran into a couple. Abe pulled Daisy closer into a sort of hug and instantly started acting giddy and romantic. Daisy found it weird, but she knew she needed to play along. However, their ruse wasn't necessary; the couple was overly infatuated with each other and hardly seemed to notice Abe and Daisy at all. The girl lifted her head and smiled momentarily at Daisy. Her eyes shone a bright gold that was nearly blinding. Daisy gasped and quickly looked away; something about her made Daisy feel uneasy. Thankfully, the couple didn't linger, and Abe and Daisy found themselves alone once again in the winding tunnels.

"Do you know where we are going?" Daisy whispered.

"Yes," Abe paused, "...and no."

"What do you mean yes and no?"

"They usually bagged me, so I couldn't see where I was going. But I think if we can get to the main hall, I can find our way out from there. The path was always the same and I counted the steps to each turn. I know if we find the hall, I can get us out of here."

"Bagged you?"

"Put a bag over my head so I couldn't see. It wasn't the most effective method, but it was the easiest I guess." Abe shrugged. Daisy wasn't quite sure what to do with the information. She paused for a moment to think but couldn't come up with a response. Instead, she focused on what did make sense and changed the subject.

"The hallways are getting wider, so I would think we are on the right path."

"Quite right."

They walked in silence for a few more moments, listening for passers-by and distant parties. At one point, they had been walking down a hall for a long time with no branches and only the occasional door. It was the widest hallway they had been in, but they still hadn't found the main hall. Abe stopped dead and pulled Daisy back.

Footsteps.

Somewhere down the darkened hallways, a person approached. As the footsteps grew louder, Daisy could hear their distinct rhythm. She felt an overwhelming fear come over her. Her heart began to race. She looked to Abe who held a finger to his lips to silence her. Quickly and quietly, Abe directed Daisy to a nearby door. He opened the door and pushed Daisy inside.

"Damn it. Not this one either," Abe yelled and slammed the door on Daisy. She was in a small room with a plain bed, table, and wardrobe. It was like her room back at Dame Agatha's. It had no personality and was simply meant to house people.

Daisy pressed her against the door listening for what Abe was doing in the hallway. Azalea must have been closer to them than expected. Daisy could hear her voice through the door almost instantly after it closed.

"What are you looking for, my dear Abe?" she remarked snidely. Daisy could hear Abe stumbling with his steps.

"The goo- good wine. The one - you, you, you always have on that big chair thing. What's it called… your big chair? What do you call it?"

"My throne?"

"Yes! That thing. The w-win w-hine you have there. I want it."

"Are you drunk?" There was a pause.

"May-be." Abe broke in a fit of giggles that Daisy found his act uncharacteristically adorable. "Pro-b-b-all-lee."

"The wife already driving you to drink?"

"No!" The humour suddenly disappeared from his voice. While he could pretend to be drunk, he did not seem willing to let Azalea speak poorly of Daisy. "She is a-maz-ing."

"I see. I have had both of you drunk in my presence in less than two days. Let's not make a habit of this. I find it annoying. Caring for others is not exactly my calling."

"Do you know what my cal… call… call-ing is?"

"I can guess."

"The good wine! Where is it?" There was an uncomfortable silence. Daisy could only imagine the look on her sister's face but pictured it was displeased.

"Purely because it is your wedding night, and I don't think you will remember the stash tomorrow… Continue down this hall until you come to the grand chamber. There is a tapestry to the left of the throne where you will find a hidden door. Pull the handle up and it will unlock. Do you think you have the capacity to remember that?"

"Probuboly nut." Abe hiccupped and proceeded to giggle. Daisy could hear as he fell to the floor in a fit of giggles. Daisy wished she could see Abe actually intoxicated, for it may be rather amusing. After a moment, Daisy could hear the steps of Azalea leaving. Abe continued giggling until there seemed a natural conclusion, and Azalea's steps could no longer be heard.

The door was flung open to Daisy's hiding spot who fell out of the room and into the hallway. She didn't realise how much she was leaning on the door until it was ripped away from her. Abe offered her a hand and helped her stand up. She brushed off her pants then looked at Abe amusedly.

"When this is over, I must get you to drink in excess. It sounds like fun," Daisy chided.

"I assure you, it is not," Abe stated with an exaggerated eye roll. "Now, come on. We've got to go before I am shoving you in another room and acting drunk again."

Abe tugged Daisy down the hall. The corridor continued widening until they reached the Grand Hall where Daisy had been chained to the floor and interrogated by Azalea. The large table still sat in the middle as well as Azalea's throne adorning the one wall. Daisy was relieved to find there was not a single person in the hall; the room was completely empty.

Abe stood beside the table and closed his eyes. He began slowly turning in a circle. Suddenly, his eyes flew open, and he pointed to a tapestry on the wall.

"There are several hidden chambers off of this chamber. I just had to get my bearings, but behind that tapestry should be the start of our way out."

They sprinted towards the tapestry and pushed it aside. Behind it was a plain stone wall with no discernible markings. Daisy looked at Abe who seemed perplexed. He started feeling the wall until he found a small divot. He tapped slowly twice, followed by three quick knocks, and one final slow tap. The wall started cracking and moving to reveal a dark passage behind it.

Most of the passages were dark in Azalea's fortress. Generally, Conductors just moved about with a fireball of their own creation which made little need for the halls to be illuminated by torches. But this passage seemed to be darker than any of the others. Not a single sliver of light could be seen; they were walking into a black abyss. Daisy lit a small spark, but even that seemed devoured by the blackness.

"Are you sure about this?" Daisy questioned nervously.

"Like I said, I was most often bagged. I couldn't see anything, but this should be correct. Stay close to me, and from here on out, do not talk. I can't lose count, or we will get lost," Abe instructed sternly.

Daisy nodded her head and clung onto Abe's arm. He began walking with purpose into the dark. As they passed the threshold, the opening slammed behind them enveloping them into complete darkness. Daisy knew she couldn't light a fireball as they did not want to give away their position, but she very much wished she could. However, Abe had only ever done this walk in the dark, so she trusted that he knew where they were going. Abe kept moving forward with long, determined strides. Daisy struggled to keep up. She wanted to tell him to slow down but remembered his warning.

After several steps, Abe stopped. They turned left and began walking again. Daisy partially expected to run into a wall or something, but with every turn and stop, Abe seemed to avoid any obstacles. At one point, the ground seemed to change from dirt or stone to wooden planks. As they walked on the wooden floor a breeze came up through the space between the planks; Daisy assumed this meant they were high, possibly on a bridge or something of the like. She held tighter on Abe's arm, endeavouring not to think about what was, or was not, below them.

They made three more turns before finally stopping. Daisy could hear Abe sliding his hand around the wall feeling for something. Eventually, his hand hit something that sounded wooden. With a loud thunk, Abe pulled whatever it was and the wall in front of them split open.

Early morning light streamed into the blackness. Daisy covered her eyes with her arm; the light was blinding after they had been in such darkness. As their eyes adjusted, they stepped out onto the dew-covered grass and into a small clearing. Tall trees encircled the entirety of the clearing aside for a small break where a path poked through. Daisy let go of Abe's arm, closed her eyes, and took a deep breath of the fresh, morning air.

When Daisy opened her eyes, Abe was staring at the sky through the clearing. The sky was starting to turn purple with the rising sun, but the stars still twinkled bright. A small tear ran down his cheek. Daisy approached him slowly and reached up to wipe away the tear. He turned into her hand and lightly kissed her palm. It was touching and sweet and an entirely different expression of intimacy that Daisy wanted to freeze.

Freeze.

Daisy snapped her fingers and the world stilled for a moment. Abe glanced at her through long lashes. He seemed appreciative of the lengthened moment. His arms tangled around Daisy's waist and pulled her closer. She breathed him in, but he no longer smelled of lavender and sandalwood; instead, he smelled of wine and vanilla. It was not the most attractive smell; however, she couldn't help but appreciate his closeness and affection. He rested his forehead against hers and closed his eyes.

"We got out," Abe whispered. "I didn't think we could do it, but we got out."

"Yes, we did," Daisy replied, but in doing so her hold on time released and the ruckus of the world surrounded them again.

"Is it hard to stop time?"

"It's not hard, but it is exhausting. Had I held that any longer, I may have passed out. It has happened before. The world doesn't seem to like stopping and certainly punishes me for doing so. I won't be able to stop time again for at least a couple days." Abe smiled. Daisy caressed his cheek. "Ambrose."

Abe sucked the air through his teeth. He pushed her hair back and held Daisy's face between his hands. Daisy wrapped her hands around his wrists to keep him close.

"Say my name again," he breathed.

"Ambrose," Daisy whispered. Abe closed his eyes and lingered in the moment.

"It sounds better when you say it." He laughed slightly before leaning forward and kissing Daisy. It started soft and gentle. He was light and stroked her cheek idly. Then, his hands slid behind her neck and the kiss deepened into a more passionate frenzy. He moaned against her mouth and then kissed her neck. Daisy tilted her head and allowed his lips to mark every inch of her exposed flesh.

Suddenly, Abe released Daisy entirely and stepped back from her. Daisy shook her head trying to clear the fog and understand what just occurred. When her eyes refocused, she saw Abe standing with his back to her. His hands were interlocked behind his neck and extended outwards with his elbows to the sky. She could hear his breathing, rapid and heavy.

"Abe?" Daisy called. He dropped his hands and looked over his shoulder towards her.

"We don't have time for this, and we really must be leaving if we are to escape at all," Abe replied. He quickly turned and grasped Daisy's hands. "I so desperately wish that things were different. I never wanted our wedding to be so coerced. I imagined this so very differently. I imagined our life together to be so different. I fear what I have brought you into and it is all my fault."

"No, Abe. You gave me the choice, and I willingly accepted. I could have left many times and chose not to. This is not your doing."

"I worry I will destroy you."

"I am not glass. I am not so easily broken. We are wed and bound. You cannot leave me now, nor do I ever wish to leave you." Abe stared deeply into her eyes. A single tear grew in the corner of his blue eye. Daisy reached up and brushed it away. "We are in this together. I promise you; we will find a way."

Abe's head suddenly snapped away from Daisy. He glared intently through the bush. Daisy followed his gaze and saw nothing.

"Someone is coming," Abe whispered. He pulled Daisy to the slide of the clearing. "You need to hide. If it is one of Azalea's followers, I can maybe convince them to leave. If they see you though, everything will fall apart."

"Why don't we just leave now? We have the opportunity. Let's go now," Daisy insisted and started pulling on Abe to leave. He shook his head.

"There are multiple steps. If they hear us, they will know we are running. I can buy you some time, Dais. I will distract them, and you can sneak away."

"No. I am not leaving you."

"Daisy. You need to go Grenich. You need to meet the Celestials. You need to save us. I cannot help you with the Celestials, but I can at least buy you some time to get out of here. Please. Just give me that."

Daisy analysed his face. She could see his concern and feel his fear. She assessed her options and realised there really wasn't an alternative. Abe was right and that sickened Daisy. She just got him back and yet… she had to leave him again.

"Promise me you will find me again. Promise me you will come to Grenich as soon as you can. Promise me you won't leave me," Daisy pleaded.

"I will find you. I will always find you, Dais." Abe quickly kissed her one more time. "Now, go. Get out of here!"

Daisy turned and started running in the opposite direction of the arriving footsteps. She couldn't look back. If she looked back, she would go back, and she knew she couldn't go back. She had to keep running.

26

In Absence

Abe quickly glanced around looking for a hiding place, but he was too far from any of the trees. Besides, Daisy getting away was the most important thing, and he just needed to give her the time to get as far away as she could. Two people, who Abe did not recognize, entered the clearing; they seemed to be in the midst of a heated conversation. Abe tried to stay as still as possible in hopes that they wouldn't notice him.

"I can't believe we have to take orders from him," remarked a young girl with black hair and dark skin. Her eyes were a startlingly red and green combo that Abe could see from a fair distance away. He wasn't sure if her darker skin made her eyes pop or if they were really just that bright. Her partner was a strange contrast. He was a tall, well-built man with a bald head and a blonde moustache. He wore a monocle over a blue eye, leaving his brown eye exposed.

"He's not even a graduated Conductor and yet we have to follow him. I get that he has some skills, but he is still an amateur. Did Gideon say why he was put in charge?" Abe's chest contracted and he stopped breathing. *Gideon? Did she just say Gideon? Was it possible that these people were Gideon's people and not Azalea's? But Abe hadn't heard from Gideon in years...Why would Gideon's people be here? Unless... Gideon had aligned with Azalea.* Abe's palms began to sweat at the idea.

"You are barely a graduate yourself, but that isn't why I don't like him. He just seems like such an ass. All that Gideon said was that he had information Gideon couldn't share with us and we were expected to follow his orders," the man explained.

Suddenly, they both noticed Abe and immediately got ready for a fight. Their hands ignited with the forces and prepared to throw everything they had at Abe. Abe could sense their power from far away, but knew he was still stronger than both of them. Abe did not prepare to fight however. He wanted to appear non-threatening and put his hands up.

"Who are you?" the woman demanded.

"I could ask you the same thing," Abe replied in a calm voice. They didn't appear to know who Abe was, which led Abe to believe they were not some of Azalea's minions. Abe had been paraded about with Azalea enough that most of her minions knew who he was. Still, Abe knew better than to trust that assumption.

"You are a Conductor," the man added.

"Yes. As are you both," Abe stated. "Are you going to attack me, or is there something I can assist you with?"

"Why are you here?" the woman asked.

"I am not going to answer any questions. Just as I assume you won't either."

There was a quick, knowing glance exchanged between the two. Abe suspected they were coordinating an attack. In one swift move, the duo completed a united attack and promptly ensnared Abe in a mix of vines and rock. He could feel that the bindings were strong, but he still knew he could break out if necessary. Yet, Abe wanted to see how this played out. This delay also gave Daisy more time to get away.

"I see you have captured me," Abe muttered, trying to suppress his sarcasm.

"What should we do with him?" the man questioned.

"Gideon stated that *he* was in charge, so I suppose we should take him back to our *leader*," the woman replied. He nodded his head and with the flick of his wrist, he began dragging Abe behind them.

As they dragged Abe on the ground, the couple continued to complain about their leader but didn't mention Gideon again. As they continued, they moved further and further into the forest and away from Azalea's underground fortress. Abe felt fairly confident that his initial assumption was in fact correct; they were not followers of Azalea. Eventually, they quieted with their complaints as they approached a small shelter.

It was relatively well camouflaged considering it was made out of local foliage. The only reason Abe noticed it was the pair of red pants hanging on the roof to dry. A small fire sparked outside of it with a pair of socks and boots beside it. Abe could hear indistinct voices coming from inside the shelter.

The couple rounded the shelter and stood in front of it, but left Abe just outside of sight from the doorway.

However, as soon as Abe could hear the voice of their leader, there was no doubt. He exploded out of his bindings. His captors immediately lit fireballs and prepared to fight. Abe quickly cast a wind gust that knocked the two strangers aside. They collapsed on the ground some twenty feet away. Abe barrelled inside the lean-to and wrapped his arms around Arlo and Evander. He moved back to take in the sight before him. *Were they really here? Was he actually looking at his studies?*

"Is it… is it actually you?" Abe pleaded. He feared this was a dream or some twisted vision, but he desperately wanted them to be here. Right in front of him. Looking at him. Lighting forces… *against him…?*

"What is this?" Evander barked. Abe took a step back and dropped his hands.

"What do you mean? It's me. It's Ambrose. Your teacher. You are my studies." Abe fumbled over his words. He had not expected hostility. Perhaps… This was some terrible vision perverted by some other person to torment Abe to insanity. "Please… please see who I am."

Evander and Arlo looked at each other in a silent assessment of the situation. Neither put down their orbs of energy, nor did they cast it against him. Abe anxiously awaited their decision. They had to see it was him. They had to see this wasn't some kind of joke or mirage. It was him. It was Abe.

"Prove it," Arlo challenged. Evander elbowed him in the side as if to say that was not what they agreed to. "What? If he is Ames, he has to be able to prove it."

"How would you like me to do that?" Abe questioned. Arlo shrugged in his indifferent manner that

Abe found incredibly annoying. He turned to stare Evander straight in the eyes.

"The last time you saw me, I gave you my journal with all the accounts of my life. The first several sections are in elder tongue, but then there are some sections in a code of my own. Near the end, there are several sections in more modern English that recount me training the three of you as well as when I was training Alina before she graduated. I imagine… you found out me and Alina's secret…. About Alina's condition and our past."

Evander immediately dropped the orb of fire he held at his side and closed the gap between him and Abe. Evander's face was mere inches from Abe's, but Abe stood his ground. Abe wasn't sure if Evander was going to hug him or punch him, but Abe would graciously accept either. Luckily, it turned out to be the more affectionate option.

Evander wrapped his arms around Abe in a suffocating and crushing embrace that warmed Abe's heart. Clearly, as much as he had missed them, they had missed him. Abe hugged Evander back and held onto him until Evander decided the hug was over.

They had never been overly affectionate people. They shared moments and understandings, but outright expressions of admiration were few and far between. Abe appreciated this more than he could explain. Tears welled in his eyes and the absence of Daisy dramatically lessened. He now had his family with him. He could do anything with them by his side.

"Where are the others? Where are Alina and Brighid?" Abe pleaded, desperate to be completely reunited. Arlo's face fell and Abe instantly knew.

"Alina and Gideon are actually the ones who sent us here. The other two are actually Gideon's students. Supposedly his best," Evander remarked with a large eyeroll. Abe could sense Evander's disapproval, but he found humour in knowing their opinions about Evander.

"You found Gideon?"

"Apparently, he and Alina have been pen pals for quite some time. We went to his secret hide out and were attacked by the Grand Master's forces."

"Alina and Brighid are both okay though?"

"Yes, they are both fine. You'd be very proud of Brighid. She has held her own very well, but Rosie was severely injured. She has pulled through and Brighid is tending to her care."

"I am glad to hear everyone is doing well, but how did you get here?"

"Alina believes Azalea had a spy in our ranks that was informing the Grand Master of our movements. During the assault, the spy was injured or killed so the Grand Master has been sloppy with her movements and plans. We were able to track attack reports to the general vicinity. We arrived here just yesterday, but it appears we are in the right area if you are here."

"Ah. Yes. I suppose I would be an indicator of that." Suddenly, something flickered in Evander and his hands reignited with balls of flame. Abe raised his hands unsure of what was happening. "What is going on Evander?"

"How do we know you aren't under the Grand Master's control?" he replied. Arlo instantly followed Evander's lead. Abe took a step back.

"You don't, but if you will allow me, I will tell you what has been going on and it may just make more sense."

Evander pondered for a moment before putting out his flames. Abe relaxed slightly. He quickly reviewed the past year including the more recent month with Daisy's capture. He explained the rune carved in his arm by Azalea and how Daisy had burned it out of him. He told them of their wedding night and marking each other with the binding rune. Lastly, he explained their escape and Daisy leaving.

They all sat in silence as the story set in. Arlo seemed completely dumbfounded while Evander appeared deep in contemplation. It was a lot of information to take in and Abe wasn't entirely sure how they would take it all.

"I believe it," Arlo announced. Evander bounced his head from side to side in consideration.

"It makes sense, but it also seems… far fetched at the same time. We sit here now and you seem like you, so I have no reason to believe it's not you," Evander stated. Abe let go a sigh of relief. They believed him and that meant opportunity.

"So, you're here, but you're obviously not supposed to be. What exactly is your plan?" Arlo asked.

"I thought your counterparts were Azalea's minions. I had to give Daisy time to get away, so I sacrificed myself to be captured. Obviously, you are not Azalea, so I don't exactly have a plan now. Daisy is going to Grenich to access the stones, but I don't know where she is now to help her. I honestly don't know what to do."

"Speaking of the others… where are they?" Evander questioned with genuine concern. Abe could see his sense of leadership overwhelming him. It made Abe oddly proud of Evander.

"I, uh... temporarily dispatched them. They are currently lying on the ground, likely unconscious," Abe replied cautiously.

"We should probably attend to them," Arlo said while standing up and heading out to look after the others.

"Any information you can give us? Anything to help the cause?" Evander pressed as Arlo exited.

"I can show you the entrance. We can watch it and track movements of forces. The inside is a maze that constantly changes. Getting in will be nearly impossible, but if you can draw them out, we stand a better chance. We will need to figure out their activities first however. Let me show you to the entrance," Abe offered.

Evander nodded and followed Abe. They walked in silence for a while. Abe just liked being in the presence of his studies. He had missed them more than he realised. In their absence, he missed them, but in their presence he realised his fondness. He wished to see Alina and Brighid as well, but he knew they were where they needed to be.

"So," Evander broke the silence. "You're actually married."

"Yes," Abe said with a large smile. He couldn't help himself. While it didn't go how he wanted, he was still happy to be united with Daisy. Perhaps when this is all over, Abe would marry Daisy again, but properly and in a way they both want.

"Did you... do you love Daisy? I thought the proposal was just a ruse to get Daisy away from her parents." Evander seemed curious, but mostly confused. Abe paused and thought about how he wanted to explain it.

"I was fond of her when I was training her, but I never acted on it. I wanted her to make her own decisions. I can see how from the outside you wouldn't have seen that. I wasn't exactly expressive of my feelings, but you never saw us alone either. I fell in love with her quickly and deeply, but I could never do anything about it. When I suggested the proposal... it was a scheme, but I think I suggested it because of a deeper desire. Over the past year, being without her, my heart grew even fonder and I cannot imagine being without her now. This is not how I planned things to go, but I am bonded to her now and I wouldn't have it any other way."

Evander nodded his head in contemplation. "Aren't you afraid of losing her? She just left and she may never come back."

"Daisy is quite capable, but there are always risks. We, Conductors, don't live a simple life, but Daisy chose this life. I don't know what the future holds, but I trust that she will come back to me. I trust that I will find her again and we will be together."

"How do you do that?"

"Do what?"

"Remain optimistic." Abe stopped and looked at Evander in surprise. Abe had never really considered himself a positive person, but in this moment, he could see it. Daisy had changed him a lot in such a short time. He didn't understand it himself.

"I don't know. I just feel it in me. I trust in her just as she trusts in me."

"I just... run away... when things get tough, I leave." Evander paused and Abe allowed him to have his moment. Evander was never one to talk about his past, so Abe just let him disclose what he wanted. Abe knew that if he pushed, Evander would shut down entirely. "I am trying not to do that now. I'm not going to run any more. That's why I am here now. I have thought about leaving many times, but I am not going to do it."

"Well, I am glad you are here." Abe put a supportive hand on Evander's shoulder. Evander gave an appreciative smile.

They continued walking in silence for some time. The birds chirped in the slight breeze. It was a gorgeous early summer day. Abe appreciated being out of the dark tunnels and in the fresh air while not being under someone else's control. They approached the clearing where Daisy had left him and a pang of sadness filled his heart.

"This is the entrance," Abe stated and indicated a rock face on a hillside.

"Thank you for bringing me here," Evander replied. "How do you get in?"

"Like this." Abe pressed several cracks and jut outs in the rock in a seemingly random order. He had one opportunity when he wasn't bagged to see how the door opened. He locked the code deep in his memories. Eventually, the rock face cracked open into a deep, impenetrable blackness. But cutting through the blackness was a dim fireball approaching them. Someone was coming and Abe would not let Evander get caught.

"Watch this exit. Track everything you can. I will try to get out information," Abe explained rapidly.

"What are you talk-" Evander paused and looked through the entrance. The fireball was growing closer. Evander looked by Abe and shook his head. "No. NO. Abe. Don't! We can leave. Right now."

"The light from the entrance will be visible. We don't have time. Just… Don't get caught. I have to keep you safe."

Abe stepped into the blackness. The wall slammed shut behind him. He stood there for a moment listening to the deafening silence. There was a small clicking further down meaning whoever was coming was even closer than Abe thought. Abe stood as still as possible, hoping that whoever was approaching would not sense or see Abe. The light was growing more quickly. Abe knew he wouldn't be able to avoid the on comer. As the light got closer, Abe instantly recognized the on comer.

Henry.

27

The Generosity of Strangers

Daisy ran as quickly as she could while still maintaining some semblance of stealth. She knew that if anyone spotted her, Abe's sacrifice would have been for nothing. She would not let Abe give up his freedom in vain.

Again…

She sprinted through the forest, pushing herself to take one more stride and another and another. When she finally felt like she could stop running, her lungs burned and her legs felt like liquid. She braced herself against a tree to catch her breath. Sweat ran down her forehead; her hair, soaked with sweat, stuck to her face. She needed to figure out her bearings. A train station would be the quickest to Grenich, but that wasn't necessarily the safest option. She would need a disguise of some sort to mask her eyes and make her less noticeably a Conductor.

Daisy located the sun and its general direction to figure out which way was north. She wasn't even sure what forest she was in to know where the nearest town was, but walking north seemed the best way to go.

The sun started to fall behind the horizon, and the air got chillier. Daisy had been walking most of the day and hadn't come across any signs of civilization. She was exhausted and confused, but kept walking north. When the sun had set and the stars were bright, Daisy finally stopped for a rest. She sat against a tree and allowed the exhaustion to overwhelm her. She was pulled into a deep sleep.

She stood in the clearing by Grenich. A knife ran against her palm, drawing scarlet blood mixed with gold fragments. She pressed her hand to one stone and was suddenly transported to the black, shale cliffs she so often visited in her sleep. The grey sky melded into a dark, angry sea. One lonely and bare tree shadowed Abe wearing only pants and an open shirt. If she walked towards him, she knew what would happen, and Daisy did not wish to see him die again. Instead, she walked towards the cliff and threw herself over it.

The air whipped her hair around her head. She watched the sea quickly approaching and knew its impact would hurt. Daisy closed her eyes, bracing for an impact that never came. The wind died down, and Daisy suddenly found herself standing. When she opened her eyes, she found herself standing in a room of all black. It was like her exam all over again, where she couldn't tell where the walls ended and the floor started. It was just endless blackness.

"Come here, my child," whispered a disembodied voice. It echoed all around her and sent a cold shiver across her skin.

Daisy startled awake. Her breath heaved as the panic of the dream filled her. It took several minutes for

Daisy to reorient herself and relax. After several deep breaths, Daisy stood, but her legs quivered. She managed to stand up and began walking in the direction of the sun. Her stomach growled in protest, and her parched lips cracked and bled. She had only consumed alcohol in the last twenty-four hours, and that did not lend well to walking for hours on end.

The sun was hot and blinding. She stumbled into a clearing and squinted angrily at the sun. The ground was hard and radiated the heat back at her. It was unpleasant, but the sun was her guide. She hated it, but knew she needed it to guide her on her way. She glared at the sun until everything became black.

Daisy awoke sometime later. The sun was lower in the sky, meaning several hours had passed. She lay on her back and watched as branches moved above her. She felt the ground sway beneath her. The rhythmic clopping of hooves lulled her back towards sleep, but she refused to give in and, instead, pushed her torso up in order to get a proper look at her surroundings.

She found herself in the back of a wagon filled with various crates. An elderly man sat at the front of the wagon reining a brown horse with a black tail. Daisy wasn't sure how she had gotten in the wagon, but she was appreciative of not having to walk anymore. Carefully, she crawled to the front of the wagon behind the old man.

"Mornin' miss. How'd ya sleep?" He had a southern drawl that was unusual for the area.

"I don't remember falling asleep," Daisy mumbled.

"I'd guessed. You had yer face in the dirt. I poked ya, but ya didn't move. Ya just lie there. I thought ya wer died."

"Thank you for picking me up."

"Welcome." He smiled over his shoulder and Daisy glimpsed two milky eyes whose colour was indiscernible. Daisy could not tell their original colour, but *wouldn't the colour of two different eyes show through?* Daisy crawled over the wagon front and sat on the bench beside him. She figured she could get a better idea of who he was if she was closer.

"Where er ya head'd?"

"Grenich actually."

"Ya a long way from Grenich, but old Delia and me er head'd to Humberg. That be mur than half way for ya." He turned and smiled at Daisy. There was no clear colour in eyes still. *Maybe they were so light, the colour couldn't be seen through the cloud?*

"If you wouldn't mind, I would greatly appreciate that."

"Why er ya walkin' ut here by yerself?"

"I… I- uh couldn't afford the train, but I needed to get there."

"Fer. Fer. Gud thin me found ya ten."

"Yes. It would appear so."

"Delia will gut ya tere. No issue. She a gud ol' gurl. She ne'er led me the wrong way. Always go where she told. Always surprise me wit her knowin'. She almost like a person sometimes."

"I am glad to hear that."

They fell into idle chit chat about the weather and their lives. He was the father of twelve and his eldest son had recently taken over the farm. He was taking Delia and what little belongings he had to his daughter's place in Humberg to live with her. She was the only one of his children willing to care for him in his old age and with his bad eyes. He did tell her he was blind eventually and that Delia had been driving this cart by herself for the last five years. It assured Daisy, but also made her weary. At the very least, he could never tell anyone he saw Daisy.

In contrast, Daisy only talked about her life before finishing school. She told him as little as she could while still being polite and keeping the conversation moving. She did tell him that she was recently married, but lied, saying her husband was stationed in Grenich and she was going to meet him there.

The sun dipped below the horizon, and Delia moved over to the side of the road. Vincent, as Daisy found out, gingerly got down from the wagon and started undoing the buckles that fastened Delia to the cart. The harness remained on, but she was free from the wagon. She graciously stepped away, gently nuzzled Vincent, and started grazing just in front of the wagon. Using the edge of the wagon, Vincent guided himself to the back and crawled up into the wagon.

"It'll be cold soon. Use this t' keep warm," Vincent stated and handed Daisy a wool blanket. He pulled out another for himself. He tossed some hay toward Delia who whinnied gratefully. He climbed down from the cart. "Cud ya take me t' some grass t' sleep?"

"Yes. Of course," Daisy said. She extended her arm which Vincent shakily took. They walked just off the road to some long grass. Vincent laid down and covered himself in a blanket. "Would you like a fire?"

"Tat be great." Daisy waited a moment before lighting a fireball and letting it adrift in the air between them. Daisy watched the fire spark, and Vincent fall asleep.

She was bone tired but sleep kept evading her. She felt alert and warry of the situation she found herself in. They were exposed and in danger. By accepting this man's incredible generosity, Daisy put him in great peril. A part of her wanted to run away while he slept, but that felt even more wrong for some reason. Instead of sleep, she watched the stars drift across the night sky in their slow dance with the moon. From the deepest black to indigo to the early morning purples, the night sky transformed to an early morning.

Vincent began stirring in the early hours of the morning as pink hues started to paint the sky. He stood up, an effort which appeared to be quite painful, and grabbed his blanket off the ground. Daisy helped him hobble over to the cart. Delia backed into the cart arms like she had done it thousand times. Vincent did up the harness then clambered up into the wagon to sit beside Daisy. She conjured an apple and placed it into Vincent's hand. He had a bright toothless grin as he thanked Daisy for the fruit.

"I rode this path a long time by meself, but I been blind for so long tat I don't know wat the path looks like," Vincent said.

"Would you like me to describe it to you?" Daisy offered. He nodded gleefully. Daisy spent the next several hours painting a picture of the surroundings. She highlighted the early tree buds in their vibrant green. Most of the leaves were fully sprouted showing a whole spectrum of greens. She pointed out the different barks and the occasional berry bush. Eventually, they came to a y in the road where Vincent again pulled over. He unhooked Delia so she could have a well deserved break.

Vincent went to the back of the wagon and pulled out a loaf of bread to share with Daisy. She had not realised how hungry she really was. Although she could conjure food, she found it always tasted unusual and the texture was off. It was never as good as food in its natural form. She once had even conjured food that was rotten, as such she tried to avoid conjuring food as much as possible.

After devouring the loaf, they headed back on the road. Several hours later, they came to a sign that stated the Grenich station was only a few miles ahead.

"Vincent, we are almost at Grenich. I think we took a wrong turn," Daisy informed him.

"No miss. We din't. I was likin' yer company and wanted t' get ya t yer destination. I em not missin' any ting by takin' the long way. Besides, I got a friend in Grenich I can visit," Vincent explained. Daisy was touched by the sentiment. His genuinely kind and caring actions were unexpected but welcomed considering all Daisy had been through.

The road became familiar as they climbed the hill to the train station. Daisy had spent so many months in that train station that it felt like returning home. She smiled softly.

"You can let me off here," Daisy stated.

"Ya sure miss?" Vincent question.

"Yes. This will be fine." He pulled the wagon over in front of the train station and Daisy climbed out. "May I ask who you are visiting while you are here?"

"Ol' Aggy. She was good t' me wife when she was alive. She runnin' some school ting 'ere now. Haven't seen her since me wife passed some ten 'ears go."

"Do you mean Dame Agatha? At Dame Agatha's School for Young Women?"

"Sounds like. Aggy loved teachin' and helpin'. Do ya know her?"

"I am quite familiar with her. I am sure she will be happy to see you."

"Cud ya give Delia 'ere the directions? She will gut me tere. No worries." Daisy walked over to Delia and said the directions to the school loud enough so Vincent could hear. He nodded along. When she finished, Vincent waved goodbye and took off down the hill towards town.

Daisy watched them go until they disappeared into the woods. She was sad to see him go as she came to find his company enjoyable. For so long, she had been on the run and afraid. Her few days of idle chit chat and niceties was like a vacation from her reality. She had appreciated the reprieve more than she could describe.

With Vincent out of view, Daisy turned back to the train station. She walked over towards the plain brick wall that hid the entrance to their old home. It was the last place she had felt truly happy. Abe had said it would be sealed once they left, but Daisy longed for one more look at the station. She placed her hand against the wall. She expected to feel the cold brick surface but was surprised as her hand disappeared into the wall. The familiar tingling sensation was welcomed. She pulled her hand back, glanced around for any onlookers and stepped through the wall.

28

Trust Fall

Evander watched as the earth swallowed Ames. In three short strides, Evander was pounding against the rocks and looking for the hidden cracks to open the wall, but nothing worked. He wasn't going to lose Abe again. There was no way Abe could be lost again. After several minutes of frantically searching the wall and nothing fruitful coming to pass, Evander collapsed against the ground and listened to the wall. It was silent. Evander's heart dropped into his stomach. *Had he failed? Was this going to be his greatest failure yet?*

Evander didn't have time to think about his failures. He needed to get information back to Alina, and he needed to set up a watch schedule to try and break Ames out as soon as he could. He quickly etched a note to Alina about the recent development and sent it off with a nearby bird. This wasn't a common method of communication amongst Conductors, but it did prove useful over long distances. Birds were faster than most other animals and typically stayed on course. They didn't require a lot of negotiation or continuous connection. Evander loved using birds but never really had the opportunity, or need for that matter, before now. Now, he and Alina sent birds almost daily with various updates and messages.

With the bird high above the treetops, he refocused on identifying features of the area. He tried to make a mind map of where he was so he could remember how to come back. The large rock to the east. The tree with the low branches that nearly hit his head. The bush with the pink roses. Just little pieces that would help him come back here. He wasn't going to let forgetting the place be the reason Ames never got rescued.

With his mental notes recorded, Evander headed back to camp. He counted paces to help with distance. He would not lose Ames again because he couldn't remember where the entrance was. The camp was four hundred twenty-three paces southwest. It wasn't far nor difficult to get to, but he knew it was well hidden.

As he arrived back in camp, Charlotte and Edward sat on stumps around a small fire, nursing minor injuries from Ames's attack. Arlo cooked something in a pot hung on a spit. It smelled delicious. Arlo was a surprisingly good cook and forager. Evander appreciated that now as they were without most of their regular resources and conducted food never tasted quite the same.

"Where did you go?" Charlotte asked with a sharp edge to her voice.

"Ames took me to the entrance to the Grand Master's hideout," Evander started.

"You mean the one that attacked us was none other then *the* Ambrose?" Edward said with thick adoration.

"Um… yes, I suppose that would be him," Evander replied confusedly. The idea of Ames being anything more than Ames was unusual. "Regardless of who he was, he's fallen back into the Grand Masters hands. There was someone coming and Ames sacrificed himself to save us. We can't let it be in vain. We must collect as much information as we can to save him and bring down the Grand Master."

He could feel his voice shaking, and the faces in front of him showed his attempts to hide his fear failed. Arlo stood and moved to place a reassuring hand on his arm.

"After the meal, I will take the first watch. We will get what we can for information, and hopefully Alina will be here shortly to back us up. We have to do what we can," Arlo added.

"Everyone will take turns on watch duty. I think we can each manage twelve hour shifts, so we don't bring too much attention to us. Essentially, one day shift and one night shift. We will find out as much as we can."

"Yes, sir," Charlotte muttered with a mock salute. Evander pretended not to care though her mockery was insulting. Evander did not put himself in charge; Alina and Gideon did. Just because he wasn't graduated didn't mean he wasn't capable. He understood why they were upset; they felt he was inferior and not trained, but Evander knew he could walk circles around them if ever presented.

Or… at least he hoped…

Arlo served the meal, and everyone ate in silence. After they finished eating, Evander led Arlo to the entrance, just as the sun was setting. They did not say much on their walk. Arlo seemed to appreciate being away from the others, just as much as Evander did. The peace and quiet was refreshing. After dropping Arlo off, Evander headed back to camp.

When he arrived, the other two were working on maintaining the camp's camouflage. They were working on making the shelter look more like a bush and hiding the signs of their fire. They always cooked their meals during the day so the fire light wouldn't attract as much attention. Evander quickly moved to hide the stumps they used as chairs and minimise their footprints outside the shelter. With everything hidden, they crawled into the shelter.

Edward lit a small fireball. It was just enough to light the interior, but not enough to be seen outside the shelter. Evander laid down on his bunk and tried to fall asleep while the other two played some game with cards and dice. Evander didn't know how to play the game, but they also didn't seem interested in teaching him. Instead, Evander focused on relaxing.

He counted his breaths and slowed his breathing rate. He tried tensing and relaxing muscles to encourage whole body relaxation. He even tried counting imaginary sheep, but sleep continued to evade him. Quiet snores could be heard indicating the others had managed to fall asleep. After several hours of restlessness and frustration, Evander crawled out of the shelter into the cool night air. The night was quiet and calm. The stars were out and shining bright. Evander appreciated their beauty for a moment. It helped to calm him. He crawled back into the shelter, feeling ready for sleep.

The next morning came early and Edward departed for his shift. Charlotte didn't speak to Evander until Arlo showed up. Arlo gave a short update about the door, but nothing of much use. He stated it was open for a while, but no one came or went. Arlo left like it was a trap and stayed away from the door, trying not to draw any attention to himself. Evander jotted the notes down and sent off another note to Alina with a bird.

The rest of the day, Evander took to foraging and collecting various edible things. In the camp. Charlotte stayed in the cabin and Arlo slept. Evander returned to the cabin with his arms full of food. The sky was darkening and his stomach was growling. Evander was excited for whatever Arlo was going to cook. He went to head into the shelter, when Charlotte exploded out of the doorway.

"Sorry," Evander muttered while stepping back to allow Charlotte out of the shelter easier.

"Right," she replied with a sideways glance. "Which way again?"

Evander pointed her in the direction and she took off without another word. Evander went back into the shelter and placed the food down. Edward had already returned and was laying in his own bunk, seemingly ready for bed.

"She means well," Edward offered from the dark corner of his own bunk. "She just doesn't get why Gideon put you in charge."

"I understand," Evander replied after a few moments of silence. He wanted to add that he wondered the same, but knew it wouldn't help his case. Instead, he moved to his bunk and laid down.

"Just show her what you got. Show her your skills and prove you should be a graduate. She respects evidence and knowledge more than she respects brute strength or cockiness. She has also not had great experiences with men, so don't take her hatred too personal. She will come around eventually... I think."

"Thanks for the tip."

Evander rolled onto his side. Edward's advice kept running through his head. He just needed to show his skills. He was sure he could do that.

With the crack of dawn, Evander was up and headed to relieve Charlotte of her duties. He peeked out into the clearing and saw no signs of anyone. He peered up into the branches looking for Charlotte, but still didn't see any traces of her. Slowly and cautiously, he stepped into the clearing. Charlotte suddenly appeared as if from thin air.

"You're late," Charlotte stated.

"Hardly," Evander replied. Charlotte rolled her eyes.

"That tree provides the best coverage and vantage point. You can see the entrance while maintaining a hiding spot." She pointed to a tall spruce tree with large branches and thick foliage.

"Noted."

"Well then," she paused, "I guess I should get back then."

"Probably wise. Arlo should be up soon to cook breakfast."

"Thanks." She took off in the direction of the camp without another word. Evander watched her until she vanished into the forest.

In her absence, Evander climbed the recommended tree. She was correct that it was the best spot. It provided significant coverage and a great viewpoint of the doorway. He nestled himself into the branches and took to watching the door.

The sun was high when Evander came down from the tree. Nothing had occurred on his watch, but he had expected Edward to come for his shift already. Thinking that they had forgotten, Evander begrudgingly headed back towards the camp.

Generally, the forest had been full of chirping birds, but now it was silent. Not even a branch whistled in the wind. As he got even closer to their camp, he could hear the crackle of fire, but it was not a campfire. Smoke started to stain the sky and burn Evander's lungs. He used the air force to clear some of the smoke, but quickly realised their entire camp was ablaze.

First, Evander thought it was Charlotte and Edward acting in retaliation. He wouldn't put it past them. However, as he walked into the camp, Evander noticed there were more than just two people. They had only been here a couple of days and tried to stay well hidden, but obviously it wasn't enough.

Evander ran to their aide, but the smoke was thick and it was hard to tell who was who. There appeared to be at least six other people meaning they were outnumbered. Going blind would not help anyone. Evander focused on putting out the blazing fire first. With one quick flick of his wrist, a water geyser burst from the ground. Everything became drenched in a loud sizzle and explosion of steam. After a few moments, the steam and smoke settled. Some people seemed dazed by the sudden change which Evander used to his advantage. He set vines to move and wrap around the two oblivious people. They squirmed against the plants but they were unable to escape. With two of the six combatants handled, Evander turned his attention to aiding Charlotte.

Charlotte was backed up against a large tree. She cast various forces to try and stop them, but nothing seemed to work. She had three Conductors circling her. Evander could see the panic on her face from afar. He jumped and used the air force to fly up and over the Conductors. He landed beside Charlotte who seemed momentarily scared, but instantly switched to relief once she realised it was Evander.

Side by side, Evander and Charlotte pushed back the attackers until they had enough space behind them to escape. Charlotte seemed to be waiting for Evander's cue. He nodded his head and punched the ground hard. A massive rock wall erupted from the ground. In the brief moment of confusion, Evander grabbed Charlotte's hand and started running through the forest.

Branches clawed at his skin and ripped his clothes, but Evander kept running. Charlotte kept up with him as best as she could. It reminded Evander of pulling Rosie through the chaos at Gideon's. Evander stopped dead in his tracks as panic clawed in his throat. He frantically moved around Charlotte and fretted over every inch of her. She swatted his hands away as he tried to survey her for wounds.

"What are you doing?!?" she cried.

"Are you injured? Are you safe?" Evander responded. He looked up to meet her eyes. Based on her reaction, he assumed that he looked like a panicked maniac.

"If we don't keep moving, I am not going to be safe. We need to keep moving." She grabbed his hand and started pulling him to move. Fear kept him planted.

"Are you injured?"

"No. No, I am not." A large rock flew past Evander's head and smashed into the tree behind him. Evander turned his head and saw another Conductor approaching. Whatever fear held him, released and Evander took off at a full sprint through the woods. Trees splintered around his head as he ran. He ducked, dodged, and weaved, trying to throw off his attackers. All the while, he kept a death grip on Charlotte. He ensured he would never let go. He would keep her with him no matter what.

Evander's lungs burned and his legs felt like jelly, but he kept moving. He wasn't sure how much longer he could last, but if he stopped, they would be captured and most likely killed. Or perhaps, Grand Master would come up with some punishment worse than death. Evander tried to keep the thoughts out of his head and focus on getting away from their attackers. He just needed to keep moving.

As the tree started to thin and Evander could run easier, a massive cliff appeared in front of them. He slid to a stop causing Charlotte to nearly tumble over the cliff. He caught her by the waist, swung her over the cliff's edge and back to the safety of the ground. They fell on top of each other. Evander peeked over the edge. There was a raging river below that Evander was not sure they could survive. Getting to the other side would be the best option. However, getting to the other side seemed nearly impossible. He could hear the others getting closer. Time was running out.

"Do you trust me?" He whispered..

"Barely," she replied.

"Well, you're going to have to trust me now." In one smooth motion, Evander rolled Charlotte on top of him and

off the cliff. They tumbled helplessly towards the raging
rapids below.

29

A Silver Owl, A Blue Fox, and A Yellow Snake

Rosie laid in bed for a few days before she was finally allowed to start moving around her room. She required assistance, and Brighid was there every step of the way. Brighid was incredible. She helped Rosie with everything. From eating to changing and washing, Brighid hardly left Rosie's side. There were even times when Rosie would wake up in the middle of the night to find Brighid sleeping in the armchair in the corner. It was nearly impossible for Rosie to find an opportunity to be alone without Brighid attached at her hip. As appreciative as Rosie was, she also longed for moments of solitude and freedom.

As they were walking down the hallway one morning, Alina came to interrupt. Alina pulled Brighid aside and spoke in hushed, excited tones. Whatever they were discussing must have been very important. When it seemed the conversation was mostly done, Alina turned towards Rosie.

"We will be moving tomorrow. We have received word from Evander that they are in the right area," Alina announced while Brighid beamed beside her. Rosie wasn't quite sure what the whispering and secrecy were for, but found it rather rude to be excluded.

"What can I do to assist?" Rosie added and stood up taller to disguise her injury.

"Get a bag packed for yourself and be ready to move tomorrow. We will head out after breakfast." Alina spun on her heel and quickly departed down the hall. Brighid bounced over to Rosie and gently grabbed her arm.

"I am so excited that we found him! We found Ames," Brighid gushed.

"Him? Only him?" Rosie turned to look straight at Brighid. "What about Daisy? Where is Daisy?"

"Alina didn't say anything about Daisy… I don't know Rosie…"

"I don't like that at all."

"Neither do I. Maybe she got out and she is with Evander and Arlo? Maybe that's how they found out where Ames is…"

"As much as I wish that were true, I doubt that as possible."

"I know, but one can hope."

They walked in silence the remainder of the way to Rosie's room. Rosie opened the door and saw a burlap bag thrown on the bed. Assuming time and agility were of the essence, Rosie guessed everyone received similar sacks to reduce extra luggage and weight.

"Uh… do you think you can pack by yourself? I've got to get myself ready and I think we could both use a proper night's rest," Brighid explained.

"Yes! Yes, please," Rosie blurted. Brighid looked a bit hurt at Rosie's sentiment. "Sorry. It's just… I appreciate your help, but I miss being able to just be by myself. I like my freedom."

"I understand. I will leave you to it, then." Brighid quickly exited out of the room. Rosie was finally alone. She quickly moved across the room and listened as Brighid's footsteps faded down the hall.

Rosie dug around the room looking for paper and a quill. She had to get a message out as soon as she could. If she didn't pass the message along…. Rosie didn't even want to think about what would happen. She eventually found parchment and scribbled a quick note: *They know where Ambrose is. They are coming for him.*

She looked over the note and played with it in her hands. *Would it be enough? Would it keep her family safe? Would it keep Daisy and the other Conductors alive?* Rosie paced the room and analysed the note. One wrong step and it would mean death for everyone Rosie ever cared about. She had already missed several days, maybe even weeks, of messages due to her injury and Rosie knew this note had to make up for it all. This simple message would not be enough.

Rosie rolled up the paper, shoved in the pocket of her jacket and walked to the door. She pressed her ear against the door and listened for any sounds of movement. The hallway was silent. Slowly, she opened the door and peeked her head out. She could hear voices coming from down the hall. It even sounded like Alina was giving some kind of speech. She had a few moments to get what she needed.

Moving as fast as she could, Rosie headed for the stairs. Brighid had given her the rough location of Alina's room and hoped it would be enough to get her there. She climbed several sets of stairs and finally came to a ladder. She called up to see if anyone was upstairs. When no one responded, she made her way up the ladder. Each rung burned Rosie's side, and she worried she would split open the wound. However, Rosie didn't have time to think about her injury. She needed information.

Finally at the top of the ladder, Rosie crawled onto the floor. She clutched her side and tried to ignore the growing wet patch. Rosie ruffled through the scattered papers, looking for anything of use. She finally came across a message from Evander. She had grown accustomed to his handwriting and instantly recognized it. He wrote a strange story about a blue fox and a silver owl that had been lost in the forest. They had been hard to find although their tracks were evident in the mud. Nonetheless, Evander had located both and stated the silver owl had left on its own to find a doorway while the blue fox was captured in a snare to allow the owl's escape.

It seemed like a beautiful story, but Rosie could read between the lines. It wasn't a very well encoded story or perhaps Rosie just knew enough to make sense of it all. She unrolled her piece of parchment and jotted down the additional details the story suggested. Evander had located Abe, but Daisy had escaped to find some doorway to another place. Abe, however, according to the story, had been recaptured or trapped but Rosie was entirely sure by who or what. That part was a bit vague. It wasn't a lot, but it was something.

With the extra information added to the note, Rosie rolled it up and tucked it back in her pocket. She winced and clutched her side. She pulled away her hand and saw redness on it. This was not a good sign. Rosie jumped down the ladder and limped down the hall. The room started to spin around her, but Rosie kept moving as best she could. She stumbled, but caught herself against the wall.

"Rosie?" called a voice from afar. Rosie's eyes were fuzzy, and she could not make out who was approaching her. She tried to stay standing, but felt her legs weakening rapidly. "Rosie!"

The ground vibrated beneath her as several people ran towards Rosie. She collapsed on the ground, no longer able to stand. She could feel hands on her body. She knew her eyes were open, but she couldn't see anything in front of her.

"She's bleeding. She must have re-opened the wound. Gideon, can you carry her back to her room?" There was an exasperated sigh. She wanted to say no, that she could do it, but as she tried to sit up, the room spun and she was knocked back down.

She could hear people talking but only caught pieces of what they were saying.

Blood.

Injured.

Help.

Lost.

Damn.

Stupid.

Things melded. She couldn't keep anything straight. There was a buzz in her ears that drowned out nearly everything.

Carry her.

Bandages.

Doctor.

She felt intoxicated and dizzy. Her head hurt. Her heart pounded.

Pressure.

Cloth.

Stop the bleeding.

Hold still.

A drum now thundered in her ears. She wanted to sleep. Blackness painted her vision entirely. Her eyes were open, but she could not see. The room spun and her stomach rolled. She wanted it to stop. She wanted to disappear…

Rosie awoke some time later with new bandaging around her midsection. She wore new clothes she didn't remember putting on, and was back in the familiar room. The curtains were drawn, but Rosie could tell it was night anyway. Everything was dark. Brighid sat in the arm chair with a candle flickering on a stool beside her. She had her knees tucked up, using them to support her head while she slept. She looked peaceful.

Rosie, again, got to her feet. Silently, she dug around in the pile of clothes on the floor, looking for her jacket from earlier. Luckily, the jacket did not get much blood on it. She dug around in the pockets until she found the piece of parchment. She opened it to make sure it was legible. If they couldn't read it, it wouldn't be worth it. She had to make sure that this was all worth it. She couldn't fail.

Rosie looked at Brighid one more time to make sure she was still asleep then she tip-toed out of the room and closed the door behind her. Brighid didn't even stir which was good. Rosie listened to see if anyone else was up, but the whole inn was silent. She walked outside, luckily, without running into anyone. She let out three long whistles of varying tones, and a large peregrine falcon dashed from the trees and gracefully landed on Rosie's shoulder.

"Tell her I am sorry it is late, and I hope this won't impact our arrangement please. This is needed information," Rosie whispered to the bird who happily chirped. Rosie looked at the note one more time. She took three deep breaths and shakily scribbled Azalea's name. She rolled it up one last time and tied a string around it. The bird grabbed the small piece of paper from Rosie, and took off into the night sky.

Silent tears streamed down her face. Her stomach boiled with guilt and anger. *What choice did she have?* She had been incapacitated for so long that only something big, something actually useful, would prevent a catastrophe. Or so Rosie kept telling herself.

This was to protect them. Her family, her friends. All of them.

This would save them all.
The end result would be better.
What else could she do?
She had no other choice.

30

Branded

Abe pressed himself against the wall as tight as he could, but it was no use. As Henry's flames cast light upon Abe, Henry immediately stopped.

"What are you doing here? How did you get here?" Henry asked. He didn't seem angry, just mostly confused. This was likely a saving grace for Abe. He had a split second to decide how to respond.

"Aza… azazie… aza-a-lee-ah said the good drank - drunk, no drink… the good drink!" Abe decided intoxicated was a good option. It got him out of his last situation. Maybe, it would work again. "She said it was in the main thingy in a secret room. I found a secret room…. Shhhh. It's a secret! But it's dark here. So dark…. Can you take me home? I don't know which way is up!"

"Alright. I was just coming to check the- uh," Henry pointed in the direction of the exit then shook his head. "Nothing. Never mind. Let's get you back."

"I have- have a quest- question for you. Have you seen me… my… partner? No, wife. I'm married now. She's my wife."

"I can't say I have. Did you lose her?"

"I was to get a beverage and she was to get food, but I haven't found her yet."

"Why not conjure it?"

"We can do that? Is that how you make fire?"

"Dear Gods…. I don't have time for this. Maybe she is back in your room, but I am sure you do know where she is." Abe swallowed hard and tried to act not effected. *Did Henry know something? Was Daisy's absence already noticed somehow? Was his drunken ruse useless?*

"Maybe! That's a good plan." Abe stumbled and pretended to use the wall to support himself. In his many years of life, he had been intoxicated enough to know how to act. He may have used the ploy more than once to get himself out of a tight situation. "Is everything spinning for you?"

"No." Henry let out a hearty chuckle. It was the most human thing Abe had seen him do. "Let's get you out of here."

"Okay, but let's get the gu-good drink first." Abe took a few more stumbling steps before Henry assisted him by acting like a crutch. Henry maintained a fireball the entire time. Abe pretended to be amazed by glowing orb and continued to ask increasingly absurd questions. From asking about large reptiles living millions of years ago to the purpose of a hat pin, Abe ensured his consciousness was scattered and random.

As they stumbled down the hallway, Abe purposely pushed them down wrong hallways and random dead ends. After what felt like at least an hour of wrong turns, a bird randomly darted in and landed on Henry's shoulder. Abe looked around trying to figure out where the bird came from. Abe knew what the bird meant and saw the note attached to its foot. Even more important was that it was a falcon. Fast birds were only used for urgent messages and could reach their intended targets in only a few hours. Henry unrolled the note and cursed loudly. Instead of reacting, Abe wanted to retain the illusion of drunkenness. Henry cursed loudly, grasped Abe's shoulder tightly, and quickened his pace immensely. Abe's attempts to divert no longer appeared to be working.

Eventually, they stumbled out of the darkness and into the Grand Foyer. Abe hoped it would be empty, but, alas, it was not. Upon her throne, sat Azalea. She wore a long, emerald silk gown adorned with gold embellishments. Her hair tumbled in thick, honeyed curls down her back. A lavish crown of gold with various jewels blended in with her hair. Her lips were the deepest red he had ever seen which made her purple and red eyes blaze from her face.

As Henry and Abe hobbled in, Azalea's eyes immediately fell on them. Abe could feel her anger and judgement weighing heavy on them. Abe just had to keep the act up. He just had to convince Azalea one more time that he was, in fact, drunk. He should have just drank an exorbitant amount then it wouldn't have mattered, but here he was, babbling and tripping.

"You are late," Azalea stated flatly. Her voice echoed with great power through the room. Abe wasn't sure who exactly was late, but it didn't seem like an ideal situation for either him or Henry.

"I found Abe in the tunnel rather scammered. His blathering nonsense and inability to walk straight made getting back on time difficult," Henry explained. Abe mustered a hiccup followed by an awkward giggle. Henry walked forward and handed her the note out of his pocket.

"Sorry," Abe managed.

"How are you still intoxicated? I saw you over twelve hours ago," Azalea demanded. She started to unroll the paper. Her demeanour immediately changed; she became furious. Abe knew he could not respond in any other way than drunk. He needed to keep up the farce even in the face of pure fury.

"I… I got -uh married. I was celebrating. So much celebrating. The wife just kept asking for alcohol, so I kept giving it. But we ran out! She was so upset. I wanted - no - needed your stash. Your delicious stash. I… I can't remember if I found it, but then there was darkness. So much darkness."

"I think you found it." Azalea laughed. Her laugh, however, was not from a person who was amused; it was far more evil, more sinister than that. "Or perhaps you found something even more interesting."

She rose from her throne and swiftly crossed the room stopping directly in front of Abe. She was a small woman, and while her stature was not overly intimidating, her confidence and power could make even the strongest man lose his nerve. Abe tried to not appear terrified or dissuaded, for he knew a swizzler would never falter. She circled him briefly, before she flicked her wrist and chains entwined Abe.

"What is this for?" he bellowed and struggled against the tightening metal. His arm was stretched before him. Azalea sliced the sleeve away from his arm, bearing the black mark.

"It's still there," Azalea stated, puzzled. "I don't understand."

"What's wrong?" Henry enquired from somewhere behind Abe. Azalea pressed the mark and tried to rub it off as if expecting the mark was painted on.

"Something… something is wrong with the mark. How else would she have gotten away?"

"It's still there, you doddypoll. Where would it go?" Abe muttered.

"Spare me. I know you aren't drunk." Azalea dug her finger nail into the mark and Abe flinched. She was certainly not being gentle. "Don't you feel a change in the connection? There has to have been a change."

"No, but I do feel this metal digging into my ribs and it hurts."

"What did you do?" Azalea's nose touched Abe's. Her eyes burned with anger. Of course, he knew exactly what had changed, but he could never tell her. Instead of his usual retorts, Abe broke into a fit of mock drunken giggles. Even if Azalea thought he wasn't drunk, Abe needed to stick with the ploy. He needed to convince Azalea he knew nothing. Azalea immediately stepped back and glared at him. She crossed her arms in a huff.

"You're funny when you're angry," Abe managed between his chuckles. Azalea lifted her hand to strike Abe.

"Miss?" Henry interjected.

"What!?" Azalea snapped.

"Could it perhaps be the marriage?" Henry offered in a voice smaller than one would expect out of such an imposing man. Azalea whipped her head towards him; her nostrils flared. Abe knew Henry had but a mere moment to finish his suggestion. Quietly, he continued: "He's now bonded to someone else through celestial magic. His finger is branded with another bonding mark. Perhaps, they don't combine well. Perhaps they can't properly co-exist."

Azalea pursed her lips in contemplation and began pacing in front of Abe while the chains tightened around him, choking his lungs. Suddenly, everything released and Abe collapsed to the ground. His lungs struggled to regain air. Eventually, he could breathe, but the air felt like fire as his chest, burning with each heaving gasp.

"Perhaps… you are right," Azalea said as she paced circles around Abe. "In the meantime, lock him up with the others. Find his wife and bring her to me immediately. She couldn't have gotten far."

"What do you mean? Who are you looking for?" Abe shouted. *Did Azalea know? How did she know?*

"You're not so clever to think I wouldn't know she somehow escaped. You pathetic weasel," Azalea tilted her head back and let out a maniacal laugh.

Henry clutched Abe's arm. The lack of oxygen made Abe feel weak. He was unable to fight against Henry as he was dragged down the hallway. He tried to take deep breaths, but it felt like a thousand tonnes sat on his chest. The halls twisted and turned. Abe's lungs continued to fail him. He even tried using the air force to fill his lungs, but not even that worked.

As they neared the bottom of the sloping corridors, Abe could hear the mutterings of others. They passed several cells filled with Conductors and even a few humans, none of which Abe recognized. Their grimy and sullen faces gawked at him through the bars. Whispering questions hung in the air, but Abe was unable to answer.

Henry came to a stop, unlocked a door, and threw Abe into the empty cell.

His lungs suddenly released and air flooded into his body. He could breathe again, but something else felt off. It was like something was missing. With the clang of the shutting cell door, Abe sat up and looked at Henry.

"I wouldn't try anything. These cells weren't built by us," Henry explained while gesturing towards the walls.

"Who built it?" Abe croaked.

"A celestial." Henry turned on his heel and waltzed down the hall, whistling some happy tune that felt horribly inappropriate in the dim dungeon.

Abe stood to analyse the bars of the cage. Along the metal were carved symbols that Abe knew relatively well. Various deities' markings etched into the metal which drained Conductors of their powers and prevented them from escaping. It would take a strong celestial to bind so many Conductors. Abe feared who Azalea had managed to recruit. A celestial willing to do this was not one Abe ever wanted to cross.

Gingerly, Abe reached out and touched the bars, which caused his skin to sizzle and burn. In response, Abe recoiled from the bars and stumbled against the wall. Again his skin was left with a horrible burning pain. He moved to stand in the middle of the room. Every wall and bar was etched with celestial magic. There was truly no way to escape. Abe walked slowly to the bed that was barely out from the one wall and curled up on it. He felt completely useless. Even when he didn't have control over his own mind, he felt more useful than he did now. His only chance at freeing Daisy had failed; Azalea knew. She knew Daisy had escaped.

Fear sat heavy in Abe's chest as he pondered his situation: *if Azalea knew Daisy had left, what else did she know?* He couldn't help Daisy now, but he only wished they had planned better. Maybe, if he had gone with her, none of this would have happened. At least, he shouldn't have gone back into Azalea's stronghold. He should have stayed with Evander and Arlo and planned an attack. Instead, Abe had failed in every way possible. Azalea knew Daisy was gone, and it wouldn't be long before she found the others. Abe knew that any chance he had had of overthrowing Azalea had disappeared.

Abe screamed in frustration, and smashed his hand against the wall; his flesh sizzled. He paced his cell, looking for any point of weakness but finding nothing useful. He listened to the sobs of his other cell mates. Some sounded young and scared while others sounded like they were experiencing complete and utter despair. Abe was desperate to do anything to help them, but everything he tried inflicted pain. He even tried teleporting himself, but that resulted in him bouncing helplessly around the room and with each contact between his skin and a wall or bar inflicted more excruciating pain. Any option he saw seemed impossible. Azalea had certainly thought of everything to keep him contained. Even when meals came, the trays slid through a tiny gap in the bars. The doors were never opened. There were several meals Abe skipped trying to figure out how to get out.

Unable to think of a solution, Abe eventually sat himself in the middle of the room and closed his eyes. He tried to block out the sounds around him and focus on his breathing. He needed to clear his head and reassess the situation.

"It's a tricky situation, these cells," said a man's voice from across the aisle. He had red hair and olive skin. As Abe stared at him, he started to seem more and more familiar. "I have seen many of you try to escape, but the bars seem to cause you so much pain. Not me though."

In demonstration, the man grabbed the bars and used them to pull himself into a standing position. He smiled softly at Abe; Abe, however, did not return this small gesture of kindness. He had little interest in talking to the man at all.

"I've seen you down here before when the young lady was in the cell. Now you are in that same cell. You had freedom which you've now lost. What did you do to get yourself locked up in here?" the man questioned. Abe sighed and stood up. He moved as close to the bars as he could.

"I helped the young lady, my wife, who also happens to be Azalea's sister, escape from this hell hole," Abe replied with clenched teeth. The man let out a slow, low whistle.

"Do you have any idea what is going on out there? In the real world? My daughter somehow got messed up in this whole situation."

"Who is your daughter? Perhaps I have news of her."

"She's just a human. She doesn't have eyes like you or powers. She's just a human."

"I understand, but that doesn't mean I haven't heard about her. I was a minion of Azalea's for some time until I broke through the bond. I may have some information to give you."

"She made some kind of deal with that woman in order to keep us, her family, alive. I can't imagine what my dear Rosette has been through..."

"Rosette?"

"Yes, Rosette Camden. That's my daughter. Do you know of her?" Suddenly, everything made sense. The man looked familiar because he looked like Rosie. Even his accent was similar to hers. He was here because of her, but that meant...

Rosie was a spy.

For the past year, Rosie would have had to give just enough information about what Daisy was doing to keep her family alive, but that also meant Daisy was in constant danger. Azalea could have taken them down at any time, but didn't. This discovery created so many more questions that Abe desperately wanted to ask the man, but everything left his mind when his cell door was opened and a beaten, unconscious body was unceremoniously tossed in.

Blood splattered on the floor when the body was dropped. Their clothes were tattered and messy. An arm extended at an unnatural angle from the body. The man that tossed the body into the cell laughed at Abe and muttered something about enjoying his *present*. Abe cautiously approached the body, unsure of who it might be. As he neared the body and saw the face, Abe gasped.

Arlo.

He remained still for a moment as terror held his heart. Abe was devastated as he cared for Arlo like a son. After a moment, Abe gingerly flipped Arlo onto his back and started assessing the injuries. It did not look good. A large wound on his abdomen trickled blood. A significant burn on his leg would certainly impede its use. Another cut on his upper arm had scabbed over. Abe ripped off the tatters of Arlo's shirt and pressed the cleanest sections to the wound on his chest. Abe tried to heal Arlo in any way he could, but he felt no connection to the forces. In this dungeon, he had no power to do anything.

He couldn't save Arlo.

Arlo clutched Abe's hand. With short breaths, Arlo struggled to focus on Abe's face. Abe could see the panic in his eyes. Abe was unsure if Arlo knew whose hand he was weakly grasping.

"You're safe," Abe lied in an attempt to soothe him. It wasn't entirely false. Arlo was at least out of battle. "You're with me, Ames. I am here. Relax."

"Ambrose?" Arlo muttered.

"Yes, it's me."

"Where am I?"

"Out of the battle."

"Where is Evander? Last I saw he ran away with Charlotte. I tried to go after them, but they were too fast and then I lost them." Arlo clutched Abe's collar and yarded Abe closer to him. "I failed."

"Arlo. I am sure Evander is fine. You need to relax."

"Edward died. I saw it happen. They just… murdered him. Fireball straight to the heart. He erupted in flames. I heard his screams." Abe could see the panic building on Arlo's face. His eyes darted from side to side; his pupils were uneven and dilated. His skin was quickly losing colour. Abe did not know how long Arlo could hold on. There was no way to prevent that in this cell. Abe was helpless. Useless. Pathetic.

Human.

"Shhhh, Arlo. Get some rest. We can talk more later," Abe comforted. Arlo nodded and closed his eyes. Within minutes, he was either asleep or unconscious; Abe wasn't sure which, but either way, Arlo was alive and with Abe. Abe only hoped that Evander was also alive.

31

An Entrance

Daisy walked through the wall. It was weird being back. When she came here with Abe in the past, the main room was always different. New furniture or pillows or even the occasional tree ensured the room constantly changed. Now, however, the room appeared nearly the same as when they all left well over a year ago.

The two hallways branched off the main room. The roof had collapsed from the battle with its rubble blocking the hall that led to Abe's room. Burnt bricks, dead plants, and boulders were scattered around the room. The signs of the water force had long since evaporated, but Daisy still remembered melting the ice wall that blocked the other hallway. The only thing that was out of place was the perfect chair sitting in the middle of the room.

The chair was brown leather with a high back and uncomfortable looking arms. Daisy had seen Abe sit in that chair many times. She had even come across him asleep in it a few times. The chair felt oddly comforting which drew Daisy towards it. As she neared it, she noticed a letter placed on its seat. A red seal pressed with a Daisy kept the letter tightly folded together. Quickly, she broke the seal and opened the letter. It was Abe's familiar scrawl. It brought Daisy back to the days of his secret notes and gifts. The message this time was not such happy tidings as Daisy was used to with his writing.

My dearest Daisy,

If you are reading this without me, I cannot imagine what has happened that I am not with you. I fear what this means for me. For us. I assume that it is not good, but if you are here, I can guess as to why.

The stones are powerful and can bestow many powers, but they also can cause great sorrow. I hope I am wrong in assuming you have come here to use the stones, but I doubt that is true. As such, let me tell you how to use them. The stones possess pure, raw power that does not wish to be taken. To begin, you must speak the elder tongue to awaken the stones. I hope you have learned how to read it in some capacity for I cannot tell it to you.

Diisa pandites ostiumi. Permittes mes transirer ins regnumi suuma.

In order to open the stones for use, you must first weaken yourself. Once you are weakened, the stones will test your intentions and your power. I don't know what comes next. I have only ever gotten to this part. I have not tested every theory of this, but I have figured out at least the basics, and I hope it is enough to aid you. I only wish I could be there to assist you through this. I hoped it would never come to this, but if you are here, there must be a reason.

I don't know what the future holds for me. I don't know why you are here without me. Right now, Alina tends to my wounds while you sleep and I write this letter. She is unhappy that I am even bothering to write this, but I feel like this all needs to be said. Most importantly, if we haven't had the time, there is something I need you to know.

I've been hiding this for so long and trying to allow you to decide for yourself. I have tried to give you space to grow and learn. I am ancient and you are so young. I didn't want to force anything on you. I wanted you to have every choice on your own accord. However, if I am not with you, you still have the opportunity for choice.

I have fallen in love with you. At first, you intrigued me, then you fascinated me. Now, I can't help but want to be with you always. I asked you to pick being a Conductor, but I really wanted you to pick being with me. I finally feel whole and at peace with you by my side. There is clarity and silence with you. You calm my chaos and I don't understand it. I hope that I have been able to tell you this in person before now and that this letter isn't my declaration of love, but if it is, know that these feelings will only grow. My love will not diminish. You are my deepest desire and I hope that we will be reunited and these words can be spoken from my lips rather than my letter. There will never be another, Dais. You are the one I was always destined to find. I will love you until the sun burns out and we are nothing more than dust in the heavens. Even then, I will find you. I will always find you and I will always love you.

Yours truest,

Abe

Daisy clutched the paper to her chest. A wave of relief flooded over her. Ever since she came across Abe under Azalea's control, she doubted his intentions, his emotions, his attachment. This letter, however, was before everything. They hadn't left. He hadn't proposed. She hadn't rewound time and made a sixth force. This was when Daisy was a student and Abe was her teacher. This was when everything was simpler. This was the proof she needed that Abe actually loved her and that it wasn't Azalea controlling him the entire time.

A silent tear trickled down her cheek and splashed on the paper. She felt sadness, but also great happiness. She missed Abe even more than she did before, but she also missed her life before she became a Conductor. Things were simpler than, although not better. Life wasn't easier, but she knew what was expected of her.

She lingered for a moment longer. While she wanted to explore the ruins more, she had a strange feeling that she should not disrupt the rubble anymore than necessary. She looked around once more, reminiscing, before leaving through the wall back to the train station.

She left the train station and headed down the hill towards town. The sun was starting to set, casting shades of scarlet and fuchsia across the clouds. As she entered the forest and came to a crossroad, Vincent and Delia were standing, seeming confused.

"Ya don't know? She didn't say nothin' aboot a turn? Me thought ya knew where ya goin'," Vincent muttered. Daisy knew he was blind, but assumed he could hear her approaching. However, he jumped when Daisy spoke.

"I thought you said Delia knew where she was going," Daisy joked. He nearly fell out of the carriage. "Sorry! I did not mean to startle you."

"Is tat ya, Daisy?"

"Yes, Vincent. I managed to catch up with you it appears. I wasn't expecting to come across you again."

"We weren't, but the road changed. Wen did this road git 'ere? Delia didn't know which way t' turn. Perhips, I shouldn't leave t' steerin' up to this ol' girl. " Delia neighed in protest. Vincent waved dismissively. Daisy hadn't spent much time around horses to know if this was a regular interaction between owner's and horses. Delia seemed almost too smart to be just a regular horse.

"You just have to keep going straight sir, but here, let me take you both."

Daisy hoisted herself up beside Vincent and gently grabbed the reins. She hadn't done much driving, but she knew the general premise. Besides, Delia just needed a bit of guiding. Their carriage bumped along the road. They remained mostly in silence. Daisy's mind was in far away places, thinking about Abe and the muddy future before her. She honestly didn't want to talk much, and he seemed to know it.

As the forest thinned, the town appeared. Daisy skirted the edge of town. Taking the carriage through the main square seemed tedious. The edge took longer, but it seemed easier. Eventually, they arrived at the gate to the manor. It was weird to be back. Daisy never imagined she would be back. She paused before clambering out to open the gate.

"Straight ahead to the front door, Delia," Daisy instructed. "Someone should see you and come to help."

Delia whinnied and started trotting down the path. Daisy watched them go until they stopped at the front door. She turned and walked along the fence towards the other side of town and the other section of forest.

The forest was familiar and welcomed. The heavy branches blocked out the last rays of the dimming sun. Birds chirped, and the wind whispered. Daisy walked down the path as though it was her home. Everything felt comfortable and known. While this wasn't home, a pang of longing filled her soul. The forest abruptly opened up, and there stood the five stones. No.

Six stones.

Six massive stones filled the entire clearing. Somehow, a new monolith had sprung from the ground since Daisy was last here. Furthermore, they had somehow spread out to form a perfect circle. Everything seemed more in balance and peaceful. Yet, fear clutched her heart.

Daisy was unsure of what was to come next. The idea of crossing into the celestial realm was horrifying. What was on the other side seemed even more dooming. Celestials and humans were not supposed to mix, and yet Daisy was going to walk into their realm to demand answers and support. The thought was enough to even shake the strongest of constitutions.

Daisy moved to stand in the middle of the circle, and the whole world fell silent. She pulled out the celestial blade out of her waist band and began to follow Abe's instructions. She sliced open her hand to weaken her body and rubbed her sacrifice across the stones. It was painful, but Daisy managed to not scream or whimper. Instead, she focused on muttering the prescribed elder tongue as best as she could. The words were hard to form and felt harsh in her throat. It was unnatural to say them.

As Daisy muttered the final word, golden flames sprouted from the ground between the stones creating a perfect circle. Daisy clutched her hand to her chest. Her heart felt like it was rupturing. Her breath was short and laboured with each inhale feeling like pure fire in her lungs. The golden flames moved slowly closer. Daisy could not move.

Suddenly, the flames made a quick jump and completely encircled Daisy. Even if she wanted to move, it would mean running through at least twenty feet of blistering hot flames. The flames started moving up her clothes and engulfing her. She expected pain and heat, but the flames were cold and soothing. They had moved all the way up to her neck and were kissing her face when suddenly the flames turned from cool to hot.

Daisy's skin felt like it was melting. Immense pain burned into her soul. She screamed out, but the sound was silenced. All she could see was gold when the flames coated her face. The fire moved into her open mouth and Daisy could feel the heat burning her from the inside as well. Right as Daisy thought she would die from heat and pain, she began falling. Light gave way to darkness and Daisy was engulfed into utter blackness.

32

Aftermath

Evander and Charlotte plunged into the cold rapids. Water instantly filled his lungs as he was tossed about in the water. He clutched onto Charlotte's arm as best he could, but eventually lost his grip. Evander tried to right himself and find the surface, but the water moved so quickly that Evander could barely move. Finding the surface seemed impossible. He was almost out of air and wasn't sure how much longer he could last. Darkness painted the corners of his vision. Time was running out.

Evander took a breath and water rushed in. His head smashed against a rock on the river bottom. Pain ricocheted through his skull. He tried to breathe again, but no air came. Just as Evander began to lose consciousness, two hands wrapped around his chest and pulled him to the surface. He tried to remain awake. He needed to know who saved him to know if he was safe, but all his attempts to stay awake failed. He plummeted into darkness.

"Evander," said a muffled voice. Something shook his shoulders which was unpleasant. "Come on, Evander. You need to wake up now."

Evander groaned and squished his eyes tighter together. He did not want to wake up yet. Everything hurt and he was sure it would be agonising once he was awake and more present in his mind.

"Seriously, Evander. We don't have time for you to be resting if we are going to save them," another voice stated. It sounded like a woman and a lot angrier than the first voice, but Evander was not conscious enough to identify who it belonged to.

"No…" he managed to groan.

"Yes. Now get up." It was a familiar voice.

Alina.

Evander opened his eyes, even though sunlight burned. He was lying on his back under a large tree. Charlotte hovered over him. Her brows were furrowed and lips drawn. Her hair stuck to her face, and her clothes were translucent. She had a large gash above her eyebrow that was still trickling blood.

"Alina?" Evander questioned.

"Yes. Good to see you awake." Alina replied. Evander pushed himself up onto his elbows. Charlotte helped him up. Alina stood at a table nearby. She seemed to be looking over some papers and barely pulled away at Evander's call.

"Is this a dream? How are you here?"

"It's not a dream. We got your message a few days back and started making our way here. Some of our scouts saw you fall over the cliff and pulled you from the water. Charlotte was definitely in better shape than you. She told us what happened, but I am glad to see you awake."

"Where is Arlo? Do you know what happened to him? I was coming back to the camp and I only saw

Charlotte and Edward. Where is Arlo?" Alina and Charlotte grew quiet. Evander searched their faces for any positive sign, but found nothing. "You... You don't know where he is."

"No, we haven't seen him yet," Alina replied sadly. "We have people looking for him, but nothing yet. Absolutely nothing."

Alina slammed the table with a closed fist. She was clearly upset. Evander managed to stand up and on shaky legs he limped over to Alina. A single tear trickled down her cheek. She wiped it away and averted her eyes.

"I'm fine," she stated. Evander was about to talk, when Gideon rounded the tree and approached the group. "Any update?"

Gideon sighed. "Yes, but not the kind you would like. We found signs of a struggle where Charlotte said he would be. We are guessing he has been taken."

"What's our next step?" Evander questioned.

"We are still all getting to the area," Gideon stated. "Once we do, we will amass an attack."

"We never got enough information to give you good insight," Charlotte protested.

"We have enough," Gideon argued. "We will make do with what we have."

"But they know we are here. They attacked us and we didn't kill them. They will report back to Azalea that we are here."

"Correction, they know you and Evander are here. They do not know the rest of us have arrived. We are coming in quietly and slowly, so we don't draw extra attention. I can assure you, they don't know we are here."

"So what do we do now?" Evander asked.

Gideon turned and pulled himself to his full height. "We train and we wait until everyone is here. Then… we attack."

326

33

Souls

Daisy blinked her eyes several times. She wasn't sure if they were open or closed because everything was black. She held her hand out in front of her face, but she couldn't even see her fingers. It was like being in the corridor with Abe again. The darkness was devouring and endless.

The air started moving rapidly. Daisy could feel her hair whipping around her face. Random flashes of light and images raced past Daisy. She couldn't make anything out, but the light was blinding. The lights flashed more frequently and grew brighter and brighter until Daisy had to cover her eyes with her arms. She pressed her forearms tightly against her eyes until she couldn't feel the air tearing at her face. She lowered her arms and gasped at the sight before her.

Daisy had been here many times before in her dreams, but this time it felt more real. It wasn't a dream, and everything was tangible. The image was etched in her mind: the black shale cliffs overlooking the grey sea, and the single dead tree off in the distance. She could see Abe's outline, but knew what going to him meant. He would die, and she would be helpless in saving him. She didn't want to endure that again. She knew the alternative meant she had to die. She turned away from Abe and ran towards the cliff's edge. She jumped off of it without a second thought. She didn't close her eyes, as she did not fear death. Instead, she wanted to look at it head on and face her fate.

As she approached the churning sea a deep voice cut through the air, "Come here my child. Join me in my arms."

Daisy looked towards the horizon, where the voice seemed to echo from. There was a ship outlined against the blackened sky. Daisy felt compelled to get to the boat, but she was falling to her death. She was helpless to move towards the ship. In a blink of an eye, Daisy jumped across the sky and was closer to the boat. She wasn't falling anymore. She blinked again and now hovered just above its sails.

It was not an inviting boat. The hull and deck were charred black from flames. There was a large hole in the boat's front hull, making floating seem impossible, yet it bobbed in the waves. A grate in the middle of the deck looked like it was made of interlinked bones rather than wood or iron. The sails on the ship were filled with holes, any other boat would have been stranded and unable to move, but the wind seemed to have no issue pushing the boat through the swell. A door to the captain's chambers hung off one hinge and swung rhythmically with the rolling motion of the boat. Shattered windows and damaged railings gave the boat a war torn appearance, as if cannonballs had bombarded it many times. The helm boasted a large white wheel.

A chill ran through her entire body as her foot touched the surface. Something came over her, freezing her in place. She pulled at her feet, but they appeared stuck. Suddenly, people started moving around her. Their skin appeared to be a ghostly white outlined with an eerie, green mist. They hurriedly moved about the boat; frantic, yet intentional as if cannons were firing and orders were being shouted, but everything was silent. She could feel their fear and sense their impending deaths. They fought their hardest, but Daisy knew they would all perish.

"Do you sense their death?" a gravelly voice echoed around her. It sounded neither male nor female. Daisy looked around for the source, but saw nothing more than the translucent bodies trying to avoid their imminent demise.

"Yes," Daisy whispered mostly to herself.

"They will all die, but this boat remains as a marker of their endeavours to survive." Suddenly, Daisy could see a dark figure in a hood at the steering wheel of the ship. This figure did not belong with the rest of the unfortunate souls. "If there is one thing I have learned about humans, it is their unwavering perseverance and will to survive even in the most dire of circumstances. It is… noteworthy…"

Daisy watched helplessly as each soul perished one by one. She watched their faces morph with pain and pure agony. She longed to help them, but knew there would be no use. They were all going to die. They all had to die. Daisy felt tormented and tortured by having to endure this event. She wanted to run as fast as possible away from here, but she could not move.

"What do you want from me?" Daisy cried desperately.

"Come here, my child." The hold on Daisy's legs released, and the dying souls vanished. All that remained was the hooded figure at the helm. Slowly and cautiously, Daisy made her way towards the other being. Her legs shook and her lips trembled, but she kept moving forward, not willing to show her fear.

"You did not answer my question."

"I do not require anything of you, but I believe you require something of me."

"I do not know who you are."

"I am not a who necessarily, but more a what."

"You speak in riddles." Daisy began climbing the stairs, and as she neared the top she noticed the wheel was made of bones. Daisy stopped and watched the figure. The hood and cloak covered nearly everything. Daisy couldn't even see hands on the wheel. It almost reminded Daisy of when Azalea stormed the train station. Immediately, Daisy's guard went up. *This couldn't be her sister, could it?* No… there was something… inhuman about them. Daisy could sense a sort of otherness to them that was not natural.

"If you look inwards, you will find your answers. You need only trust yourself."

"What are you?"

"Think Daisy. Where are you?"

"The Realm of Celestials."

"Then what am I?" the voice hissed. It seemed irritated that Daisy couldn't piece things together.

"A celestial."

"You learn." Daisy moved one step closer. The figure released the steering wheel, and they were immediately transported to somewhere new. They stood atop a silver disk with two holes in the middle. Little lines of various shimmering colours extended every direction from the disk. Daisy reached out to touch one, but as she neared one, a wave of guilt overcame her.

"Where are we?" Daisy enquired.

"In your words, my home."

"This isn't much of a home."

"We don't live as you do. We all live to serve a purpose."

"And what is your purpose?" The figure turned and reached out to touch one of the lines. The light dimmed and the line turned black. The figure lifted the line and dropped into one of the holes.

"Each of these lines is a soul. I collect the souls and deposit them into their rightful afterlife. Either good or bad. Their faith decides the rest."

"You… you are… you're the … Grim Reaper then." A coldness captured Daisy's throat.

"I go by many names. Hades, Diablo, Kali, Hel. A great many options depending on who you are and what you believe in. I take the shape of whatever you expect me to look like, which may be why you see the Grim Reaper before you. However, in the most simple form, I am the Deity of Death."

Daisy stared Death in the face and questioned its motives. It seemed factual and straight forward. It was neither friendly nor malicious in its demeanour, and yet Daisy feared it like nothing else.

"Why am I here?" Daisy asked while trying to keep her voice still.

"You called on me. Why should I know your motives?"

"How did I call on you?"

"You did the ritual and passed my test of death to allow you to fully cross into my realm and now you are here. So, why do you disturb me?"

"I have come for information."

"What kind of information do you require?"

"What am I?" Daisy blurted it out without thinking. This thought had not plagued her mind until now.

"You are many things. You are a human. You are a Conductor. However, you are also a Celestial."

"How can I be a Celestial?" Death was quiet for a moment and seemed to assess Daisy. What exactly Death could be looking for, Daisy was not sure.

"Deities can interact with the humans on your mortal plane in two ways. The first is possession, which often kills the host, and we are trapped to look as someone else. The second, which is preferable, is taking a temporary human form. Some deities have become trapped in their human form, which is why many avoid it. Both have drawbacks, but both allow us to interact with your mortal world. We bore and tire as our existence is taxing, and we often need reprieve. Entering your world and interacting with those we govern gives us the opportunity to be temporarily free."

"What does this have to do with me being a Celestial?" Death held up an empty sleeve, but Daisy understood the suggestion. She needed to be patient, and Death would explain everything.

"I once journeyed to your land as my temporary form and came across a young woman. She was the image of beauty, but had a short temper and fiery attitude. I watched her many times. She was lonely and afraid. I grew fond of her and longed to meet her. So I did. She was brilliant and witty. I greatly enjoyed my time with her, but she was bound in contract to another. She was being raised to be wedded to a boring thing of a man. I wouldn't stand for it. Just a few days before her wedding, I stole her away in the middle of the night. We ran to a church and were wed. We consummated our marriage and enjoyed one night of pure bliss. However, my temporary form was weakening and eventually died. The woman cried, but could not tell anyone about me. She knew that if she did, she would be cast aside in society and left to die. Instead, she kept me a secret and wed the other man she was legally obligated to wed. No one but the priest who married us ever knew I even existed. She lived out her life relatively peacefully, without me in it any further. I tell you this story, because this is where you came from. The woman in the story is your mother, and, by the story, I would be your father."

The room fell quiet. Daisy had to process the information. Somehow, her mother had fallen in love with Death and created her. Somehow, she was the daughter of Death. It seemed impossible and unusual. Yet, she stood in front of Death now. Death seemed almost human. He described the story with such tenderness that Daisy knew it had to be true. It just felt so terribly wrong. Of all the Gods that she could be connected to, Daisy never imagined it would be Death.

"You are my parent..." Daisy whispered mostly to herself. It was a lot to take in and did not make much sense. She was trying to pull the pieces together, but this was beyond anything Daisy had expected.

"In rare cases, Celestials procreate with humans and create a Celestial hybrid. Some call these demigods. You would be one of these rare cases," Death offered. Daisy paused and contemplated the information. It made some sense into what Daisy was, but there was one glaring issue Daisy needed to figure out.

"What about my sister? Is she also not a Celestial?"

"You're sister is even more unusual. It seems, when you transfer Conductor energy into a Celestial foetus, the embryo can't sustain it and must split into another being: one pure of Celestial force and the other human, but your sister was already a Conductor. As such, you came out a god and she came out a Conductor. You are a most fascinating quandary." Death almost seemed excited to tell Daisy this information. There was an eagerness and pure intrigue. It was like Death had long wished to discuss this with anyone, and Daisy was the first person to ask.

"So I am human and Celestial, but my sister was just human. Correct?"

"Yes, when you split, your sister retained the human qualities, and you became pure Celestial. When you became a Conductor as well, you became an even stranger combination. We've only seen this one other time in your history to date, where a Celestial, human, and Conductor have mixed into one being."

"In my history?"

"I exist throughout time. I collect souls from the Black Death, the World Wars, and the Intersection simultaneously. I am not linear, but ever existing. As such, I know the history of this world at all times. This occurs in your timeline in the future, but has only occurred once in your past."

"How do you know that?"

"When Celestials mix with Conductors, your magic grows. You can suddenly do more. We call it an *emergence*. You call it a new force."

"You mean the mind force? That was the last time it had occurred."

"And now you. You made a time force."

"Why did I make a time force? Shouldn't it be more death-related?" Death inhaled sharply; it almost seemed Daisy had insulted Death, but that seemed almost too human. Death slowly reached out and grabbed a handful of strands. They all twinkled before turning black. He deposited them into one of the holes. He cleared his throat and turned back to Daisy.

"An emergence is never certain, but it more often has to do with balancing the forces. Your forces hold the world in balance, and an emergence sets them off. It has to eventually go back. I don't think your parentage had much to do with your force. I believe having a counterpart to the mind force was more important. That is why you created the time force, the mind's greatest enemy. It wears away memories and deteriorates thoughts. While perhaps not the most direct connection, it is logical. You were needed to restore the balance in the world, my child."

"Please don't call me that. It is... uncomfortable." Death stood in silence, staring at Daisy. Daisy swallowed and tried to keep her gaze level with Death. Everything about this situation made Daisy want to run away.

"I understand, but I know that is not the only reason you are here. A history lesson is not the primary reason for your journey to my home."

"You are right."

"What is that you require?"

"We are at war, and we are losing."

"I know. I have collected many souls from her wraith. She is recruiting."

"Recruiting?"

"Your Grand Master has recruited Celestials, and brought them down to her battle though their temporary forms are faltering. They will have to return to their realm soon, but I do not believe they will stay away for long. Hence, your war is tilted, and I assume you've come to realign it."

"I must know how to defeat her." Daisy stamped her foot with frustration. She needed to know, and it was weighing heavily on her soul. Death fell quiet. Daisy could sense Death's eyes assessing her, determining if she could handle the information. To show she could, Daisy rolled her shoulders back, stood tall, and lifted her chin. She tried to limit evident body shaking, but she knew her fear was palpable.

"I know of two options, neither of which are easy or wise, and I cannot make the decision for you," Death whispered, "You, and only you, can make the ultimate decision."

"What options do I have?" Daisy demanded.

"The first option is a transference. Just as Azalea has done to foetuses in the past, the same process can be completed with two Conductors that match power types. Another fire-mind Conductor could have Azalea's essence imbued into them, but Azalea will die. You would be transferring a great deal of power, and, if the host is not strong enough, they could also die."

"So, the death of two souls to potentially save the world. Does the alternative involve less death?"

"Yes and no. The second option is only an option because of your unique abilities. You can go back in time and stop the emergence of the fifth force."

"How would that fix this?"

"The forces would not become unbalanced, and you would realign Abe and Azalea to work together likely. I am not entirely sure of the outcome, but it would prevent Azalea's power from growing as it has."

"And how would I do that? How would I stop the emergence of the mind force?"

"There are several ways to do that. You need to only change the correct moment in time to stop the emergence. There are three points in time that I believe could change the future. Firstly, you could stop Azalea from learning of transference and overwriting a Celestial offspring. This would prevent the first true emergence of the mind force. Alternatively, you could stop Abe from falling in love with Isabetta and creating the Celestial offspring that Azalea later overwrites. Lastly, you could remove Isabetta from Abe's life all together."

"You're suggesting murdering Isabetta?"

"You are a child of Death, and she has already died. The only thing you would change is *when* she dies. However, you could just prevent her and Abe from meeting in the first place which would prevent you from needing to end her life."

"Not murdering anyone seems like the better option. Does it not?

"It does, but there is one more thing. By changing the course of history, I do not know what will happen to you. There have been very few cases of time travel, and even less that have changed history so dramatically. I do not know what will happen to you. You could cease to exist entirely. You could be a source of endless torment for those who knew of you. Or, nothing could change. Everything that you endeavoured to do could prove futile. As you can see, changing the future is a tricky mission that I do not know enough about to truly help you."

"Changing the past has no guaranteed outcome while completing a transference has a clearer outcome."

"Yes, that is correct."

"What if I make no choice? What if I do neither option? Is there no other way to beat her?" Death reached out and put a supportive hand on Daisy's shoulder. She expected it to be cold and unwelcoming, but instead found a soft, comforting grasp that felt like home.

"Even killing her where she stands will only put her back into her elemental essence which is even more dangerous. Her essence must be contained or altered. There are only those two options, and you must choose."

Daisy moved away from Death and watched the shimmering strings of life around her. She wanted to hold one, to feel the power within it, to disappear into the life of another. She reached out to grab a strand, but ended up collapsing on the ground in a mess of tears. Death's arms wrapped around her. Daisy sobbed into the heavy cloak, almost forgetting it was Death that comforted her.

"I know," Death cooed while stroking Daisy's hair. "I know the weight that sits on your shoulders. I know the pain you feel."

"How do I decide? How do I make the right decision?" Daisy muttered.

"You can't make the right decision. You can only make a decision. I never intended for you to be burdened with my purpose, but you must decide, and it is never an easy decision."

Daisy sat on the ground for a long time as Death comforted her. She ran through her head every possible outcome that she could see. She had to make a choice, but there was too much unknown. Eventually, Daisy picked herself up off of the floor and slightly out of Death's grasp.

"Whatever you choose, my child, I promise you there is a more positive future awaiting those who survive. While I cannot see what those futures will be, I do not fear either choice you make. You will make the correct decision." There was a heavy pause as Daisy weighed her options. While the weight of the world fell squarely on her shoulders, she found a small glimmer of hope in Death's words: either decision would ensure a brighter future for those who survived. She continued to ponder, struggling within herself to find an answer. After a few moments, Death broke the silence, "So, my child, what do you decide?"

www.ingramcontent.com/pod-product-compliance
Lightning Source LLC
Chambersburg PA
CBHW071406200726
48294CB00002B/299